MEMBERS ONLY

A NOVEL BY
Patricia Welles

ARBOR HOUSE *New York*

TO BARBARA FRIEDMAN
AND GARY WILLIAM FRIEDMAN
WITH LOVE

A Jew who cannot laugh at himself is not truly a Jew.

—Chasidic proverb

MEMBERS ONLY

CHAPTER ONE

Buddy Schwartz, still a bull of a man at sixty-three, splashed Aramis under his armpits and thought of his daughter-in-law's *tush*. Soon he would be seeing the lovely sculptured mounds outside on the Crestwood Hills golf course.

Whenever he gazed at those sculptured mounds his thoughts ran to golf. For nearly a decade he had associated Dodie's *tush* with the wonderful, miraculous game of golf. She was the best woman golfer he had ever known. The only reason he had invited his older son, Hank, to the Pro-Am charity event was so that he would bring Dodie. The three of them were partnering with Mickey McHale, the professional, who had taken time off from the tournament to attend the important charity event. The Police Athletic League would be the beneficiary. They had actually been invited to the posh country club and were to attend the extravagant catered party when the golf was ended. He hoped they would behave, but he had a lifelong prejudice that *goyim* did not behave when the champagne was free.

Buddy looked behind him, making certain he was alone, then gazed at his naked body in the mirror of the men's locker room. He was proud of his body. It had been good to him, having been denied only one coveted prize—Dodie. For a decade his alluring daughter-in-law had been the object of his reveries. When he made love to his wife, Rose, he thought of Dodie. She had been the spur to his sex life all these years. Every woman paled beside her. He had never understood why she had married Hank. Such a *shnook*. He, Buddy, was so much more the man. Why couldn't she see this? Endearing pats on her famous behind, affectionate remarks, extravagant gifts—nothing seemed to pique her interest. He might as well be invisible.

He had even given her blue-chip stocks for her birthday, hoping this would get the result he yearned for, but all she did was smile and say, "Thank you, dad." He hated being called *dad*. So impersonal. And it put the relationship on the wrong footing.

He now knew he was never going to have her, and there were days when his frustration was vented in violent fantasies of exterminating Rose and Hank with a five-iron. But of course he knew he would never do that. He was a basically good and kind man, he told himself, just a little horny and wild for his daughter-in-law. He had long ago realized he would have to make do with the odd *shikse* girlfriend for extramarital sex, with Dodie always in his mind's eye as he *shtuped* away with her surrogate. Nevertheless, he was looking forward to the day spent with Dodie, he admitted as he put on his white golf pants and pulled the Yves St. Laurent cashmere sweater over his thick, gray hair.

Glancing at himself in the mirror, he decided he didn't look any more than forty years old. He had no gut, nothing sagged. He was more fit than his sons. Ben was only thirty, but he could not compare to his father. Not on any level. Buddy was slimmer, smarter, sexier and a lot richer. As for Hank, he too was lost in the shadow of his father's success, and he had the beginning of a potbelly. In a few years his fat would hang over his belt if he weren't careful. He didn't even get any exercise from golf because he preferred to be driven around by the caddy. Buddy, on the other hand, never rode, and this gave him an extra opportunity to be near Dodie. Unlike most of the women at the club, she enjoyed walking the course.

Sometimes he wondered if the walking had something to do with being only half-Jewish. His wife never walked any more than was absolutely necessary. Even when they parked in front of the movie theatre she expected to be delivered to the door. If she could not find a place in the parking lot by the market she came home and had the groceries delivered. Walking was anathema to Rose. God forbid she should whittle down those overwhelming thighs.

Dodie was half-Jewish, but not Jewish in the part which counted—the mother. To be truly Jewish meant that one's mother was Jewish. Dodie's mother was a Polish woman who had worked as a maid for Pop Margolis, Dodie's paternal grandfather. Buddy and Pop had been students together at Michigan State way back when. Even their families had been friendly, going to *shul* together, but when Rose and Buddy climbed the ladder to success at Crestwood Hills Country Club they had left the Margolis family way behind in Oak Park in a small, undignified house.

And then, twenty years later the gorgeous Dodie appeared at the club as Hank's date and with a handicap that almost made her professional. Buddy Schwartz was excited. He remained excited when she grew even more stunning and desirable year by year. When she had married Hank, he was shocked, totally shocked. She was either naïve, crazy, or possibly both to have settled for Hank. She did not seem to have any awareness of her charms; the shiny, waist-length hair, the firm breasts, the *retroussé* nose, the soulful eyes. And those cheekbones! And how about her

11

voice, all soft and whispery. Her glorious attributes seemed endless . . .

What the hell, she made him feel alive even though he couldn't have her. He pulled on his new golf shoes with a sense of anticipation. How lucky he was to know such a woman. The time it took to cover eighteen holes would be spent with this queen.

He stood up, feeling he was six feet tall (although he was only five feet seven), and strode down the mahogany panelled corridor to the main dining room where everyone was waiting.

He automatically searched for Dodie as he looked around the room, and was surprised to see his wife was there, seated at a table with Hank and the pro. Before them were platters of scrambled eggs, apple dumplings covered with powdered sugar, rye bread cut thin, brioche warmed to taste, sausages for those who didn't keep kosher, jelly doughnuts, pancakes and Nova Scotia salmon. In the center was a vase of freshly cut roses.

Buddy sighed. He hadn't expected Rose to join them, and yet there she was, eating all that food. And Hank next to her, doing equal justice to the elaborate breakfast. But no sign of Dodie.

He was about to creep away, forgetting the cup of coffee he wanted, when Rose saw him and smiled.

"Hello," Buddy said politely, hoping his disappointment did not show. "I thought you'd stay in bed, Rose."

"I followed you in the Porsche, dear," she said, giving him the enigmatic smile she had been practicing for thirty years. She would do nothing to alienate a husband who had provided so well for her all these years. No matter what he did to her, she would never hurt his feelings. She had endured years of aggressive sexual advances which she deplored, but he would never know her true feelings about this. You did not bite the hand that fed you.

Buddy glanced at McHale, who was sipping at a scotch.

Buddy hated anyone to drink, especially an athlete. People who drank were weak.

"You okay, McHale?"

"Sure thing," Mickey answered. He was about to feel even better. Another couple of drinks and he would feel like a winner. He knew he would beat his hosts without half trying, although he was not sure about the daughter-in-law whom he had seen play the day before.

Buddy frowned. He preferred a thief, a pimp, a pederast, anything to a drinker. The merest whiff of alcohol made him sick. He glanced at Hank, barely able to hide the look of contempt. Hank looked away. He knew his father's opinions. He finished a thin slice of rye bread, then summoned up the courage to look his father in the eye, hoping the expression of respect on his face would put his father into a better mood.

"Guess I'll sit," Buddy said.

Hank stared at him, the father whom he believed he adored. This was the man his analyst said he feared in a most profound way. For years he'd had a recurring dream of a man running after him with a meat cleaver. Doctor Goldman insisted this was his father. Hank refused to believe such nonsense. At forty-two Hank still had the same dreams, only now Dodie brought warm milk when he woke up sweating in the middle of the night. He had quit analysis when Dodie entered his life, which had proven to him that he was ready for marriage. Everything had turned out fine, except that Rose did not like her.

"Where's Dodie?" his father said casually.

Hank studied his father for a moment. Even if Rose did not like Dodie, his father liked her enough for the two of them.

"Where's Dodie?" Buddy repeated, a wave of anxiety coming over him. The day had begun normally, only now he had a sudden peculiar feeling that something unpleasant was going to happen. A sinking feeling assailed him.

Maybe Rose was going to take her place? Of course, that's why she was here, dressed in her fashionable golf attire. He was not going to get to view those sculptured mounds today . . .

As if reading his mind Rose said, "I'm playing with the Beitners and the pro from Cincinnati."

"Oh, you're not taking Dodie's place then?"

Rose smiled placatingly.

"I have no intention of taking Dodie's place," she answered softly. And Dodie was not going to take her place, either. She had decided when she first set eyes on Dodie that the younger woman was competition, strong competition. She knew damned well that Buddy was mad for women, any woman. Throughout the years she had endeavored to put Dodie in her place without anyone knowing about it. The situation was known only to herself and Dodie. The outside world would never believe what passed between them—and the outside world would never know. The other ladies at the club thought they enjoyed the most wonderful mother-daughter relationship. In public Rose was always affectionate to her daughter-in-law. However, in private she had told her in no uncertain terms that all Buddy wanted was to lay her.

"See," Rose had said, "he's a typical man. He just wants to get into your pants. He's not better than other men. Just because he's your father-in-law and a Schwartz, don't think he's so swell. You let him near you and you'll be out of here in two seconds flat."

Rose never shouted; she always spoke quietly to Dodie, who seemed terrified of loud noises. She had discovered early on that Dodie was no fighter. To Rose's way of thinking, Dodie was dull and colorless, but she never pointed this out to Buddy. Let him have his fantasy. Dodie had understood and accordingly treated Buddy with no more than polite attention. She did not want to be thrown out, sent back to the life of poverty she had experienced before

Hank came along to save her. She had no money of her own, just what the Schwartz family had been good enough to award her, perhaps twenty thousand altogether. Rose had even offered her tuition to college as a method of keeping her under control, but Hank had decided that since he had not gone to college his wife should not go either.

Rose soon perceived that her darling son Hank was running around like his father and this worked for her, too. She quickly relayed the information about Hank to Dodie, swearing her to secrecy and threatening to throw her out of the family if the secret was revealed . . .

"You're going with the Beitners?" Buddy said, "oh, that's good, wonderful, Rose. Isn't the Beitner woman the one who works? The good-looking one with the hair pinned up?"

He recalled a shapely woman who was, rumor had it, a stock-broker. She was attractive, but when Dodie was around, all women were eclipsed.

To his joy he saw Dodie coming towards their table. She was wearing a handsome Ultrasuede pants suit befitting that marvelous *tush*. He stood up to greet her.

"Dodie, good morning!" He grinned, pleased that the object of his fantasies had finally arrived. Buddy fastened his eyes onto Dodie's hips, which were swaying towards him. He had built Dodie and Hank a seventy-five thousand dollar pool with cabana just so he could glimpse her thighs as she dived into the sapphire blue waters.

He gazed into her dark eyes as she stood by the table. Her beauty was unreal. She looked like a classic painting, a Goya he had seen in Madrid. In the last few months he had taken to sending her select bits of pornography; stories and pictures. The very idea of her looking at those pictures and reading those words with her own exquisite, mysterious eyes gave him a thrill. He hoped she might guess that he had sent them.

Lately, Buddy had come to the conclusion that if his

money could not ultimately get the attention from Dodie which he craved, then life really was not worth living. He had thought it all through many times. He was going to write a larger share for her into his will and send her a copy. Fifty thousand just was not enough. He would ask Jerry Fryman, the family lawyer, to amend his will. And if that didn't get to her . . .

"The caddies are waiting. The golfers are on the links," Dodie said in her breathless voice.

"Let's go, then," Rose said, smiling for the dining room.

"Ready, sweetheart?" Buddy asked, coming out of his reverie.

"I've been outside for ages," Dodie said. "We've got only five minutes to get to the first tee before the shotgun goes off."

Mickey and Hank got up. Rose grabbed a last slice of rye bread. Buddy followed behind Dodie, trying to conceal his excitement.

Outside the caddies were waiting. Buddy's bag was custom-made pigskin and had cost him over a thousand dollars. Dodie's clubs were relatively modest and encased in a dark leather bag. Hank and Mickey used ordinary white vinyl. Rose, her designer bag already on the go-cart, walked away from the foursome to her own group awaiting her at a different hole.

"A tough course," Mickey said cheerfully, wishing he had ordered another scotch. He didn't feel up to form. "Who's the architect of this course?"

Buddy shrugged. His only interest now was Dodie. Art and architecture would have to wait.

"Jenkins, I think," Dodie said.

Mickey nodded, looking off towards the first hole which he had played the day before.

"It's a bitch," he said as the shotgun blast resounded nearby. He walked over to the plush green of the tee area and gazed around. He put the ball down and swung at it with what he considered to be poor form. The ball swung out at an angle, just missing the sandtrap.

"Not bad," Buddy said, gripping Mickey's arm. He liked touching such successful people as a professional golfer. He had to admire the guy. It was a tough business.

"I haven't been the same since Miami," Mickey said in a dispirited voice.

"Hank, you going next?" Buddy asked as he looked around for Dodie, who was staring into the distance as if she were in another world. Yet when she walked towards the tee she became alert, so alert that he wondered if her air of permanent distraction was some kind of an act.

"No, Dodie goes," Hank said. "Dodie!"

His sharp voice caused Dodie to look around suddenly, and catching his signal, she moved rapidly to the tee. She chose a wood club that she considered the correct one for the hole. The caddy, standing near her, looked on admiringly. He had seen this woman play many times throughout the summer, and never badly.

Dodie drove the ball almost two hundred yards so that it landed three feet short of the first hole. She quickly smiled but did not look around for approval.

"Great shot," Mickey shouted, "Great!"

Hank just nodded. He was not an affectionate man. Dodie had discovered this on her wedding night when he refused to make love to her. She had believed his reluctance to touch her was out of a reverence for the sacrament of marriage, only to discover it came from fear—that and the idea that it was somehow dirty to make love to your wife. Yet she knew that he was fooling around—his mother had made this clear. After five years of marriage, Dodie had given up caring. She was actually relieved to have him out of her bed and in the guest room. Now she had a nice king-size bed all to herself and the demon lovers who came to her unexpectedly in the night and sometimes during the day. Increasingly during the day.

For the past few years, Dodie had lived her sex life in her head, creating romantic fantasies . . . a nude man bearing roses . . . a pair of young boys wearing fur coats . . . boxes of Godiva chocolates being spread across her belly and plucked off by a handsome blond man wearing jackboots. He would sing in a velvety baritone, kissing her earlobes and promising her a castle on the Rhine if she would offer her virginity. There was a quasi-brutal quality about him but just before she was seduced the fantasy ended . . .

"Terrific," Buddy applauded her shot.

She glanced furtively at him. He seemed to be adjusting something in his pants, a strange gesture which embarrassed her. Buddy often embarrassed her. She knew he had sent her the pornography, but the books made her feel soiled, not sexy. Still she could not utter a word for fear that Rose would send her packing.

Suddenly, she realized Buddy was staring at her with an almost rapt expression on his face and she looked away, wishing she were somewhere else. Hank, approaching the tee with trepidation, would blame her, as he always did, for his poor showmanship. As usual, he would be many strokes over par. She closed her eyes to blot out Hank and his father . . . Sometimes, Dodie almost wished she were back with Daddy Margolis and her mother Shirlee, even though their religious and ethnic differences prevented them from ever getting along. There had been a lot of shouting in that household, but it was something she could cope with. There had been a certain amount of whispering she never understood, but she had always taken comfort in the simple fact that the arguments were out in the open. There was nothing insidious going on, or was there? . . . Maybe Shirlee and Daddy were no better than the Schwartz family after all . . .

There had to be something more pleasant to think about. Later, she thought, there would be a party, and Dodie liked parties. She could get lost in the crowd. The usuals would be there—poor Doc Matthews and red-haired Jerry Fryman, whom she did not trust. He was the Schwartz family lawyer and was at every party the club gave. Dodie had heard he was a womanizer, though he was best known for his jogging around Palmer Woods in the early morning hours. She supposed Jerry considered himself an intellectual because he went to Harvard Law School and owned two Dobermans. They snapped at everyone and relieved themselves on his Persian carpet, but he was devoted to them.

She was grateful, at least, that he had done Hank's will. After two years of subtle suggestions from Dodie, Jerry had agreed to do the will for nothing. He had always been polite to Dodie, yet she wondered if he really liked her—well, liked her for herself. She knew he liked her as a potential client. Dodie was an heir to the Schwartz millions and he knew this perfectly well. There were no grandchildren to inherit, only Hank, his brother Ben and, indirectly, Dodie herself.

She wasn't sure if Jerry knew that she was aware he had borrowed from the Schwartz family to finance his numerous business schemes. First, a resort hotel in a racially-troubled Bahamian island, and then a health food franchise that went instantly broke because the customers got food poisoning. Jerry was also a gambler, planting himself at the card table in the men's card room almost every weekend.

The club's card room contained the same male and female faces with hardly any variations. Mostly, they were the older and richer members of the club, the ones who didn't give a damn if they came away a few thousand poorer. The men's card room in particular was the scene of many a thousand, or a ten-thousand, changing hands. The members vied for the greatest casualness when they lost, however secretly embittered. Although a big loser, even Jerry had managed to make losing an art. In a sense he was the best poker player of the group because he outbluffed everyone. Inside, though, his stomach turned over at every penny he felt he had to give away. His *kishkes* ate themselves up when at the end of a month he tallied up the money he no longer had, though his losses were open to conjecture—no one really knew. Dodie sensed that he was a loser in more ways than one, and for this she felt sorry for him. Though it was said he had a good law practice, she doubted it, thinking that his gambling debts and unlucky business ventures had to be wiping him out bit by bit . . .

Dodie suddenly was again aware of Buddy in front of her. He had turned to her and flashed a smile. Nervously, she smiled back, tucking her hands into the pockets of her Ultrasuede pants suit, and nodded briefly at the caddy who was following along a short distance behind to hurry him up. The caddy, a college student, interpreted her nod as flirtation and self-consciously cast his eyes down. Dodie smiled widely at the misunderstanding and thought of Dickie David, perhaps one of the sweetest men at Crestwood Hills. Dickie paid attention to her in a special way so that she could tell he liked her as a person. And when his wife was not around he was affectionate, patting her arm and sometimes kissing her cheek in a fatherly way. Dickie was a fixture at the club, possibly one of its richest members, having struck it big with gold bars in the seventies. Dickie made the club his second home, attending every function, party, golf meet, bar mitzvah, bas mitzvah, swimming contest, wedding and birthday party.

Unfortunately, Dodie had to deal far too often with his wife, Beverly, who had always made Dodie feel small and insignificant. Compared to glamorous Beverly—who at a rumored fifty-two was as alluring as a young maiden—maybe she was. Everyone more or less understood that Beverly slept around, though with whom was uncertain. Each wife thought it was with someone else's husband.

Dodie did not delude herself—she knew Hank had been in bed with Beverly, and so had Buddy. Now Beverly was casting her eyes on Ben, the thirty-year-old pot-smoking youngest Schwartz, who hung around Wayne State University signing up for classes he never finished. Few in the community even recognized his existence. Beverly was among the handful who seemed to have an empathy for him. Or was it that she had an inexhaustible hunger for anything male? . . .

"Damn." Hank exploded, his early morning temper tantrum beginning. Dodie could have easily predicted this behavior. His ball had flown past the flagstick and into a clump of trees, no doubt exacerbating his customary outburst on the golf course. He ranted. She was aware that the other members with their families and friends standing on the sidelines could hear him, or if they could not, they could imagine what he was shouting, having heard it all before. Hank was notorious for his bad temper, both on and off the course.

A few moments after his son's invective permeated the air, Buddy began to comment on the drive. As usual, this would continue for the rest of the game. Buddy's life seemed to be enhanced by a running emasculation of his son. No professional ever played twice with this father-son team. Dodie dreaded the Pro-Am charity events, but of course, being a fine player, she had no choice but to appear.

Hank had now reduced his outrage to mutterings which could be heard by only the immediate group. He blamed the mishap on his father. His father had sneezed on purpose, breaking Hank's concentration just as he was teeing off. He did it every time.

Abruptly, Hank realized he was berating his father, whom he adored. He stopped and gazed at him with contrite eyes. "God, dad, I'm sorry."

The tone of his voice caused the caddy to look up with

interest. He had frequently seen violent behavior on the golf course but had rarely heard any sniveling apologies for it.

"Like hell," Buddy said, grabbing his number-two wood out of the caddy's hands. "*Shmuck,*" Buddy mumbled, moving quickly away from Hank. Though he saw himself as a loving, peaceful man, sometimes Hank made him feel aggressive, particularly on the golf course. But words were enough. He could chew him out, berate him, put him down with words. If only the kid would get that look off his face. Buddy hardly knew how he could spend all day with him, but Hank *was* his son, a Schwartz. They even looked alike. Who else should work for him? A stranger? Some *goy* who didn't understand the intricacies of the building business? It was not an easy business, in many ways a fringe business, where he was forced to deal with lower-class hoods. Too bad the other kid, Ben, the *shnook,* the ingrate, couldn't have pulled himself together to work for his father.

Buddy looked around the golf course. On such a glorious day he shouldn't feel angry, yet he had the distinct feeling that things were beginning to fall apart. There was inept Henry . . . the pro who drank . . . a caddy who probably played better golf than he did . . . and Dodie, who seemed not remotely interested in him . . . He gazed down at the ball he had placed on the tee, aware that Dodie was near. He could smell her perfume, breathing deeply the rich odor. He knew it was the smell of *Bain de Champagne,* as he had given it to her for Christmas. There was no smell like it in the universe, except the heady aroma of a woman in the act of sex. He inhaled deeply, a resurgence of vitality pushing through his body.

"Ouch!" Buddy yelled suddenly in pain. It felt as if a wasp had stung him. For a moment he was in such pain he did not notice the remarkable shot he had made, almost a hole-in-one. He clutched at his leg.

"What's wrong?" Dodie asked, stepping over to him.

"Dad, dad," Hank said, a note of panic in his voice. "What's the matter? What happened?" Dodie observed that Hank's face was still red and sweaty from his temper tantrum.

"A wasp," Buddy gasped, staring at Dodie. She was next to him, a look of sympathy on her beautiful face. "Maybe a bee," he added, "I don't know. Something stung me."

"A bee sting," Dodie said. "Some people are allergic to bee stings. I hope you're not one of them, Buddy."

"Better now," Buddy said. He did not wish to appear cowardly in front of her. Just a little sting, nothing spectacular. He had not been attacked by a nest of hornets.

"Are you okay, dad?" Henry asked anxiously.

"Maybe we should stop?" Dodie said.

"Nah," Buddy grunted, "let's get the show on the road. I'll be okay."

Dodie stared uneasily at him, her dark eyes searching his face.

"Really?" she said.

"Wait a sec, wait," Hank said, "let's check it out. That bee could still be under there, dad." Before his father could protest or move away, he had stooped and began to put his hand up his father's leg. "Maybe he left the stinger in? Sit down and I'll see," Hank insisted.

Buddy swatted at his son's head as if he were the bee.

"Out of there, boy, I'm okay, what do you think? Doesn't hurt, I'm fine, let's play!"

Mickey ran over to investigate. He had been standing by the first hole when Buddy's unexpected swing resulted in a near hole-in-one.

"You damn near made it," he shouted. "What's going on?"

All eyes turned mid-westward. With Buddy leading, the four ran the rest of the way to the first hole. Buddy's ball

23

was resting on the lip of the hole. He had not noticed the cheering crowd. Nothing had penetrated except the sudden pain from the sting.

"Terrific," Hank said, feeling ambivalent. His father beat him at everything—craps, chess, gin, clabiash. It would never be any different.

"Super," Mickey said, slapping Buddy heartily on the back.

Buddy looked at Dodie for comment. She smiled, showing her white teeth, her dimpled cheeks, her shining eyes. He wanted to hug her—he had an excuse—but everyone was looking and the news would get back to Rose. Actually, he felt rewarded simply by her appreciative smile. One day he could get her in the women's dressing room, or take her by surprise in her swimming pool, the one had had given her . . .

"Hey, shouldn't I have been next?" Mickey said. "I'm the pro here. I know this little lady is a good athlete and this shot is fine but I was next."

"You went first, don't you remember, Mickey?" Dodie said.

"You'll get your turn again," Buddy added, wishing his eyes were laser beams to get rid of everyone but himself and Dodie.

"What's the matter, dad?" Hank asked, as his father clutched his chest, grimacing in pain.

"Ugghh . . ." A strangulated sound emerged from Buddy's mouth. He suddenly could not breathe. He opened his mouth wide and then sank to the ground, his left arm squashed under him, his right arm in the hole.

"Get up, dad," Hank begged.

The caddy thought the elder Schwartz was joking. He was always horsing around. But Buddy did not move.

Mickey McHale bent down and touched his shoulder. "I hope I didn't do that with the smack, old buddy," he said. "Can I help you?"

24

"Oh, my God," Hank gasped, "get a doctor, hurry up!"

"Maybe it's the bee sting," Dodie said, "some people are allergic to bee stings."

For a second no one moved, then Dodie began to run toward the crowd, the others close behind her.

"Daddy," Hank murmured, "daddy." As he ran toward the group of people standing on the sidelines, he felt a terrible sinking sensation in the pit of his stomach. He stopped short, shouting for the others to go on, and decided to run back to the collapsed figure.

Clumsily, Hank gripped his father's head with one hand and with the other tilted his chin up, pressing his mouth down, attempting what he thought, in his panic, would be the kiss of life.

CHAPTER TWO

Doc Matthews pronounced Buddy dead at the first hole. An ambulance was called, the body removed to the funeral home. Doc could find no mark of a bee immediately and therefore marked the death certificate "heart attack," which it appeared to be. Hank made the funeral arrangements by telephone. He did not tell the other members of the club his father had passed on until after the party for the charity event and the Police Athletic League. Mickey McHale got drunk and had to be carried away, and Rose Schwartz broke down at six o'clock, wept openly, and went home.

Ben Schwartz was called from Crestwood Hills and told that his father's funeral would be the next day. He was expected to wear a tie and get there on time.

Hank ate too many hors d'oeuvres and wondered why he had not got along better with his father. Now that Buddy was gone he missed him horribly. He felt helpless and alone. How would he run the business without his father's screaming help which he had grown accustomed to through the years? His mother was hopeless at business and there were no partners. He cried silently to himself in the men's card room, empty except for squashed and evil-smelling cigar butts that overflowed in the ashtrays.

That evening Hank stayed in his parents' mansion off the Wabeek golf course, to which they also belonged. When they weren't engaged in Crestwood Hills functions, they could always be found on the links at Wabeek. An expensive community of massive homes, lavish condominiums and elegant apartments, Wabeek was only a few miles from Hank's conservative mock-Tudor home. Hank loathed staying away from his own house overnight, but this certainly was an exception. His mother desperately needed him. Ben had never been a comfort. Yet Hank secretly admired his younger brother's rebellious spirit. He had to admit that Ben had done everything imaginable to irritate their parents unnecessarily. He even smoked dope in the house, the aroma filling the numerous rooms and passageways of the enormous Schwartz mansion. Rose would have a sneezing attack and escape to her suite of master bedroom and gigantic adjoining bath, which contained an original Picasso from his Blue Period . . .

Tonight, seated in the imposing and stylish living room, Hank looked sadly from Ben, who was puffing on his pipe, to his mother, dressed in her new pink bathrobe and crying. Ben had not even attempted to put out the pipe, although Rose had made the request several times. The atmosphere was charged with a mixture of whatever evil-smelling thing Ben was smoking plus guilt, grief and mutual recriminations. Hank felt horrible.

"I don't understand why something wasn't done for dad," Ben said crossly.

"We've gone into that already," Hank replied.

Ben shrugged. He was sitting in a red velvet chair regarding what was left of his family. Overweight Hank and overweight Rose.

Ben had the Schwartz look, the curly dark hair, the olive

skin, the heavy beard that needed daily shaving. But he was taller and slimmer than his brother and with a straighter nose and thinner lips. Like most of Crestwood Hills Country Club, the entire Schwartz family except for Ben was obsessed with their waistlines. The money Ben's parents had spent on efforts to keep themselves attractive was enormous. Not content with Pritikin, Scarsdale, Rubin, not content with the odd fast, the giving-up of late-night *noshes*, not content with avoiding ice cream and potato chips and caramel corn, they were forever signing up for classes to keep slim. Usually, when the first session was over, both of them dropped out, having had enough. Buddy's continuing battle with the bulge seemed to triumph, and he looked reasonably intact for his age. Rose, though, had been defeated years ago. She had been thinking of a face-lift, perhaps a trip to Brazil for some further tightening. Body sculpture, they called it. Now Ben did not know what his mother would do—without Buddy she would be at a total loss. They were so dependent on each other, or so he believed.

Rose had the consolation of being an extremely rich widow. She could certainly afford a trip to Brazil now. Ben felt a tug of guilt at the thought. He glanced at his mother. She did not know he had seen his father early in the morning—if she knew she would have mentioned it. Ben had stopped over to the house for money, having run out of his monthly stipend some two weeks earlier. Buddy had been furious. It was not easy to explain to him that the price of pot had gone up and that restaurants, gasoline and women were costing him a mint.

"I'm flat broke," Ben had said. "So what else is new?"

At first his father had refused him entry into the house, but finally he relented and shoved two hundred-dollar bills into Ben's hand with a warning to stay away . . .

"Your pipe is making me ill," Hank said gently, feeling his nose beginning to itch. "Please, Ben," he said, smiling affectionately, "can't you get rid of it? Mother doesn't like it, either."

Ben arched his dark brows. He was far better looking, younger and brighter than Hank, and Hank knew it, or suspected it. But he never felt resentment, even though Ben always got the beautiful women. As children it was Ben who was sought after for sports and who was elected class president. In a way Hank felt relief when at twenty-three Ben turned hippie and was cast out of the family. He even suspected his parents had cut Ben out of their wills, effectively turning over the family fortune to him, and because of this almost certain knowledge, Hank allowed himself to feel a sense of pity for his brother. He would, after all, be the one who had to protect his baby brother in the coming rough years ahead. It would be Henry who would be taking care of Ben . . .

Ben smiled back and continued to suck on his pipe. He did not like to be told what to do.

"I'm in a good mood, that's all," Ben explained.

"How can you be in a good mood?" Rose asked in amazement, her eyes red and swollen from tears.

"Oh, sorry, mom," Ben quickly said, feeling embarrassed. He sighed heavily. He had a penchant for saying the wrong thing at the wrong time. He crossed his blue-jeaned legs and pulled at his yellow shetland sweater, a decaying hand-me-down from the dim past.

"When is the will going to be read?" he asked, apparently without shame.

Hank gazed at his brother, wondering what demon prompted him to ask such an impertinent question right in front of their mother.

"*Oy*, this is my son?"

"Wills aren't read any more," Hank said, "it's not like Agatha Christie."

"I don't like her books anyway," Ben said.

"I'm going to bed. I'll take some sleeping pills. Pick me

up at nine tomorrow, Hank," Rose said and stood up.

Hank got quickly to his feet and rushed to his mother's side.

"Mom," he said, "mom, I wouldn't leave you alone, you know I wouldn't."

Tears flooded Rose Schwartz's green eyes. "You're a good boy," she said. She glanced at her younger son, and without saying another word left the room.

Hank turned to Ben.

"Jerry has their wills, of course," he said archly. "I'm sure you'll got a copy in due course."

Ben got up and stretched.

"I think I'll split," he said.

"We'll see you at the funeral. Ben, please, try to be on time, won't you?"

"Yeah, sure," Ben said and left by the back door, the sickly sweet aroma of the pipe remaining behind.

Hank sat on the couch feeling morose. He tried to think straight, clear his thoughts of the oppressiveness that hung over them. His father was gone. The unbelievable had happened. Big, strong, important Buddy Schwartz was gone and not coming back this time. It wasn't as if he went to Ohio on a business trip, or took one of his ladies to Miami. No, this was it, the long goodbye. How was he going to manage?

His thoughts wandered from his father's death to other subjects equally dispiriting. Since his wedding night his marriage was in name only. He could not allow himself to be attracted to his wife, feeling inordinate guilt when he so much as stroked her. Somehow sleeping around with other women lifted any guilt feelings he had. The only problem was actually finding the other women. There seemed to be fewer and fewer. Beverly David had dumped him for Ben, reminding him yet again that he was the unattractive brother.

Recently, Hank had found he had to buy women in order

to have any sexual liaisons. The women were not exactly hookers—he did not feel attracted to women who sold their bodies for sex. Mostly, the women were secretaries or telephone operators, or anyone whom he could pick up at a singles' bar. However, he had to spend considerable sums of money on them to keep them interested. Dinners at fancy restaurants, perfume, candy, sometimes a quick trip to Toronto for the day to buy Wedgwood china, cashmere sweaters and woolens . . . It was not ennobling.

Then, there was his private relationship to his mother, as opposed to the public one. From the outside they seemed close. But this was mainly a display for the members of Crestwood Hills, Wabeek neighbors and the congregation of the temple. As soon as they were alone his mother would start haranguing him about Dodie. She seemed to want to alienate him from his wife. At first Hank protested. He tried to defend his wife, but he tired easily. And his own unhappiness caused him to engage in senseless arguments with Dodie. He began to view her as an object like a heating pad. At times he even moved her into the guest room just before retiring, so she could warm up his side of the bed. Then, he moved her back to the master bedroom. He began picking on her just the way his mother picked on him. She wore too much makeup. She wore too little. Her hair was too dark. Her breasts too firm. And then the golf. He criticized her golf technique whenever possible. Her form was improper. Her hands were not placed on the shaft in the right manner. He would come up behind her as she was teeing off and distract her.

Hank was amazed at Dodie's ability to concentrate on her golf game no matter what distractions he provided. She ignored everything except what she was doing. For Hank, whose attention span was no greater than a child's, Dodie's fervent interest in golf seemed impossible. He decided there was a cool, detached side to her no one knew about.

He did not really want to think about all of this. Depressing thoughts overwhelmed him, and he did not know how to cope with them.

He tried not to think about his dead father. He needed him, and now who would help him? He had no real relationship with Dodie and his mother could not abide him. He began to cry.

"Goodness," Rose said sharply, standing in the doorway of the living room. "Stop mooning about like that, Hank." But Hank could not stop his tears.

The doorbell rang and Rose ran to the front door and looked through the peephole. The rabbi was standing outside, his hat in his hand. She yanked open the door and threw herself into his surprised arms. "Oh my God, rabbi!" she cried.

Rabbi Stone retrieved his hat, which she had crushed, and then gently tried to push her away. He invariably felt awkward when he was alone with a woman who was not his mother. He touched his hat nervously, wondering when she was going to invite him into the house.

"Thank you for coming, Rabbi Stone," she cried.

The rabbi nodded, relieved to see her son, Hank, sitting in the living room. "May I come in?"

"Of course," Rose said. The truth was she had never really taken to the rabbi. There was something squeamish about him she did not like. He was supposed to be in his thirties but looked older. Once she overheard Dodie telling Hank that the rabbi was handsome. That had settled the matter for her.

"Your husband promised for the building fund," the rabbi stammered, realizing immediately he should have waited longer to say such a thing. Rose's face went pale and she frowned.

"Come in," she said, slamming the front door behind him.

"I don't suppose he said anything before he died?" the

rabbi continued. He had just seen Doc Matthews's car pulling up in the driveway.

"Hank, get over here," Rose snapped. "I'm going to bed."

She, too, had seen the arrival of the other car. She disappeared down the hall, leaving the rabbi standing at the door, his question about the building fund having gone unanswered.

The doorbell rang again. The rabbi, not knowing what else to do, opened the door to find Doc Matthews, the look of a grieving spaniel plastered on his round face. Beside him stood Dodie Schwartz and Jerry Fryman, who was rumored to have lost five thousand dollars playing poker over the weekend. They exchanged greetings, the rabbi sidling away in the hope he could avoid being touched. He dreaded direct contact, but Dodie was grasping his arm firmly. If only he could have been an orthodox rabbi instead of a reformed one, he would have had a good excuse for not touching. Even the most perfunctory touch made him skittish. In order to conceal this phobia he slid away from people as if he were in a perennial hurry. So far it had worked. . . The rabbi was known for having a high energy level.

The rabbi stared at Dodie's striking designer clothes. She was exquisitely dressed as always, her outfit highlighted by her dark hair, olive skin and strange, mysterious eyes. She was without doubt the most interesting looking woman in Crestwood Hills, not to mention his temple. The rabbi looked over at Doc Matthews. He stared at Doc's hand coming his way, allowing it to remain in his own longer than he would have liked out of deference for the feelings of those grieving for the dead. He thought that he had tried hard to love Doc, one of God's misfits. Doc's face was jowly as well as paunchy; he was a curiously misshapen person.

"I must see Mrs. Schwartz before she retires," the rabbi

explained, loosening Doc's grip. He managed to escape and trotted off after Rose.

"Well, then, come on, let's go into the living room," Dodie said, leading them into the empty living room.

"Hank must have gone to his old room. He sleeps a lot when he's at his parents'."

"Where's mom?" Hank asked, emerging from the hallway. "Hi, Jerry, Doc, thanks for coming."

"I think Rabbi Stone said she went to her room," Dodie said.

"Don't know for sure," Jerry added. He had a neat, precise way of speaking which he felt made him appear trustworthy. His voice had brought him success in his law practice.

"She must have gone to bed," Doc said, "she's whacked out, isn't she, Hank?" He followed Hank out of the imposing living room and down the hall.

Dodie glanced hesitantly at Jerry who was sitting down, playing with his mustache. He was invariably polite but she was not sure if he liked her. He did not pay attention to her the way she wanted. His eyes averted hers as if he were either afraid or not interested enough to look at her. She wanted to befriend him. She would like that more than anything. She needed friends, particularly male friends . . .

Once when she and Hank were first married and their King Charles spaniel, who had since died, was vomiting for two days, she had called Jerry for help. He had got rid of his client and rushed over to their house to advise them. She would never forget this unexpected kindness. Since then he had barely looked her way except to be courteous.

"I wish you liked me," she said out loud.

Jerry looked startled. His hand dropped from his mustache and he stared at her for an explanation. When she said nothing further he perceived that she was not aware she had said anything. She was a flake, he thought, constantly

34

preoccupied and jumpy, the sort of gal who would jump on a chair if she saw a mouse. Yet there was something attractive about her helplessness. Beautiful knuckleheads like Dodie Schwartz had an appeal. So did sexy-looking manipulators, or women interested in art; any woman, in fact, could be attractive. He sighed. Bright women did not like him. A bright girl tired of him within two weeks.

Dodie felt uneasy. Jerry was not talking to her. He was sitting there silent as the walls. Was he shy?

"Did I say something?" she asked.

"No, I don't think so," he said.

"Sometimes I talk to myself," she said.

He watched her full lips as she spoke in her childish, breathless manner. Hank was a disgrace. Here he had this sweet, adorable wife and he was making a fool of her, taking up with anything that came his way. Jerry believed that Hank was always successful with his women just as Hank believed that Jerry was. He did not blame Hank for having extra women. What he did not like was the fact that Hank was a married man. It was all right for Jerry to want any female who came his way. He was single. It was not necessary for him to have loyalties to one woman . . .

"My dad taught me not to trust lawyers," Dodie was saying apologetically. "Lawyers are shrewd . . . I mean you do owe the Schwartz family a lot of money, don't you, Jerry?"

Jerry was stunned. He blushed and for a moment fumbled for something to reply. He did not know that Dodie was aware of the Schwartz business ventures.

"That's right, Dodie, but don't worry your little head about it."

He laughed sheepishly, remembering the four hundred thousand dollars Hank had given him to act on his behalf in a silver shipment deal. Sooner or later, he was going to have to confess to Hank that the shipment had been hijacked in, of all places, Connecticut.

35

"I'm not a business expert, Jerry, but since Buddy's death I've figured you must owe Hank, or Buddy's estate, right?" She smiled at him, hoping his pale blue eyes would rise to meet hers, but he was gazing at the carpet, apparently deep in thought.

Dodie had liked science and business at school, taking as many math courses as the school offered. Her goal had been to be a science major, but having no money to go to college had discouraged her. When she met Hank she was working as a waitress in a Big Boy restaurant.

Jerry slowly raised his head. His eyes met hers for a fraction of a second.

"Yes, that's correct, Dodie," he said, gazing at her in a state of semi-shock. He did not like the idea that Hank might have been talking to her about their business deals. She seemed to know something—but did she know about the silver shipment?

"Are you involved in the Schwartz office in some way?"

"Oh, only vaguely," she said, rising, then excused herself and left the room. Jerry wondered where she was going. To say goodnight to her mother-in-law, perhaps? He stared at his feet, which were encased in three hundred dollar shoes from Milan. He never stinted on these things, liking to be well-dressed in the conservative fashion befitting his law practice.

He got up to look around. Where was everyone? The house was quiet. He wandered down the hallway toward the bedrooms. Buddy, poor old Buddy had died before his time, but what the hell, he died well, having made love to the ubiquitous Beverly David the evening before. The untiring Beverly had confided this morsel to Jerry via telephone, though her real reason for calling Jerry at home was to find out in her not-so-subtle fashion whether Buddy had left her anything in his will. He had not. Everything was left to Rose and Hank, with fifty thousand for Dodie. Ben had been cut out, something which bothered Jerry enormously. How was Ben going to live? His part-time job at the Humane Society barely paid his rent. Jerry felt that his friend was entitled to his share of the Schwartz millions and had tried to convince Ben of this on numerous occasions. He and Ben had been close since the discovery of their mutual love of animals, and now they had even shared the same woman—Beverly. Now Jerry was puzzled by the fact that Beverly had also bedded Buddy the night before his death. Beverly had explained that she had picked that night to tell Buddy about Ben, but never got around to it. Buddy went to his grave not knowing he had been pushed aside by his son.

Jerry had always been envious of Buddy's money, believing he ought to be just as rich. The other men had made their millions young. Why hadn't he? He did not have sufficient luck, he thought, but he knew his day was coming.

All Jerry's friends seemed to live more opulently than he did. Buddy had ordered a one hundred thousand dollar custom-made car, a Rolls. When the car had arrived he decided to keep it in the garage because he had no immediate use for it. The car was equipped with a bar, a refrigerator, a fantastic stereo set with short wave to Europe, two telephones—one a hot line to his office and one a hot line to Beverly—and seats that could be made into a bed. The back of the car was separated from the chauffeur by a smoked glass panel to insure complete privacy.

In fact Buddy liked driving his Cadillac, his Porsche or his Mercedes himself, thinking a chauffeur was a waste. But he kept a man on his payroll to drive him just in case the need might arise. The man sat in one of the rooms of the Wabeek mansion playing gin rummy all day, hoping to be called. What Buddy essentially wanted him for was one night in particular, the Halloween party at the club. Buddy had always dreamed of arriving at the club on Halloween in a Rolls, and then stepping out dressed as Count Dracula.

Jerry grimaced. Buddy would not be going anywhere now except in a hearse. He glanced into the library half expecting to see Buddy in there. Where was Dodie? He needed to talk to her. Had Buddy told her about the large sums he had lent him? Did Rose know he was up to his ears in gambling debts? Did she know about the poker? Did both of them know that Buddy had actually given the okay to Hank to release four hundred thousand dollars for the silver transaction? Had they kept records, or was this under-the-table money?

Doc, Hank and the rabbi were gathered in the library around the television set, feeding their obsession with Jack Nicklaus. Jerry was not a golfer, preferring such pursuits as the art museum for Sunday brunch with Bach, and sometimes afterwards, a stroll through the galleries accompanied by the most lovely gal he could find. The Midwest was a far more cultured place than people realized. Certainly the area around Wayne State University offered many cultural pursuits and that was where the pretty girls went also. And if you really wanted to go out of your way, there was the Cranbrook Music Guild in the winter. He had never met anyone attractive there, but there was always hope for the future. If one felt like driving, the Detroit Symphony offered an array of women at the intermission. He had once met a girl who sold lingerie, and took her to three more performances before she rejected him.

He continued on down the hall, treading softly. Dodie could have gone to the powder room. If only he knew the right one, there were so many. She was nowhere in sight.

The Schwartzes' Wabeek mansion was a fantastic maze, and Jerry had got lost there often. There were too many rooms, too many nooks and crannies. There were a dozen bathrooms, three pool-table rooms and all kinds of other game rooms dotted around the establishment. One wing contained an entire amusement arcade with computerized game machines, fortune-telling machines, machines that actually gave cash prizes. The house had been a lot of fun before anyone had died.

In addition, there were two in-ground swimming pools, one which was always hot, with the steam rising, and the other cool and the size of a tennis court. There was a floating bar in the hot one. Then there were the rooms off the swimming pools, the Jacuzzis, the saunas. Each room contained vending machines that offered everything from piping hot coffee and beer to pizza and even chicken soup.

As far as Jerry knew, Rose and Buddy merely went from the kitchen, where they dined on an ordinary butcher block table, to their bedroom, where the wall-sized home entertainment unit was installed. Although Rose protested, Buddy enjoyed dirty movies. Occasionally, the rest of the house was used by family or friends, and, of course, whenever a party was given, the entire house was ablaze with thousands of colored lights. The Schwartzes had been excellent hosts, opening their mansion to their friends. This included the music room where Buddy kept every kind of musical instrument he had ever heard of. He had hired a student at the University of Michigan to research ancient instruments, and his collection of international instruments occupied a room of their own. His guests could beat congas, blow eighteenth-century trumpets and sing at a specially constructed stereo Dolby sound stage equipped with an engineering studio for recording. Or they could waltz to a full orchestra in the ballroom, even boogie in the bar while drinking to an elaborate system of disco music and strobe lights which had cost fifty thousand to put in.

Jerry searched up and down the corridors for Dodie. She could be hiding out in any of these rooms, and he was getting tired of looking. The person he desperately wanted to talk to was Rose. Her room seemed a playing field away. He looked around. The hall was deathly quiet. He walked

39

through the interconnecting rooms and chambers until he saw what he believed was the door to the master suite. Quietly, he opened it.

He had found the right room. Rose was stretched out on the bedcovers, her eyes closed, her arms at her side. But he began to shake. Dear God, he prayed, don't let Hank discover about the silver shipment until I can make some sort of restitution. Staring into Rose's pale face, a thought crossed his mind. If Rose Schwartz did not exist, there would be one less person to know about his mistakes.

CHAPTER THREE

Ben Schwartz moved over to the passenger seat of his Volkswagen Rabbit and lit a joint, inhaling deeply. Beverly did not understand the joys of marijuana, being of a different generation. She was his first older woman, however, and he liked it. His annoyance at her dislike of dope had diminished since he seduced her. Before, she had belittled him for liking drugs. Now she no longer cared what he did.

He stretched his legs. His intention was to arrive late at the Fox and Hounds restaurant. He was going to remain at his parents' home until it was time to meet Beverly, but he had not enjoyed the tone, the ambience—death was not exactly invigorating. He had once loved his father, although there was no way Ben knew to convince his father of this. Buddy had considered him a bum, a *shnook*, a freeloader, and their relationship had disintegrated. But he had done what he could, and when he realized that there was no way for him to get through to his father, he had protected himself by pretending not to care.

Glancing at his watch he saw he had fifteen minutes

before Beverly. Time enough to get absolutely stoned.

Beverly liked to eat before she participated in sex. Usually she ordered something light like fish, either plain broiled trout, or pike. She said it gave her energy, determination. Ben smiled to himself. She was a four-orgasm woman, something new and exciting in his thirty-year-old life. He did not know exactly how much older she was, but she had to be fifty, judging by her twenty-four-year-old daughter, whom he did not particularly like. The daughter could not compare to Beverly, who was sophisticated and worldly. She made him feel good, fed his ego, stroked his soul. Age did not matter. He considered Beverly the sexiest woman imaginable. She was lovely, an expert at sex and an expert at making him think he was the best lover in the world. No wonder men liked older women, no wonder books were written about this wonderful phenomenon. He adored hearing her talk about her previous lovers. This was nearly as good as making love to her. And he *did* admire her looks. She was slim and had perfect breasts and streaked blond hair. She had class.

Ben sucked on his dope, trying to keep his thoughts away from his father and on Beverly. He did not realize, or notice at all, that she had a remodeled nose, a breast reduction, the loose skin and bags removed from around her eyes. Nor did he understand that she spent a large part of her day exercising to keep her figure from sagging. Perhaps it would not have made any difference anyway, as he thought he was in love with her. At thirty Ben had not settled down. His part-time job at the Humane Society was all the work he had ever done except for working summers for his father, which he detested. He took classes at Wayne State University, yet had no thought of obtaining a degree. He was in no hurry. His interest in humane ways of killing animals had been his chief concern for the last few years. Once in a while he thought he might like to be a vet, even if it was nearly impossible to get into veterinary school.

The Humane Society had promoted him to injecting the animals. He knew how to inject so they would not suffer. He would have liked to discuss his views on euthanasia with Beverly, but he detected she was not that excited by them. The only member of his family who had ever shown any interest in the subject was Dodie.

What Dodie needed, he thought, was a good affair. Beneath that little-girl voice there had to be a woman inside some place. He would like to turn her loose and see what would happen. She might come out sounding like Beverly, sounding like a grown woman.

He looked again at his watch. Only two minutes had passed. He leaned his head against the seat and shut his burning eyes, a by-product of too much dope. He was feeling chilly this September night, and wound up the window to shut out the breeze. Then he resettled himself and shut his eyes again. He snuffed out the joint, then put the remains of the roach into the glove compartment. If he swallowed the roach he would immediately be in a fog, and he wanted to be alert for Beverly. She deserved so much. He had been in love with her for several weeks, for him a long time. He had never before really loved any person, only stray dogs he had brought home. Women were far more intriguing than puppies. Did she love him? She had never said so, but she had sworn to get rid of her other lovers. Could he trust her? He had not much to offer her except his body. He was only a mere student without wealth or ambition. He did not aspire to climb the social ladder like her friends and his relations. Look at her husband or his father.

Ben felt a twinge of guilt thinking of Buddy, but he quickly shifted back to Beverly and her husband. Dickie was a sweet man, although he spent all his time at his boring investments. Soon Ben would have money of his own . . . Buddy's death could be understood as a harbinger of things to come, too, good things, things that would benefit Ben.

"You will inherit a fortune," Beverly promised, "you're not poor, dummy, you're rich. So don't act poor." They had been in bed together, and he would never forget that afternoon of drama. Not in a lifetime . . .

"You could inherit a fortune, baby. You could have your money soon. . . ." She had whispered in his ear that she adored him, that she worshipped him. He was her best lover, the most ardent and successful. She told him she would leave her husband if he had the money to support her lifestyle . . .

"Think of the scandal, darling, how marvelous!" She had stared intensely, flashing her green cat-eyes and for an instant he felt he would go mad with desire. She *must* love him. At that instant he would have done anything for her, robbed the Chase Manhattan, sailed the ocean in a rowboat, blown up the Renaissance Center, anything. He felt like Hercules.

"We'll travel," she had said dramatically, "I've been to Europe twice but never with you. Oh God, Ben, take me, take me, darling."

Then she had her orgasms, a veritable pageant. This was an occasion in Ben's life—he had never slept with a woman who came the way Beverly did. She seemed to get everything out of it there was to get. She laughed, she cried, she screamed. The experience was amazing and wonderful and one that Ben wished to repeat as much as he was able . . .

He was trying to recapture that moment when he gradually became aware of a tapping noise on the window of his car. He felt an unwillingness to open his eyes. Not yet—his thoughts of Beverly had not been finished . . . It was Beverly who had informed him that his father had cut him out of his will. Jerry must have told her in one of their weekly gossip sessions.

When Ben first heard this news he was shocked, never dreaming his father would go so far as to disinherit him. And when Ben sought out Jerry and learned that his mother and father had dovetailing wills, effectively cutting him out altogether, he was in a state of panic. But he was not going to let this get in the way of his feelings for his parents. With all their problems and counter-viewpoints he still cared about them in his own way. While they were still alive he might even let them know he cared. Maybe. Still, whatever positive feeling he had towards them was never going to stand in his way of inheriting the money which was rightfully his as their son.

He tried to avoid thinking about the problem but Beverly constantly brought it up. She insisted she could no longer ignore his poverty now that he was in love with her. He was a prisoner of poverty, not able to move to a better apartment, not even able to leave the vicinity of Wayne State University. His car needed spark plugs, shock absorbers, a lube job. He could barely afford to drive to Crestwood Hills to borrow money. And then she would nudge at him about traveling. How about Europe? Didn't he realize what he was missing all these years? How about the Chateau country in the Loire, which he had never seen, only read about? Paris? There was also the Italian Riviera, the East African game reserves. She began to bring him travel folders to encourage his interest in obtaining money. The Gritti Palace at Easter. The Dalmatian Coast in August. The superb art collection at the Hermitage . . .

Beverly liked to go in style. She had plenty of money from her husband on a daily basis, she explained. Divorce was different. Women got "rehabilitation" money and that was all. Alimony was a thing of the past. She might be awarded the house and a small property settlement. Dickie

45

was glad to put their daughter through school—she would be nicely provided for, but not Beverly. She would be out in the cold with just her five fur coats to keep her warm. And Ben, of course.

Once the issue of money had been successfully raised, Beverly continued pushing it. She knew that the Schwartz fortune was in the neighborhood of fifty million, give or take ten million. This would make life splendidly comfortable. The Schwartz money could provide beautiful rooms with large beds, furs in excess of the five she already owned, jewels and endless holidays in foreign lands. The idea of being ensconced in her very own Swiss chalet in Gstaad, possibly next to Elizabeth Taylor and Audrey Hepburn, women of her own generation!

"I'd like to buy you a wardrobe in Rome," Beverly had mused one evening while they made love in a chair.

Ben had not liked the suggestion. He rather liked his old clothes. They were as much a part of him as his interest in animals. Nothing would get him rid of his jeans, and tattered pea jacket. When she had seen the frightened look on his face she had wisely amended her suggestion to a reference to *The Roman Spring of Mrs. Stone,* a novel about an older woman and a young man falling in love. This reference to literature had impressed Ben. Here he was having sex with a potential intellectual.

The disagreement about the clothes was their only one so far, mainly because Ben's wishes prevailed. He could be stubborn when he wished—he was not a Schwartz for nothing. The evening had ended with Beverly crying into the bedspread, apologizing for broaching the subject of his clothes . . .

A loud, incessant tapping on the window forced Ben to finally open his eyes. He looked up to find Beverly standing beside his car.

"Ben, open the damned door, what's the matter? I've been here ten minutes already."

46

Ben reached over and unlocked the door. He glanced at Beverly's carefully made-up face and tried to clear his eyes. He blinked several times to focus. She seemed to be wearing a light coat with a hood and sandals. She seemed shorter. She turned around. From the back it did not even look like her. Ben could not understand the clothes women at Crestwood Hills wore. Evidently, they thought their getups were attractive. The nails puzzled Ben the most. He would never get used to Beverly's carmine claws. . . .

"Beverly?"

"Come on, let's go inside. I've been banging on the car for ages. God, I'm starving."

"Hey, wait," Ben said, suspicious.

"What?"

She turned and looked him in the eyes.

"How do I know it's you?"

"It's me, silly, doesn't it look like me?"

"No, I don't think it's you."

Ben tried to get back into his car but she grabbed hold of his arm.

"It's me, honey, honest, look at me."

Ben stared at her then began to nod his head. Yes, it was Beverly, or a reasonable facsimile.

Beverly smiled, realizing he was stoned. She bent and whipped up her coat, revealing tanned, bare legs and a pair of white lace bikinis.

"Look familiar?"

Ben giggled and followed her into the restaurant.

The restaurant was the kind Ben hated. The place was filled to overflowing with younger singles, people of his generation and maybe a little bit older, the newly divorced. Most were aspiring business types who would probably envy anyone who belonged to a country club. It was a medium-priced restaurant known for its dim lights and atmosphere of genteel promiscuity. The entrance was crowded with people waiting for tables. The bar was overflowing with smokers and talkers and drinkers. Ben did not like the look of it but Beverly proceeded past everyone to the back of the restaurant.

"The table is in the last little nook," she said, smiling at him over her shoulder.

Beverly brought him to this particular restaurant because she was certain she would never see anyone she knew there. Her friends ate at the club or at home, and rarely ventured forth to local restaurants. She did not mind if she came across acquaintances. She regularly introduced Ben as her cousin from Toronto.

"Wanna fight?" Ben asked.

"Sure," Beverly said.

Ben trotted obediently after her and held her chair as she slid into it. He then lit her cigarette and sat down.

"I'm not hungry," he said, watching her look at the menu.

Beverly shrugged. He needn't eat as long as he could perform. She had been looking forward to his performance all day. The fact was that Ben had a chronic erection—there was nothing like a younger man for self-fulfillment. Far more interesting than Dickie, or any of the other older men. She should have discovered them sooner. And now that she had Ben, she had begun to wonder about much younger ones, the boys in their twenties, or even younger. Wouldn't it be amusing to have a nineteen-year-old, and why not? She knew she looked good.

She had gone to the hairdresser in the afternoon to have her hair lightened just a little. The two-part operation was tedious but necessary. She enjoyed talking to her hairdresser, a *fagola* from Mount Clemens from whom she learned all her politics. Usually Beverly took along her mail to open, a book to read and letters to write. She spent at least five hours being gone over. There were the legs to wax, the pedicure, the massage, the manicure, the makeup and the hair. Today was just a special two-hour trip for a

48

quick lightening of her fading streaks. She did not want to lose Ben to some grasping, hungry woman . . .

"How do you feel about the election?"

"Huh? Election? Or did you say erection?" Ben asked, picking at a piece of cold cauliflower from a plate of crudités which the waiter had set down in the middle of the table.

"Presidential *elections*," Beverly laughed.

Ben stared at Beverly's nose, which he adored. She looked like an older Tatum O'Neal.

"And are you going to take some political science courses next semester, Ben?"

"Yeah, good idea. Maybe I'll take some economics, too."

Beverly nodded.

"Good thinking," she said, "excellent, sweetie. You'll devastate them. Especially now that you're going to be a very wealthy man."

"I am?"

Ben gawked at her with love in his eyes. She had ordered monkfish and was slowly eating each forkful. What a wonderful, intelligent woman.

"Eat faster," he said, "I've an erection."

"Hard-on," she said, "Or are you into Emily Post?"

Ben laughed and took her hand, sliding it onto his thigh.

"I'd like to have you on the table," he said, "we could do it right here. We could do anything together, Bonnie and Clyde." He gazed into her cat-eyes.

"Let's go to the Jockey Club," she murmured.

"What's the Jockey Club? A racetrack?"

"Miami, darling, the two of us, Tristan and Isolde. The devil and the flesh."

"Yeah?"

Beverly removed her hand from his knee and continued to eat her fish. Each meal was figured out ahead of time for calories, vitamins and energy. She needed the fish. When she finished she would take two Naturades and three calcium-magnesium tablets. She ingested somewhere between thirty and forty vitamins daily and did it in a careful, organized way. Ten minutes after she ate she took bone meal and then vitamin C and a B–6.

Ben tried to focus. The restaurant was too warm. He felt as if he were slipping into a warm sleep with a warm woman.

"You're passing out, darling," Beverly warned and pinched his arm.

"Have some coffee," she said, "you'll feel better."

She pushed a cup at him and he raised it to his lips and drank purposely. He began to perspire. He felt hot, clammy. There was, obviously, no air conditioning. He felt himself shake. Beverly, who had not yet noticed his shaking, spooned crème caramel past her red lips and thought about the number of orgasms she was going to have soon after dinner was over.

"I've got to go," Ben said, suddenly standing up, scattering the silverware across the table and onto the floor.

"My God, what's wrong?" she asked, now aware that he was actually ill. The next moment he had fallen to the floor, joining the salt and pepper shakers and the empty coffee cup.

"Oh, oh," Beverly moaned, anxiously looking around the room for help, and saw that a young blond man was making his way quickly to her side. She prayed she did not know anyone in the room. No reason to draw attention to herself.

"I'm a doctor," the young man said, pushing her away. "Did he drink too much? Is there a history of heart disease here, or diabetes?"

"Drugs," she whispered, tears appearing in her eyes. Maybe the idiot had overdosed. How could she tell?

"We'll get an ambulance," the doctor said, taking over. He instructed the waiter whom to call, then began attempts at reviving Ben.

"Straight to Beaumont," he said.

"Beaumont, yes, fine," Beverly said, relieved he was helping her. She wondered if she could slip away unseen. "I hope he'll be okay," she mumbled.

"We'll see. I've got a good heartbeat. Yes, I think he'll be coming around. I don't believe it's a heart attack. Did he eat today? Yes, I think your son will be okay."

CHAPTER FOUR

Doc Matthews persuaded Dodie to meet him by the Crestwood Hills pool at nine-thirty, even though it might appear odd that she was out swimming the day of Buddy's funeral. Doc thought it seemed normal; he came to Crestwood Hills each morning for a swim before he went into his office. He didn't think anyone would really hold it against her. Buddy was her father-in-law, not her husband. And after all, Buddy had always wanted everyone to have a good time.

"I'll have an orange juice, please," Dodie said to the attendant. She was sitting on the edge of a deck chair waiting, wondering why Doc hadn't come to the house to speak to her. Well, she had plenty of time—the funeral wasn't until eleven. She had brought a black dress and pumps to the club and left them in her locker.

Hank thought it bad taste to go to the pool at the club. He screamed at her, "Why can't he use our pool?"

"He doesn't like our pool," Dodie answered sweetly. This was true and Hank could not debate the point. Although his father had spent lavishly on the pool, he had decided to make it only five feet deep, wanting to protect Dodie from drowning. It was not ideal.

Hank had watched without much interest as she got into her baby blue one-piece suit which showed off her firm body. All he wanted to know was which outfit she had selected for the funeral . . . Dodie had little choice. Her black silk dress with the décolleté front was all. She had thrown out all her depressing clothes recently and had begun to collect bright Yves St. Laurent numbers which made her feel happy. Hank was going to be surprised when he got the bills, if he actually got them. In the past they were paid automatically by the building firm's accountants. But why shouldn't she have gorgeous clothes like the other women at the club? They lived for their clothes. Marilyn Kanterman had several closets filled with clothes in a house she rented for that purpose—the house was furnished only with clothes. Marilyn's furs occupied the entire re-frigerated living room.

Dodie had already started buying her fall wardrobe. She had ordered some fancy numbers which she had seen at the club—a bright taffeta harem skirt with a spangly black sequined top. She had ordered two velvet dresses, one with a large white lace collar, the other without. Black velvet seemed to be in and she wanted as much as she could get. Then there was white velvet. A French designer coat for eight hundred dollars caught her fancy at Saks. The price seemed right. The coat was fitted, yet flared and bordered in red. All the new clothes were sophisticated and fit well. She thought she might look good in them . . .

The attendant walked into the clubhouse to get the or-ange juice and Dodie was alone by the pool. Not many people came here this early. Fastening back her thick black hair with an elastic, the image of Buddy falling at the first hole sprang into her mind. She wished the image would disappear but she couldn't get it out of her head. Last night she had dreamed about him and the feeling of being frightened remained. She had not yet thrown out the last batch of pornography, the literary legacy of the late Buddy Schwartz. She could not imagine why she was holding onto it, yet she felt a certain reluctance to get rid of it.

She looked up at the sky which was still bright although summer was clearly at an end. The weather could suddenly change, and then the bleak empty winter would soon follow. She did not like Michigan winters; the dull routine of the club and the same old restaurants with the same old people. So predictable. The tedious Sunday brunch at the club. Everyone seemed to love it but she—to Dodie each party, each dinner, was just like the one before it; only the table decorations were different.

She marvelled at the members' obsessions with parties, especially parties with a special motif. The Gershons had given a party in honor of their son's getting into Harvard. Everyone had to come dressed as a student. Cheap wine and cheese were served, and everyone had to leave by eleven. And this was a party given by a surgeon whose income was over four hundred thousand a year, not to mention his investments. His wife, a wealthy lady in her own right, wore a cable-stitched red sweater and corduroys although it was June. Then there were the Cohens, who had given an outdoor garden party fit for a sheik. They had pitched two giant tents under which were catered tables that almost sank into the ground with the opulent display of food. The tents were decorated like harems and beautiful girls served in exotic Middle Eastern costumes.

All the female members of Crestwood Hills were constantly planning the affair to outdazzle all affairs. Between their weddings, their bar mitzvahs, their lavish dinner parties, the women were busy. It was a way of life.

Dodie had never really felt like a member of Crestwood Hills. She had always been an outsider of sorts, a person who did not belong. She detested that which everyone else seemed to crave—the sameness, the unchanging routine.

No one seemed to notice her attitude, which made her feel even more the interloper.

Abruptly, she sat up. Had Po Lee, her Chinese maid, remembered that the trays for after the funeral were to be delivered at noon? She had better call her. But first a quick dip in the pool.

She dove in quickly, feeling the cold but refreshing water on her body. She swam a lap, then floated, letting her long hair drift slowly out of the elastic.

"Hi, there."

She looked up, expecting to see Doc, his bathing suit hanging around his belly, a pathetic look on his face. Instead she saw Dickie David smiling at her.

"Hi."

"I didn't expect to see you," he said, "but it's nice. You're so young. You *should* enjoy yourself."

"Thanks."

"How come you're not at home in your own pool?" he asked, sitting at the edge and dangling his feet in the water. He grinned at her and watched her side stroke. She was a good athlete. He had known about her golf prowess for a long time, as well as her excellent form on the tennis courts, and he could see now that she knew how to move her body through the water.

"It's too shallow," she called, as she swam down towards the other side of the pool. He was a nice man with pleasant eyes. She liked him for being pleasant on all occasions and for ignoring the fact that his wife, Beverly, slept with all his friends.

Glancing back at him she thought he was attractive for a man his age. He was tall, about six feet two, and with the undulating muscles of a swimmer. He was standing up, watching her.

"I may join you when I get the courage," he yelled.

She waved her hand and dove under the blue water.

For years Dickie had admired her. She was a lovely

young woman, the kind of person he would have wished his daughter to be. Instead, his daughter had an unpleasant way of expressing herself. She was liberated, she told him. She swore, she drank, she ran around when she wished. She lacked the feminine grace he loved in a woman. Dodie had a natural charm which seemed to elude most of the women he encountered . . . He saw Dodie was looking at him and, flushing, decided to dive in.

She at once thought there might be something unseemly about the two of them alone in the pool. Up until now she had regarded him only as a friend.

"Oh, no," she murmured to herself. Against her will she began to envision them in a more comfortable position . . . she was nude in the pool . . . she looked towards him . . . he was swimming to her in his old-fashioned swimming trunks which reminded her of her father. He was smiling . . .

This bizarre phenomenon of spontaneous fantasizing about sex had assailed her ever since Buddy had sent her those awful words and pictures. She had studied the bits of material carefully, and found that they were stimulating in a way that upset her, although there was nothing she could do about it. Her thoughts just came to her from the deep and there was no way of stopping them. It was like a hunger that could not be quieted. . . .

"Hey, Dodie," Doc Matthews called, his high-pitched voice invading her fantasy. He stood at the side of the pool dressed in his funeral suit.

Dodie glanced quickly at Dickie, who was still some distance away and floating, only gradually making his way towards her.

Doc nodded to Dickie and bent to talk to Dodie.

"I need to talk to you, dear, I think it's important. I've already talked to Hank. Can you come out now, dear?"

"Sure, Doc."

Dodie swam to the ladder and climbed out, shaking off

the water. She reached for her white terry cloth robe, suddenly feeling self-conscious. She noticed that Doc was gazing at her chest, and she felt inexplicably inhibited. Buddy's pornographic pictures and stories had not yet helped her overcome an anxious feeling when men viewed her body. She knew she was supposed to take pleasure in it, but in fact she felt painfully unattractive when a man looked at her with interest. By refusing to look at her, Hank had not helped matters. She had come to interpret her husband's apathy as a lack of sex appeal or beauty on her part.

"Should I dress, Doc? Or is it urgent?"

Doc perched on a chair and gazed down at the half-filled glass of orange juice which Dodie had been drinking earlier.

"I hope that dead fly floating in there isn't an omen," he said grimly. He took a deep breath, then cleared his throat. Dodie was his ace in the hole, and he was counting on her.

"Some folks have said I should have reported Buddy's death to the medical examiner . . . uh, coroner."

"The medical examiner? Whatever for?"

"The medical examiner investigates all deaths which aren't natural, or don't seem natural, like murder or suicide."

"Really? There's a television show like that, and the medical examiner is Jewish."

"Uh huh," Doc acknowledged, "and there's a medical examiner in Oakland County. Not far from here."

"I thought Buddy died of a heart attack," Dodie said.

"Uh huh."

"Then why report it to the medical examiner?"

"He had no known history of heart disease. Besides, I wasn't that positive. It *seemed* like a heart attack."

Dodie smiled gently, the dimples appearing on either side of her mouth. The members of the club did not want any scandal, but neither did they want any mystery. Many of them wanted to know more details about the death, such as what brought on the heart attack, and why was it so quick?

"People die of heart attacks every day who have had no previous history, right, Doc?"

"Oh, yes, certainly, but some members of the club insist that it's strange I didn't report it."

"A man dies of a heart attack," Dodie murmured, ". . . it happens every day."

"Hank doesn't want any scandal, Dodie. He already told me that. It might get into the papers."

"Yes, it would. All the papers. After all, Buddy Schwartz is, or was, one of the richest Jews in the Midwest."

"Yes," Doc agreed, hoping that Dodie would have this in mind when he asked her for money. He was working up to it, screwing up his courage in order to ask her for a large sum, one that would bail him out of his most pressing financial problems.

Unfortunately, he was not the type to come right out and ask for money. He felt ashamed and frightened to be in such an ignominious position. And he had only himself to blame . . . he couldn't really blame his ex-wife *all* the time for the fact that his friends, patients and relatives had dropped him . . .

Dodie flicked the fly out of the glass and emptied the remaining juice on the lawn. Why was Doc so concerned? He had already examined Buddy and indicated heart attack on the death certificate. Case closed. The medical examiner would only create a scandal that would besmirch the Jewish community and cast a gloom over life at the club. What in heaven's name was he considering? To go to the medical examiner's office meant to admit something was fishy. Why would he want to do that?

"Let sleeping dogs lie, Doc," she advised.

"How about the bee sting?" Doc asked nervously. "This could get around. People will want to know about this. Was he allergic to bees and that sort of thing. I only found a tiny mark and that was after looking a long time. Almost looked like a pin prick not a bee, so . . . ?"

Doc looked miserable. He did not like writing things on death certificates when he was not totally certain of the truth. Well, he was certainly not going to bring back to life Buddy Schwartz, to whom he owned money. Anyway, he had not really liked him in years. Buddy was a thieving fellow, whose claim to fame was his ill-gotten gains, like so many of the members of the club. . . .

"Of course, it's up to you," Dodie said hastily, rubbing her hair. It would take at least twenty minutes to blow-dry her hair unless she shook it dry in the sun, and then it would take an hour. Since Doc had arrived early, there was plenty of time. She could languidly dry it outside.

"Up to me?" Doc questioned, his sadness disappearing. He suddenly felt a great power come over him. Since Sheryl had left, this feeling had vanished. He had felt emas-culated when his two sons had taken his wife's side. Was he experiencing male menopause? His self-doubt, his loss of ego was perpetually on his mind. When he looked into a mirror he saw a wrinkled old man. But at this moment Dodie had suddenly restored some feeling of potency to him. Something was up to *him* to decide. He had the power to call in the medical examiner, or not . . .

"Is she speaking to me?" Dodie said, looking at the uni-formed figure of one of the club's maids who was standing at the clubhouse, shouting and waving her hands. She ran down the tiled walkway towards them.

"Emergency," she screamed at Dodie, "come fast here, missus."

"What's wrong?" Dickie called, scrambling out of the pool.

"Your husband, ma'am, he called. Get to your mother-in-law's house fast. There's an emergency, he sure was crying on the phone."

"Crying? I'll take you, Dodie," Dickie offered.

"I can manage," Dodie said anxiously. She moved swiftly towards the clubhouse.

"I'll meet you there," Doc called.

Dickie rode in Dodie's Cadillac Seville, while he tried not to see that she drove erratically, twice almost losing control of the car.

When they arrived at the Wabeek estates, Dodie noticed that Doc Matthews's car was blocking the driveway in just the same position it had been in last night. She felt disconnected, disorganized. Her hair was soaking. She had hurriedly thrown on her funeral dress.

Dickie gazed at her turned-up nose and thought she was beautiful.

The front door was open. There was a bustle of activity near the master bedroom.

"Back there," Dickie instructed.

Doc Matthews, his jacket off, his shirt sleeves rolled up, was administering to Rose, who lay on top of the covers, her arms at her side. Hank hovered at the side of the bed.

"Is she sick?" Dodie asked.

"Sick?" Doc answered. "She's *dead.*" He glanced up at Dodie. "Dead as a doornail," he said, turning to Dickie, whom he considered one of his closest friends. Dickie had been the one to recommend Jerry Fryman to him when one of Doc's patients died for no apparent reason. Jerry had the whole mess covered up with just an exchange of money. Doc would be forever grateful to Dickie for referring him to Jerry.

"Dead?" Dickie said in a shocked voice, watching Hank cry. He stared at Rose Schwartz's face. He had seen her only yesterday at the Pro-Am charity party. She was drinking a glass of champagne, standing close to Hank, her look-alike. They had the same brown eyes fringed with dark eyelashes, the same jutting jaw, the same full lips and, unfortunately, the same convex stomachs. Hank was not

60

much taller than his mother and, slouching next to her, appeared the same size. Dickie had observed that they were quieter than usual and attributed this to the fact they did badly on the golf course. It was not until later that he learned they were silently grieving over the loss of Buddy. To Dickie's mind, however, the family's treasure was Dodie . . .

"Dead?" Dickie repeated, as if he did not know what the word meant.

"Oh my, I *am* sorry, Hank," Dodie said. "My God, it must have been the death of Buddy. I've read about this sort of thing. They needed each other, I guess."

Doc grimaced.

"Yes, a heart attack," he murmured.

"What does that mean?" Hank spoke angrily, having not yet come to terms with the fact that his mother was gone. Couldn't Doc do anything? He felt an intense desire to grab him and shake him into doing something. Now Doc was sitting comfortably on the edge of the bed—he was used to death.

"They were in love," Doc confirmed.

"Mom didn't die from love," Hank whined, his fighting spirit having suddenly dissipated. He really felt like going to his old room and crawling into bed, pulling the covers over his face—a couple of hours sleep might make him see everything differently. He tried to avoid looking at his mother's limp form. Her body seemed dead, but not her face. The face bore the same vexed expression he had seen last night. The remains of her makeup, which she had not removed, were still there. He half expected her to suddenly wake up and start haranguing him.

"The rabbi said he was going to make a claim against my dad's estate, maybe that's what killed her," he said.

"Shhh," Dodie said in an attempt to quiet him. "What kind of claim, dear?"

"The building fund, that's what kind of claim. Dad promised the temple a hundred thousand for the building fund."

"Get in touch with your lawyer," Dickie said helpfully, backing out of the room. Death made him ill, he wasn't used to it. That was no longer Rose Schwartz on top of the bed. There was just a corpse. He thought he might throw up.

"I'll put heart attack on the death certificate. Looks like a heart attack to me. Better call Kaufman's to postpone the funeral," Doc said.

"Postpone?" Dodie said, thinking of the funeral trays that were going to be delivered to her house at noon. She must telephone Po Lee, who was probably wondering what to do next.

"Twin burials," Doc said. He had an eye for expense. Everything reminded him that his debts were killing him.

"I think it's peculiar that Mom and Dad died this way . . . so close together . . ." Hank said, his eyes brimming with tears. "I think we should report this," he said.

"I can assure you this is a natural death," Doc hastened to say. "She apparently died in her sleep, not a bad way to go. After all, she was in her sixties . . ."

"Maybe you're right," Hank said, backing down, "we don't want any scandal at the . . . the . . ."

"Club," Dodie said firmly.

Hank nodded, a fleeting image of the other members coming to mind. The blond heads of the women, the bald ones of the men, the younger members, some of whom were years younger than himself, flashed before him. They always seemed to be fresh out of the bath and the hairdresser's and the department stores. Hank loved this about the other members of the club. They were extremely careful about the way they dressed and presented themselves to the outside world, even if the outside world meant only the hundred other members they had known all the days of their lives. The members of the club looked as if they had just stepped out of fashion magazines, and he was proud of them. They were people who had arrived . . .

Now he could see them all clearly, the image stronger. But what was wrong? And the thought sprang to his mind: Hank Schwartz had sullied Crestwood Hills—he knew this was what they must be thinking. His family had brought disaster to the club. There would be a blemish on the temple and on Jews in general. The world would scream "Unnatural." Had his parents been murdered? . . .

"Nothing terrible could happen to them," he blurted out, overwhelmed with a feeling of guilt, "they were too . . . ah . . . too . . ."

"Rich," Dodie said.

"I wasn't going to say that," Hank muttered, wiping at his tears, "I was going to say nice, or good or something like that."

"Sorry," Dodie said, gazing compassionately at him. She had never seen him in quite this mood of contrition. She had seen him during his tantrums, and she was used to those lashings and vile comments. This, however, was a new Hank.

"Words do not cook rice," she said, thinking aloud about Po Lee and the funeral trays.

"What?" Hank asked, looking confused.

"I mean action speaks, doesn't it?" Dodie said, "I'll call the funeral home. I think we must settle all this." She touched Hank's shoulder. "We'll go now. You'll want to say goodbye to your mother alone. We understand."

Dodie looked at Doc for affirmation. He was staring at Rose's hand and was not listening.

"Doc," Dodie said louder, "we're going now. You and me, okay?"

"Oh, okay, if you say so," Doc said, rising from the bed. He straightened the handkerchief in his breast pocket and took a last look at Rose Schwartz.

Dodie grasped Rose's cold hand in her own. "We've already said our goodbyes, Rose," she said quietly and let the hand drop back to the bed.

Hank watched them leave, horrified they had left him alone with his mother again. You couldn't pay him to touch her. He stared at her for a moment, allowing the guilt to sweep over him.

Nothing had been resolved.

CHAPTER FIVE

When Ben woke up in a bed in Beaumont Hospital's emergency room, he was confused. Had he had a heart attack, too? He had not yet been informed that his mother, Rose Schwartz, was lying next to his father at the funeral home. As he would be unable to get out of bed for several hours, it made no difference. The funeral, he decided, would have to proceed without him.

Eventually a nurse came to look at him, a schoolmarmish look of disapproval on her youthful face.

"You've been here all night," she said. "We've no beds for the likes of you. The doctor said you can go home soon. This afternoon, maybe. Meantime, buster, you just lie here. Your mother's going to visit. That's what she said."

Ben touched his head, wondering where the headache began and where it ended. His head throbbed horribly. "Give me some aspirin," he begged.

"I think you've had enough of those kinds of things," the nurse said, pulling the drapes across his side of the room. He closed his eyes, trying to remember what happened. He and Beverly had been eating dinner somewhere. He couldn't remember any more. He fell back to sleep and began to dream . . . He was in his parents' home, and they were arguing. Buddy was ranting and raving, his usual performance. Rose was standing in her pink bathrobe, waving dollar bills around. When he looked closely, they turned out to be thousand-dollar bills. He made a grab for them, but his father made a grab at the same time and they ended up fighting on the floor, when Beverly ran into the room to separate them. . . .

He awoke, feeling cold, miserable and alone. Slowly, he got out of bed, testing each leg until he was certain it would stand firmly. He was getting out of here—this wasn't jail and they had no right to keep him.

He looked around for his clothes. The hospital gown, wide open at the back, would not do. He quickly found his clothes in the locker and began to get dressed when the nurse entered.

"Oh no, you can't go," she said firmly, "the doctor didn't say so."

Ben pulled on his jeans, zipped them up and fished around for his wallet.

"My wallet, baby, where is it?"

He flashed his best Schwartz grin. Reluctantly, she left the room and he followed her out to the nurses' station. She handed him the wallet.

"I better get a resident. No one's here just now. They'll be back real soon. Can't you wait a little? I'll catch hell."

" 'Bye, babe, thanks," Ben said, walking out the door to the stairway.

He would either have to call a cab, or get someone to pick him up. Maybe Beverly? She was the one who got him in here. She ought to be waiting at the entrance for him with a chauffeured limo. He found some change and called her from a phone booth. No answer. He called Jerry, but his answering machine was all that greeted Ben. In disgust he called his brother's house. Po Lee answered.

"They at funeral," she said, "you don't know?"

"Oh, of course, my dad. I ought to be there, too."

"Your dad, yes, and your mom."

"Oh, okay, Po Lee."

"You don't know news, you bad boy."

"I never understand you, Po Lee, learn English."

Po Lee began to cry into the receiver. "Your mother at funeral, too," she wept.

"Bright, real bright," Ben muttered, and hung up.

He supposed he ought to find a taxi and go directly to the funeral, only there were no taxis around and he detested funerals. They were so embarrassing, so phony. He *did* have the excuse of being in the hospital, although he could not reveal how he got there. Neither could Beverly. Their plans had to mesh carefully, no backlash, no repercussions. He was the heir to the throne, as Beverly had so often said, and there weren't many ahead of him. Why ruin his ascension?

He decided to run over to Thirteen Mile Road and hitch to Woodward. From there it was not far to the Fox and Hounds restaurant. It took him two rides, a proposition from an older man with graying hair, and a garrulous student. His car was exactly where he had left it, the sun beaming down on it. He got in, cranked down the window to let in a breeze, revved the motor. The gas tank was at empty, as usual. He bought some gas at the nearest station, then made a decision to drive immediately to the funeral home regardless of what he looked like. He knew his clothes were crumpled and dirty and that he needed a shave, but he knew it would be better to put in an appearance. Some time in the future, and probably not very far away, he might need someone who had seen him there. A dutiful son, a loving boy . . .

He passed a Big Boy and realized he was hungry. Nothing equalled a nice fat, juicy hamburger when you were really starving. Unfortunately, there was no time. He

67

would have to wait for the hot knishes and the meatballs served after the funeral service. He reached into the glove compartment to give himself a treat. He took out the old roach and swallowed it. If he had to go hungry he might as well be high . . .

To his surprise the parking lot was full. He had assumed he would arrive just as the funeral was ending. He parked and proceeded to the side entrance, hoping he could make a discreet entrance, but still manage to have people notice his presence.

Walking down the hall he saw a group of people at the end of it. When he got there he saw they were the overflow from a room in which sat a large coffin. He entered the room, squeezing between two fat ladies, to make sure he was going to be properly seen. There did not seem to be any seats in the room.

After a few minutes a man got up and left the room. No one moved towards his seat. Ben sidled into it, now congratulating himself on his appearance. His parents' friends were more or less used to the way he dressed, and perhaps on this occasion would not hold it against him as they had done in the past. He could recall several occasions when he was asked to leave Crestwood Hills because of his sloppy appearance. On the last two occasions it was Buddy himself who had evicted him, claiming that his presence was a blight on the club . . .

"This is a *shande*, a *shande*," Buddy had yelled unceremoniously. Then he had taken him by the elbow of his torn sweater and escorted him to an exit.

"Don't ask the Oriental kid for your car, get it yourself." He had deposited him out on the grass and without looking back had slammed the door in his face. Ben had sat there five minutes, laughing and shouting and generally carrying on. Eventually, the laughter ceased and he went to look for his car in the large parking lot, where it was by far the oldest vehicle. Virtually every car in the lot was new, ex-

68

pensive and large, all of which, in his own manner of re-verse snobbery, Ben disapproved.

Since he had sat down at the funeral, Ben kept his eyes lowered out of respect and because he was feeling ex-tremely stoned on his empty stomach. Now he lifted his eyes and began to look around. Next to him sat an unfamil-iar woman who had red hair and wore a feathered hat. On her right hand was a large emerald. Her husband was cry-ing into his necktie. Ben looked further down the row. He didn't know anyone in this row, but that was not odd because there were many members of Crestwood Hills whom he had never met, and even if he had, would have promptly forgotten. They were not his style. He had never seen any one of them in rotten old jeans.

He sighed. A couple of children in front of him got up and wandered out of the room, their mothers following. He watched them go. He didn't know them, either. He looked up to the front of the room. At the podium an unfamiliar man was saying something about the deceased.

And then he realized. He quickly left his seat.

Ben was too stoned to feel embarrassed. He had walked into the wrong room at Kaufman's; some other funeral was taking place, no doubt simultaneously. He made a brief investigation down the hallway and saw that no one he knew from Crestwood Hills seemed to be anywhere.

Back in his Volkswagen he decided he would drive to Hank's house where surely everyone was stuffing their faces with the best kosher knishes that money could buy.

Po Lee greeted him at the door. "You hang up before I say they all here."

"That's okay. I was sick. Tell everyone who asks I was sick, Po Lee."

"Okay."

Po Lee, dressed in a light green maid's uniform with matching cap which made her look exactly like a nurse in a psychiatric ward, politely backed away. She did not like

Master Ben. Once he had asked her to buy some drugs for him. He had assumed that because she was Chinese she would have access to opium. Her pride was insulted and she had never trusted him since.

The Schwartzes' living room was filled to capacity. Ben looked around for Beverly. He was dying to know what exactly happened last night.

"Oh Ben, for Christ's sake," Jerry Fryman said, grabbing his arm, "where have you been?"

"At Beaumont, sick as a dog."

"You weren't at the funeral. You know, of course?"

"Know what?" Ben asked, scanning the room for his consort.

"Couldn't you have worn a suit? That looks terrible. You were wearing that last night—"

"They don't give out suits at Beaumont Hospital. Sorry, Jer."

"But you know?"

"Know what? Have you gone bonkers? Know what?"

"Your mother is dead," Jerry said in a flat voice, his usual semi-theatrical tone gone. He searched Ben's face for a suitable reaction.

"She's been like that a long time, so what else is new?"

He strode quickly away from Jerry, who had tried to hold onto his arm to speak more. Ben's stomach would not allow further conversation. He had to fill it, or die himself.

Beverly, wearing a chic black pants outfit, accosted him before he could get even a tiny hot dog into his open mouth.

"What are you doing?" Her eyes penetrated his as if he were doing something wrong. But what? He was confused. Would she deny him nourishment?

"You collapsed last night," she said, bending toward him in a conspiratorial manner. He glanced around him to see if anyone was watching him.

"It's those drugs you take, honey, you mustn't. You'll get us into trouble. Why weren't you at the funeral?"

"I was," Ben said, popping the tiny hot dog into his mouth and thanking God he was not such a health nut as Beverly.

"You ought to be careful, Ben. Understand?"

"I'm perfectly all right, it's all the others."

"Damnit, Ben, that doctor knew you. He said he went to Cranbrook with you. Doctor Levine?"

Beverly pouted in spite of herself. She had gone out on a limb for Ben and he didn't seem to notice. Or care.

"What doctor?" he asked blithely, reaching across her for a hot meatball. "I don't remember him," Ben said munching. He spotted Hank making his way toward him, an anxious look on his face. Ben hated confrontations with his brother. Hank always lost his cool and shouted. Ben did not want to hurt his feelings, which was so easily done with Hank. He won every fight with his brother without even trying.

Hank now stood in front of him, his cheeks pink, his eyes teary.

"I should have saved her. I might have prevented the whole thing. It's my fault. I failed her . . ."

"I'm sorry," Ben said.

"You don't know what I'm talking about, do you? You're too stoned."

"Dodie? She left you?" Ben said.

"Mom's *dead*. We just buried her," Hank said, tears welling up in his eyes. "She died last night."

Ben stared at him in disbelief and for a moment was unable to focus on the reality before him. And then, tears streaming down his cheeks, he hugged his brother to him as they both cried tears of fear and guilt and sorrow.

CHAPTER SIX

Tim Levine, the medical examiner, sat at his desk reading the pathology report from his colleague, Doctor Mills. What had caught his eye was the line:

Due to the unexpected deaths of the senior Schwartzes within a short space of time, Doctor Matthews, their family physician, has asked that a postmortem be performed to rule out foul play. The deputy medical examiner, Doctor Fenton, did not think there was evidence to support a postmortem but Doctor Matthews insisted. The body has been moved to the morgue.

Tim put down the report and stared out the window at the parking lot. Little activity took place down there. He might as well be facing a brick wall. Why couldn't an attractive woman, or two or three, walk past? He suddenly thought that he had not gone out with anyone in a couple of months. Between his job as a medical examiner of Oakland County and his private practice in internal medicine he was too busy, too exhausted and possibly too depressed to hunt for women. His friends constantly begged him to let them introduce him—even his sisters and brothers were lining up lists of ladies. But he wasn't really interested . . .

Every woman reminded him of Patti in one way or another, and he compared every woman to her unfavorably. She was lovely, tall, graceful, with a fine way of expressing herself even when she was angry at him, which was frequent. She had an Irish face and a temper to match. Tim had never seen such an interesting face as Patti's. Her eyes were hazel, large and round with dark lashes. Her nose was just a little bit crooked, but small and sprinkled with tiny freckles. Although in the summer her pale skin burned and her freckles multiplied, she was still charming. The contrast between her ivory skin and her ebony hair was devastating.

Tim Levine's parents, though, were not too happy with her religion. A lapsed Catholic, she had no intention of converting to Judaism or anything else. Tim respected her ideas and loved her. The only problem was she had not loved him enough to remain in Michigan.

The shock he had felt at her departure eventually turned to numbness and then to a terrible feeling of betrayal. He wondered if he would see her again. Since she vanished he had lost interest in the opposite sex, as if every woman would do the same rotten thing to him. Patti had left him for a woman's movement, and he heard she was living on a commune in California with a group of professional women. She had opted for independence, leaving him bewildered, stranded.

He no longer had a tennis partner. He did not like golf anymore, nor the winter sports they had once shared. He had taken to going to movies and, finally, he knew that what he needed was a murder to cheer him up. He was happiest when he was invovled with postmortems and could determine the actual causes of death, when he could

73

say what the murder weapon was or the modus operandi. With Patti's help he had solved six murders in Oakland County since he took the job as medical examiner. His parents were not thrilled with his choice of career; still they had to admit he was using his medical knowledge, and although not solely in private practice, it could have been worse. Tim could have been a cop.

If his parents had not pushed him into medical school, goaded him into accepting a scholarship, he would have been with the Crestwood Hills Police, certainly one of the best police units in the Midwest. Compared to the other adjacent police forces such as Birmingham and Bloomfield Hills, the Crestwood guys were by far the best. He adored and worshipped them, having idolized them since he was a child, when they had solved the case of the disappearing twins.

Actually, Tim felt more a slave to his part-time medical practice than to anything else. He saw as few patients as possible, only enough to maintain his relationship with the other doctors with whom he shared offices. Often he assigned his own patients to the other doctors, who never seemed to object.

Glancing again at the report he wondered why Doctor Mills did not write down the age of the deceased parents. He disliked such vague expressions as "short space of time." Meaningless doctor gibberish. Tim had always respected Patti's precise way of expressing herself. She had chosen the right profession, although she would have made a damned good medical examiner. At Princeton she had debated. At the University of Michigan Law School she had achieved law review, while taking special courses in criminology and forensic medicine. He really missed her and their shared interests. Was he ever going to find another woman as exciting?

74

Chapter Seven

The death of Rose Schwartz obliterated any need to question Buddy's untimely departure, one justifying the other in the minds of the members of Crestwood Hills. They could talk of nothing else. It was almost as if an Egyptian monarch had passed into the nether world bringing his slaves, his household goods *and* his wife with him. It gave Nettie Rosen the idea of having a fantastic, posh Egyptian Rosh Hashanah party in her home in Palm Springs, ferrying the guests by chartered plane for the weekend.

Henry and Dodie declined the invitation as did the close friends of the Schwartz family.

Doc liked to say that the shock of Buddy's death was just too much for his unfortunate wife. She did not want to live without him.

When the will was read and it was found that Buddy had cut out Ben Schwartz and left the fifty thousand to Dodie, tongues loosened even further. No one expected Buddy to leave a penny to Dodie but they all had to agree that he did seem to like Dodie. Didn't he build her a swimming pool so shallow she *couldn't* drown?

Everyone had known he would cut out the *shnook* Ben, because soon after he made that particular will the word leaked from Jerry Fryman's office, who had a way of letting things get out when they weren't supposed to.

Hank had been left a fortune, though how much had not yet been determined. He had debated whether to hire other lawyers, but had decided to let Jerry work off some of the debt to the Schwartz estate by retaining him. Ben had done nothing thus far to contest the will, and Hank, for whatever reasons, did not seem worried.

Eventually, the intense fuss, the talk and gossiping over the elder Schwartzes' deaths died down. Warm September gave way to cool October and autumn and the fur coats emerged. Dodie wondered if she and Hank ought to move into the Schwartzes' Wabeek home. It seemed not a bad idea, but Hank said he preferred his own bed. Dodie did not quite understand; nevertheless, she agreed to remain in the mock-Tudor . . .

Hank entrenched himself in the company business, and soon admitted he needed Dodie's help. She was excellent at math and was very organized. He brought her right into the office, sat her in front of his double-ledger bookkeeping accounts and set her to work. Every day including weekends, she went to the office. Po Lee ran the house. There was no time for domesticity, so they took their meals at the club whenever possible. The books were in an appalling mess and needed her constant attention.

One Sunday Dodie examined her nude body in the mirrored closet in the master bedroom. She no longer felt unattractive. She gazed wistfully at her reflection. Was she pretty? She was not certain. Maybe her hips had got too thin? Constant work had caused her to lose some weight. At five feet six and one-half inches she appeared fragile. She scrutinized herself. Did her breasts seem too large now?

She decided she would not really know herself until she fell in love and had an affair. And with this new knowledge she wore her beautiful designer clothes to the office, although no one but Hank was there to see her.

Dodie was bored and she felt sorry for herself. Life seemed to be passing her by as in a very slow dream. She had no close friends—the women at the club did not like her. They made her aware of her background, so seemingly different from their own. They asked her where she had gone to school and what her father had done. She felt like a pariah. They were the women who as girls had expensive cars in high school, stereo sets at ten. They summered at lovely camps in Canada, or in the upper peninsula, and went to Europe with their parents. Dodie had enjoyed none of this, growing up instead in a tiny house with no money for such luxuries.

She had no male friends, certainly no lover. It was a shame because now she had a little money of her own and felt somewhat independent. In fact, she would not know how to go about getting a lover . . . This was on her mind this Sunday as she dressed for the autumnal day. But what to wear? She looked through her closet, examining the clothes she had put into plastic bags. Eventually, she decided on gold velvet pants with a matching silk blouse, red lizard boots that attempted to look western, and a red belt with silver and gold studs on it. She slipped the belt through the loops of her pants and looked at herself in the mirror. The red was really closer to a burgundy, she decided, selecting her wine-colored coat to throw over her shoulders. She was in a definite clothes mood. Whenever she felt the urge to spend money she instantly wished to spend it on beautiful clothes. Beautiful clothes made her feel luxuriant. And what was wrong with that? She could afford anything she wanted.

The Somerset Mall was open on Sundays and she decided she would shop at Bonwit's and Saks and have a peek at Claire Perrone's boutique, perhaps even drop into the fur store across from it. She knew she wanted to buy some cashmere sweaters and try on some jackets at Roberts Furs. Why not? She had paid her dues . . . She felt unexpectedly good. Today would be a day she rewarded herself. No work. She was going to refuse to go to the office, no matter what noises Hank made.

Brushing her long hair vigorously and pinning it up into a bun with a large gold clip, she thought how delightful it would be if she were meeting some charming man for tea. She slipped her recently-acquired diamond stud earrings into her earlobes and smiled hesitantly at herself. She did not look bad at all.

"Where you going?" Hank demanded, peering into the bathroom. He stood in the doorway wearing his blue terry cloth robe, the one that had belonged to his father.

"Shopping," she said gently, hoping to avoid any unpleasantness.

"Spending more money, huh? Can't get enough, now that my dad left you a little money."

"That's in a money-market certificate, dear," she said calmly.

"So now you're out there charging up a storm."

"You'll inherit a lot of money. You can afford it." Dodie patted her hair in place, avoiding his eyes in the mirror. She felt more courageous recently in dealing with him, resisting his need to dominate and control her.

"Jerry's coming here to talk about the money we lent him. I'd like you here," Hank said petulantly.

"What time?"

"Soon."

"I won't be gone all day," Dodie said. He needn't worry, she thought. Jerry would be seeing her soon, but on her own business.

"Shop another day," he suggested.

"No, today is my day; tell Jerry to come over later to-night."

"Doc said he was coming over later."

"When?" she asked.

"Tonight."

"Good, tell him to stay to dinner."

"We're going to the club for dinner. It's special, a sort of Chinese party for one of the members."

Hank flounced out of the bathroom. Lately, he thought, she was too assertive, and he didn't like that. She needed to be put in her place. On the other hand, despite his squawking, she ought to be allowed to shop and spend—she was the wife of a rich man and in the eyes of others her expensive clothes made *him* look good.

He went into the kitchen and felt a surge of pride. His kitchen was a showcase. People gasped when they saw it. Instead of the usual table there was a counter where everyone sat. The kitchen had cost ninety thousand dollars five years before and was the only one like it in the Midwest. It had been specially done by a famous architect. None of the other members could boast of anything remotely resembling Hank's kitchen. The kitchen was Hank's very own "thing." Each member of the club had his own "thing." Marvin King had a custom-built Porsche which cost fifty grand. In the winter Esther Winer wore only ermine underwear made in Paris. Minnie Blau had three hundred and fifty-eight pairs of handmade shoes and Sam Schostein had two mink-lined raincoats and thirty-five Borsalino hats from Italy.

Indulgence was acceptable and self-indulgence the rule. Hank had his kitchen and no one could take it away from him.

"I forgot to tell you," he yelled, "the rabbi is coming over tonight to talk to us about the building fund."

He did not listen for her reply. Peering into the refriger-

79

ator he found some salami and brought it out.

"What's that stuff on the top shelf?" he yelled again.

"My face creams," Dodie said quietly, causing him to jump. She was standing behind him dressed in a new wine-colored coat he had not seen before.

"They have to be refrigerated, don't touch them." she said, "They're hormones."

"I didn't know you took hormones," Hank mumbled irritably. "Don't worry, I won't eat them."

He turned towards her but she had already gone. He could hear the sound of his father's Rolls as she pulled out of the garage.

Chapter Eight

"I'll take two packs of those stickers," Tim Levine said, pointing to the "Hello Kitty" packets which he was buying for his niece Nicole, a seven-year-old blond terror who looked like him. Being the only child in the entire Levine family made her more important. She had two aunts and two uncles who were continuously thinking up delightful surprises for her. Tim had recently discovered she collected stickers.

He paid the saleslady, then left the Crown House of Gifts, Nicole's favorite shop, and wandered into the center of the mall, where the piped-in music of Henry Mancini could be heard. In the dead of winter a band concert took place in the mall in the Fountain Café, but now it was too early in the season. Every Christmas since Nicole was born he had taken her to the mall to see the decorations. What difference did it make, their being Jewish? Christmas was for everyone.

He glanced at the tables in the Fountain Café. Was he hungry? What he really wanted was ice cream and that place was further on. He had plenty of time to ramble around the mall window-shopping with his ice cream, or maybe he would window-shop and then sit down with a banana split. He could not decide.

He walked along towards Bonwit's, looking at the passing parade of pretty women, well-dressed and well-groomed. They *were* pretty, yet his thoughts constantly reverted back to Patti, the deserter. She could not really commit herself to a man, and he felt sad about it. When was he going to get over her? He needed a therapist, but had no time to go searching for one. He had gone so far as to look up Doctor Goldman's phone number but had never made the call for the appointment.

He stopped at the Claire Perrone boutique and looked in at the gorgeous, glittering clothes. Patti never shopped in such a place. She liked simple plaid skirts and ribbed sweaters. In the summer she wore shorts. She dressed like a student, underplaying her sexuality—a perennial Princeton girl. At thirty-one she still wore knee socks.

He glanced over at Bonwit's. Should he go in? He might have a look at their kilts, but he knew this would make him feel worse. He needed nothing himself, having plenty of clothes for the life he led. If he belonged to a club, a country club, for example, he would need other things but that was hardly likely, not with the money he earned.

Maybe he should visit the children's department? He might find a little kilt for his niece. Children looked adorable in kilts. He started towards Bonwit's when something caught his eye. He stopped, froze. Opposite, on the other side of the mall was a fur shop. Inside was a graceful-looking woman, her dark hair adorned with a gold clip. For a moment he thought she was Patti. What a fool—Patti was in California. She hated furs anyway.

Nevertheless, he found himself walking across the mall to take another look. Miracles did happen. Maybe she had come to Michigan and had followed him into the mall and this was her crazy way of attracting his attention . . .

82

He peered through the window for a closer look. The woman's back was to him. She was trying on a short white fur jacket. He moved so he could get a better look. No. He felt disappointed. Not Patti, but someone pretty with dark hair like Patti's. But there were no freckles, no white skin. No, she was really nothing like Patti. But, wait, even if she wasn't Patti, she did have olive skin and lovely, curious dark eyes, with a nose that turned up in a patrician arc. He stared hungrily at her through the glass. She had a terrific figure.

Despite his shyness he opened the door and walked in. A tall man sat watching tennis on a television set. The salesman waiting on the girl turned to greet him.

"Are you together?" the man smiled.

Tim felt ridiculous. He shook his head.

"No," the woman said.

"What can I do for you, sir?" the man asked.

Tim shrugged, not knowing how to extricate himself. He glanced at the dark-haired woman. She was smiling, showing a dimple. He *had* to meet her.

He leaned forward and whispered into the man's ear.

"I'm actually with her," he said, "it's just a little joke. I'd like to see a nice . . . mink."

"We only have nice minks," the man said, turning and winking. He went to a rack and took a fur coat off a hanger.

"This color would be excellent with her coloring" the man said, smiling.

Tim heard the woman ask if the white jacket looked good. Stepping over to the long mirror where she was looking at herself doubtfully he said, "Beautiful, it's beautiful. You should have it."

He had the urge to whip out his checkbook and buy it for her, only he probably did not have that kind of money in his checking account and would make an ass of himself.

Dodie glanced up, startled. There stood a handsome blond man with what appeared to be curious violet eyes.

83

He was about her age, maybe a few years older.

"Yes, you think?" She fixed her childlike gaze upon him.

"Definitely your style, you should work here as a model."

Dodie flushed with pleasure. He was looking at her as if she were the most attractive woman in the world. Together they stood there, their eyes locked.

"I think *you* should work here," the furrier said amiably.

Dodie fumbled for her checkbook and without thinking wrote out a check for five thousand dollars.

"I believe you know the family," she said, "I forgot my driver's license. Wait, I have some credit cards. Are they all right?"

"Certainly," the man said, taking them and disappearing into the back of the shop.

"Would you care for . . . an ice cream?" Tim asked nervously.

"I would," Dodie nodded, "but I've got to go now. It's been nice to meet you, really . . . ah . . . lovely." Dodie stared at him. She felt an urge to reach out and stroke a strand of his blond hair. He reminded her of her high school heartthrob, Sydney Bergman, who was of Dutch descent. He was the high school athlete, the boy every girl wanted to date and few actually did. He was devoted to his studies, his music, his athletic activities which were many and varied. She had daydreamed about him all through school, imagining herself as his girl, his lover, his wife. Unfortunately, he had not bothered to look her way. Later, she learned he had become a doctor, married an artist, and was living in California in a house he had designed himself.

She suddenly felt embarrassed. She did not know this man, after all. She blinked and for a moment imagined him kissing her in the fur vault. She could feel his firm, strong body pressing against hers, pressing her into a long sable coat. . . .

When her credit cards were returned with the box containing the mink jacket, she smiled coyly at Tim and departed. She liked him, but today her mission was private. She needed the afternoon for herself.

Tim looked downcast after she left.

"I thought you were together," the furrier said, a twinkle in his eye, "thought you were playing a little game. You're sure that's not someone you know?"

"We were just pretending," Tim said, feeling foolish.

"I think she went to Bonwit's, go after her," the man suggested, looking toward the other man. "Right, Bobby? Didn't she say she was going to Bonwit's?"

Tim shut the door behind him. Instead of pursuing the lovely woman he would have an ice cream. She probably thought he was impertinent anyway. Maybe he was. He had sounded absurd.

He walked toward the ice cream parlor, thinking he was an idiot. She was probably married. What he desperately needed, he thought to himself, was a good murder case to solve.

CHAPTER NINE

At four o'clock Dodie felt it was time to drive over to Crestwood Hills for tea. Her five-thousand-dollar jacket and the cashmeres she had carefully selected at Bonwit's were in the back of Buddy's Rolls. Now she would have to phone the bank in the morning and tell them to cover her check, somehow. She did not have the funds in her account yet, but as Hank Schwartz's wife she would be extended credit. She need not tell Hank.

She thought it amusing how she drifted by Roberts Furs and saw that adorable jacket in the window, and just the perfect size for her. She couldn't wait to show Beverly David and see the look of envy on her face. Beverly, with all her sophisticated manners, sardonic humor and attempts at being a wit, was no different from all the other women at the club. She bragged about what Dickie gave her, flashed it around. Everyone knew Dickie was generous because Beverly told them so.

Dodie sighed. Hank had been far too busy lending money at usurious rates to bother with his own wife. In going over his books she had discovered it was not only

Jerry who had borrowed. Doc Matthews was in for one hundred thousand at an exorbitant interest rate. He still owed most of it . . .

Dodie gave the massive Rolls to the parking attendant and hurried inside to see who was there. She checked her coat but kept the box containing the new jacket and wandered around the various rooms until she decided Beverly must be the card room. It gave Dodie pleasure to know that Beverly, whom Hank had bedded probably dozens of times, now knew that Dodie knew. Dodie had made a point of letting Beverly know she didn't give a damn. Furthermore, Dodie had made a point of telling Beverly that she, Dodie, was driving Buddy's Rolls, the priceless car that Beverly had constantly admired out loud at all the Crestwood functions, as if she hoped Buddy would give it to her.

Dodie had been aware of Hank's girls for a long time, thanks to Rose, and although she had been jealous at first, she soon resolved the problem by becoming more involved in her own fantasy life, thus cutting out the cold reality of her loveless marriage.

Beverly was indeed in the card room, sprawled over a chair, a cigarette dangling from her coral-red lips.

"I'm knocking," she said, letting the ash fall across the table. Everyone hooted with laughter except for Mignon Teedberg who never laughed at anything unless it was a joke she had just told.

"Hello, girls," Dodie said, putting down her package.

They glanced up and nodded.

"Well, hello," Beverly said, a snide tone in her voice. "What have we here?"

For a moment Dodie felt like running out. She always felt intimidated by Beverly and she had not come here to let herself be put down. Was showing the coat worth it? She glanced at her Cartier tank watch. Too early to go home.

Forever inquisitive, Mignon eyed the package.

"What's that?" she said, pointing to the box. She was a

recent member of the club, having been a schoolteacher until she met Herb Teedberg, a retired millionaire. They talked baby talk to each other and Mignon, who was much younger, bragged about the excellence of their sex life. She made the other members uncomfortable with her graphic details. No one really liked her center-stage performances, but she was tolerated because of Herb and because of their respect for Laura, his first wife who had died. Mignon liked to announce that Laura's funeral was so popular they held it over a second night. She told this joke frequently.

"I've got a darling mink jacket," Dodie said, unwrapping the box to show off her purchase.

"Nice, cute," Beverly said in a condescending voice, looking sideways at Dodie. She was pretty, but there was a screw loose somewhere. She was so vague and uncertain when she spoke. Since her in-laws popped off she was beginning to look anorectic. Hank was probably driving her crazy, too. He wasn't exactly God's gift to women.

The other women admired Dodie's coat and when she felt she had her fill, she excused herself and went into the grillroom and ordered a pot of tea.

She nodded to Gloria Brown who was with her brother, then settled down to drink her tea, stretching out each moment, savoring her new-found freedom, hoping no one would approach her.

Meeting the handsome blond man in the fur shop had boosted her ego enormously. It was exciting to know that a man could be attracted to her. Clearly, he had found her interesting. She wondered if she would ever see him again. She was silly not to go for the ice cream but she had things to do which could not wait now that she had decided to carry them through. He was definitely the sort of man she liked, tall, slim, good-looking, fair, and with an apparent lack of inhibitions. If she were to undress in front of him he would really look at her body, unlike her husband, who averted his eyes. What would it be like to sleep with him?

She decided to go home. Get through the evening some-how. She expected the following weeks to be isolated, the winter lonely as ever, but there was some comfort in the prospect of spring.

She waited for the Rolls in front of the club. To her surprise Jerry Fryman's Porsche pulled up. She had not expected to see him.

"What are you two doing here?" she said, looking from Ben Schwartz to Jerry.

Jerry held out his hand as if to say, "Let's be friends." Ben said nothing. He wore scruffy, faded jeans and some kind of anorak from the fifties. Would they let him in? The members of the club were painfully clothes conscious. Clothes were constantly the subject of conversation, and not only among the women. Everyone knew everyone else's wardrobe, and each female made certain that she *never* wore the same thing twice to a Saturday evening party. Scruffy jeans were definitely out.

"It's my gin game," Jerry explained, "Ben had nothing to do and was visiting my Dobermans. He can watch our game."

Ben stuck his hands in the pocket of his plastic anorak and regarded Dodie. She seemed surprised at seeing him— or maybe annoyed? She looked a little different than when he last saw her at the funeral party—happier.

Dodie looked at them, sensing something was going on between Ben and Jerry, but she couldn't quite figure it out.

"I can't believe they bet so high," Ben finally said, feeling obliged to say something to his sister-in-law. He didn't want her to think he thought about her at all, and his silence might lead her to think he was harboring some-thing. He wasn't stupid. In fact, he felt that she might have had something to do with being cut out of his parents' wills. But how could he prove it? He had gone over the matter endlessly with Jerry and they could find no grounds for collusion. Dodie had gained only a minimum from

89

Buddy's death and nothing thus far from Rose's estate. . . . For a moment, Ben stared at her in silent enmity.

"Nice seeing you," Jerry said, motioning to Ben to follow him inside.

Dodie stepped into the car, waved and drove away. She turned on her favorite phone-in radio station and drove home. As she approached her still unpaved road she had the same sense of freedom she had experienced at the club. She glanced up ahead at the house, situated at the end of a cul-de-sac. She had never liked the house, Hank having insisted on his own decorator. There was nothing in the house of herself except the sunken bath where she luxuriated daily. She would like to sell the house one day and buy one she really loved. She would decorate it herself in yellow and pink and wine colors, those colors she liked in French Impressionist art. And then she would have vases of fresh-cut flowers in every room, soft music on the stereo and track lighting. Plants were important, too, because they were life and she could talk to them when she felt lonely. Hank had forbidden plants, saying he felt they reminded him of dying.

There were many changes she would like in her life. If only she had the daring, the capacity for action. Sometimes, she had doubts that she would ever be able to change her life. Even with freedom, money, a degree of good looks and good health, could she really get what she wanted?

She saw Doc Matthews's car in her driveway and pulling up next to it, parked and got out, taking her box with her. Before she could put it down to open the door, Doc had flung it open and was standing before her, a flushed, anxious expression on his face.

"Now we'll *have* to call the police. It's Hank," he puffed, "I found him . . . I swear . . . I found him dead . . ."

"What happened?" Dodie asked calmly, her inner detachment taking over to control her pounding heart.

"What happened?" Doc repeated, incredulous.

"Is an ambulance needed?" Dodie said, the realization not yet sinking in that Hank, too, was now dead.

Doc nodded his head up and down like a puppet on a string, his mind racing. His debt to Hank was obliterated along with Hank.

CHAPTER TEN

There were so many people at the Ira Kaufman funeral home that if poor Hank had not already been dead the crowd would have suffocated him. The coffin was closed in an effort to avoid offending the sensibilities of some of the members of Crestwood Hills. The medical examiner had performed an autopsy, and having found nothing bizarre or remarkable, pronounced Hank dead of natural causes. An embolism to the heart had killed him. Just what had caused it was still not known.

All the members of Crestwood Hills who were not already settled down for the winter in their resort hotels and condominiums came. Even some of the members of the two less distinguished clubs, Frankwood and Somerset Cliffs, came to honor Hank Schwartz, who had died before his time.

Doc Matthews spread the word that there must be a congenital problem among the Schwartzes. When Dickie David objected, pointing out that Rose and Buddy were not brother and sister, and therefore unrelated genetically, Doc brushed over the statement.

"Ben may very well have the same defect."

Ben, who sat in the last row in order to remain as unobtrusive as possible, did not appreciate the nervous stares from the other funeral-goers. He knew perfectly well what they were thinking. He had been convinced by Beverly to buy a suit and a tie for the occasion and sat uncomfortably, counting the minutes until the service ended.

But the service had not yet begun, the people had walked to and fro in front of the casket, murmuring in scarcely secret voices that Hank had *really* died under mysterious circumstances. Since Hank's death, a feeling of paranoia had descended over each member of the club. The gossip and conjecture were endless.

In the darkened chamber next to where Hank lay sat lovely Dodie wreathed in a black cloth coat. As Hank's acquaintances and numerous business associates marched past, she glanced up, daubing at her eyes which were itching and burning from a new mascara. She was relieved it was nearly over. The worst had been Hank's body lying at the morgue for two days. The medical examiner, a Doctor Mills, who was none too compassionate, had gotten her over there for questioning, only afterwards admitting that Hank had died from natural causes. The whole humiliating experience had shattered her self-confidence. Keeping it out of the newspapers took some doing, too, but Jerry had handled that nicely. In fact, he seemed to be paying a lot more attention to her now that Hank was dead.

Dodie gently wiped her eyes with a lace handkerchief, her thoughts wandering to her inheritance. Feeling guilty, she tried to push such thoughts from her mind. Poor Hank was barely in his grave and here she was pondering such crass items as money. Poor Hank did not live to see his millions spent on what he really loved—other women. The week before he died Dodie had found a hotel bill in his jacket pocket from the Somerset Inn, where he had obviously been with a girl.

Rabbi Stone stopped by the darkened chamber to greet Dodie, hoping she would not lean forward and grasp his hand.

"I'll start the eulogy soon," he whispered, "come and sit with the others now."

At a word from him, the twins Del and Danto Tannenbaum, Hank's poorer relations, whom Dodie had never before met, came to escort the young widow into the chapel. The Tannenbaums were now Hank's only living relations other than Ben. They lived in Dayton, Ohio, and never came to visit. They had each sent two dozen roses, although everyone had been told not to send flowers but to make a contribution to the Heart Fund. They were sweet, she felt, even if Ben said they were ingratiating.

As she sat down in the front row, a twin on either side, the idea came to her mind that they were in a sense "heirs-in-law." They could not directly inherit from Hank unless he put them into his will, but if she or Ben were to die they would inherit the Schwartz fortune. She glanced at Del's beaky nose. Did he know about this? She glanced at Danto's same beaky nose. Did he know?

The rabbi addressed his soothing words to Dodie. The eulogy was quiet, low-key, in an attempt to avoid any emotional displays. Rabbi Stone forced his eyes over the captive audience. Why were so many of the members of his temple and Crestwood Hills, where he was a lifetime member, so unattractive? After a few minutes he found a way of secretly glancing over everyone so he was not exactly looking directly at them. He had only recently given Hank's parents the same funeral in almost the same words. Who would remember? Did anyone actually listen?

Evidently, the widow and Doc Matthews opposed autopsies. He had heard Dodie say, "Jews do not mar the dead. Let them rest in peace, poor souls."

The rabbi could not recall this statement from Jewish history, but perhaps the young woman knew something he

94

did not. Her father was possibly from an orthodox background. The statement sounded religious and impressed Rabbi Stone, who was not used to members of his flock philosophizing. Since she had uttered this remark he looked at her with new interest.

"Buddy went to his grave unblemished except for his appendectomy scar. Rose had only the mark of her gall bladder operation. Their vital organs were intact and it's better left that way," Doc Matthews was heard to add to Dodie's statement.

Why should the rabbi interfere? He was not a policeman, and he did hope to collect for the building fund. Also, the medical person from Oakland County had looked into the situation, hadn't he? Hank had died of a heart attack as the result of an embolism.

"Hank was a good man," the rabbi said to the mourners. "He died before his time." The worst death was the untimely one, the rabbi thought, thinking about himself and hoping he was going to die a handsome old man, attended by his congregation. As the rabbi spoke about Hank Schwartz, his eyes swept over the room.

Dodie found it hard to concentrate. Ben's head rested on his arm, which was flung over the back of the bench. If the rabbi did not get quickly to the end of his speech, he might have to get up and leave, which would look bad. He did not like to sit in one place for too long. He had tried unsuccessfully to get Beverly's eye, but she was doing her grand performance, snuggling next to Dickie and weeping into a Kleenex.

Dodie's thoughts began to wander. Buddy would be furious if he knew Hank had gone. He was a founding member of Crestwood Hills and expected life to treat his family better. It was Buddy who had decided women should not be members of the club. There was a tacit understanding among the members, all men, that women ought never be allowed to join. According to the rules, women must never be allowed in tight-fitting pants or shorts on club premises. A wife was only a guest of her husband, who was the real member. A divorced wife had no privileges at all and was denied membership in her own right. A widow was allowed to assume limited membership rights only until she remarried. Buddy had invented these discriminatory rules and Hank had followed in his footsteps. She glanced down at her wedding band. Hank was gone. Did everyone expect her to be next?

She looked at the rabbi, uncomfortable with the thought that he might address himself to the question of multiple deaths. Studying his face, she wondered why God had made him so good-looking. He had a mass of curly dark hair and greenish eyes which never quite focused.

"Hank was only forty-one at the time of his passing," Rabbi Stone said. "He had everything to live for, a sweet wife, a wonderful home, a devoted brother . . ."

At the last words Ben sat bolt upright. Did he hear correctly? He tried to get Beverly to look at him. She was several rows down and he could see her profile. There was not a crack, not even the smallest suggestion of a smile. Then, surreptitiously, she turned and glanced his way, her face a mask. But her eyes were communicating. The eyes went from him to Dodie and back again . . .

"Hank Schwartz was loved by everyone," the rabbi said, attempting to shorten the eulogy. There was still the tedious journey to the cemetery and the cold graveside ceremony ahead of them. More than tears he hated the Michigan weather, the snow, the sleet, the rain . . .

Dodie looked at the rabbi, trying to push away a sudden fantasy which had taken over her body and mind. She thought she saw him blush, and this blush strangely catapulted her into a brief but intense image of his body pressed against her sleek, slim form . . .

She touched her wedding band. She was no longer Hank's wife. Nor was she a daughter-in-law anymore. She was a widow and alone. Realizing that the rabbi had stopped talking and that everyone had stood up to go, she tucked her handkerchief into her handbag and got up. A tear came into Dodie's eye. She was free. She could no longer be controlled . . .

"Oh dear," the rabbi said, stopping in front of her, "you're not crying, are you?"

CHAPTER ELEVEN

Hank's *shiva* was held at Crestwood Hills Country Club so that any member might give his or her condolences to what remained of the Schwartz family. Nat Kanterman, the serious, ultra-rich president of the club claimed it was a landmark occasion. No one had ever before held a *shiva* there. Members wandered into the main dining room, where there were tables laden with enough food to make a king gasp. They ate, talked, sat for a while and then disappeared.

The *shiva* was only three nights in the tradition of reformed Jews, which most of the members of Crestwood seemed to be. The last night Del and Danto stayed close to Dodie as if now there might be a significant connection between them. Ben appeared during the final hour, just before the waiters began cleaning up the mess. Dodie was surprised to see him looking so clean and well-groomed.

She really wanted to leave. She was tired, and felt like a hot bath and a relaxing hour under her perfumed Porthault sheets from Paris. Unfortunately, Jerry Fryman loomed in front of her and began to talk.

"Are you listening, Dodie? Will you be in my office in the morning?" he repeated.

She nodded and smiled vaguely. He smiled back and headed for the bar where Beverly was having a nightcap. As he moved away from her, Dodie stared at his back in wonder. He was neither tall nor handsome nor really very rich, yet he was supposed to be a ladies' man. What did they see in him? Hostesses vied for his company, ran after him, made fools of themselves for him. He was in constant demand.

Yes, Jerry was living at the right time, the right decade, when bachelors like him were considered modern-day Casanovas. Twenty years ago he would have been pitied and scorned for not having a wife. It was not fair—single women were not treated the same. They were excluded because hostesses found them threatening. Would she get any invitations if she was without Hank? Now she would find out. She glanced around as if to determine how she would be treated by some of the members who were now downing the last portions of stuffed pasta shells, smoked salmon and hot meatball canapes. Her eyes met Rabbi Stone's, who reddened when he saw Dodie looking his way.

"Dodie?"

She turned to see Dickie David. He looked deep into her eyes, happy at last to comfort her in her bereavement. She looked more beautiful than ever, he noted, as he reached over and brushed his lips across her soft cheek. For a moment their hands touched and a spark of excitement rushed through his body. He glanced furtively around to check whether Beverly was in the vicinity.

"I wish I could help you," he whispered. "Is there anything I can do?"

Beverly, having seen the little kiss from across the room and perceiving that her husband was enjoying himself, pushed her way through the throng. Hank's death put Dodie in a new light—she could become a menace to the wives at the club. Certainly she was one of the more alluring women. She might become an unwanted attraction. Her beauty and look of utter helplessness could detract attention from Beverly, and Beverly did *not* want competition. She had always been one of the more glamorous ladies of the club. And then there was Ben. Her affair with him was still in the beginning stages, and she was not yet totally certain of his devotion. He might stray, and a pretty sister-in-law could tempt.

"I know you must feel awful, honey," Beverly said, slipping her trim body in between her husband and Dodie, ignoring Dickie's annoyed look.

Dickie frowned. His wife had made the space around him somehow smaller. He moved back so he was pressed against the windows. Sometimes he felt an urge to hit her, although he never had.

Beverly spoke affectionately to Dodie, though both realized it was an act. As Beverly chattered on, Dodie thought about how hungry she was. The table looked appealing, overladen with food. She did not expect to be hungry. Would anyone care or think less of her—the widow—if they saw her eating? . . .

She did not have the nerve to eat, even though she suddenly felt faint. Out of the corner of her eye she spied Doc. He was sitting alone at a table, undoubtedly trying to avoid his ex-wife and her husband, the heart specialist. Poor Doc. She felt so sorry for him. He had lost his looks along with his money; it had seemed to happen overnight. One day he had hair, no paunch and stocks; the next day he was bald and penniless. The sagging jaw, the terrible bags under his eyes gave him a perpetually drained look.

Dodie knew a lot about him, even the details of his divorce from Sheryl. Doc had a way of relating extremely personal information when he was examining you. His children were grown up and lived in New York and had lives of their own. Each one was financially better off than Doc.

"I've a headache," Dodie said to Beverly. "Must go, dear."

She slid out of Beverly's grip and headed toward the powder room. She really needed to eat something. She needed her strength for her daydreams, if for nothing else. What would her mother think if she knew about her constant fantasies? Behind her mother's steel-framed glasses were mad-looking eyes. The hooked nose, the small lips, the skin wrinkled from anxiety had given her the look of a mad peasant. Did *she* have sexual fantasies?

Dodie opened the door to the powder room. Beverly had beat her to it. She was inside, standing at the long mirror and putting on eye makeup. Beverly smiled into Dodie's unfathomable eyes.

"I think it's odd the way they all died, Dodie. I know you don't want to discuss it. I know you're upset, but maybe there should be an investigation?"

Beverly patted turquoise eye shadow on her lids, then took a good look. She did not like to stand next to Dodie in the mirror. The contrast was too severe. The girl was at least twenty years her junior—no one could expect Beverly to look as young.

"Dead is dead," Dodie said nervously. Hostile situations were beyond her control. The anger of other people made her feel hopelessly frightened.

"I must pee," she said, "could you go away?"

"There are a number of toilets," Beverly answered, noting the pathetic quality in Dodie's voice. She sounded like a child asking permission.

"I can't do it when anyone is around, it's sort of a phobia, I guess."

Beverly shot her a disbelieving glance and slammed the powder room door, passing Doc on her way down the hall.

"The girl's a little nutty," she said.

Doc tapped on the door.

"Come in," Dodie called.

He opened the door to find her applying lipstick.

"I understand you've got a headache. Want some Tylenol? I'll go look for some."

"Yes, okay, thanks, Doc."

"Dodie, I know this sounds strange, but I could get into trouble. This whole thing . . . the three of them, well, it's bizarre. I understand," he said, "that Hank found some dirty stuff in your dresser, some pictures and things. Pornography."

"Who told you?"

Doc smiled nervously.

"Hank."

"Is this blackmail?" Dodie asked.

"No, of course not."

"Why mention it then?" Dodie asked.

Doc shrugged. "Thought you'd like to know. And when you're ready to start dating, you will let me know first, won't you?"

Dodie stared at him, her eyes opening wide. Her stomach churned at his suggestion.

"I'd do anything for you, Dodie."

"I know, Doc, I know."

CHAPTER TWELVE

Tim picked up the report. Hank Schwartz died at forty-one of a heart attack, at that age pointing to a congenital defect. Poor slob. The cause of death had been listed on the postmortem report as "embolism to the heart."

Feeling restless, Tim got up and walked around his small office. Hank Schwartz had been a wealthy member of the Jewish community, a fairly small community of money which was mostly confined to the Birmingham, Crestwood Hills, Franklin areas with some few exceptions. Tim recalled seeing notices in the local papers of the man's death. He himself probably knew a number of people who had known the family and who might be able to shed further light on their history. His sisters, for example, knew Doc Matthews and his ex-wife. These connections were usual. Everyone was connected one way or another, either through school days, college, or through marriage and friends. Even the Jewish guys who married Gentiles remained as part of the Jewish community. Usually, the men married outside, not the girls. Jewish girls seemed to want their husbands to be Jewish. His sisters did. Tim thought this limiting—how many Jewish men could there be? Certainly not enough to be divided between the Gentile women and their Jewish counterparts.

He stared out the window. A woman was getting out of her car with her two kids and a dog. Was she bringing the dog into the medical examiner's office? Did the unknown "Madame X" have children? She could be married. No one that attractive would be single. Except Patti, of course, who did not wish ever to marry.

On impulse Tim reached into his desk and brought out some photographs of Patti. There was a certain resemblance between her and the girl he had seen in the mall that Sunday afternoon. He studied the picture carefully. The images he had in mind just after he left the fur shop had somehow driven out the image of Patti. The new girl had replaced Patti's face, her body. He felt confused. He put the photograph away and thought about "Madame X." He thought about her dimpled smile, her slow, sweet manner of speaking. He had always had a passion for dimples and this woman had an ingenuous quality of pronouncing words, almost like a child, that was captivating.

Patti would probably not like her. She had always believed women who bought furs were criminals and should be sent to prison—Patti was an environmentalist. He had respected her for her views. She had an opinion about everything. And therefore he had allowed her to help him solve his murders. This had actually excited him as much as anything else about their relationship. They were a sort of unofficial partnership. She was especially brilliant and incisive when it came to the modus operandi. God, he missed her. He would rather think she missed him, too, and was now devoting herself to work just the way he was, than dwell on the possibility of her being unfaithful.

He got up from his desk. There was plenty to do.

He walked into the outer office where his caramel-skinned secretary, Leona, was carefully applying nail polish. Leona had large blue eyes which appeared to be hyperthyroid; her nostrils flared dramatically and her full lips were covered in a magenta lipstick. She explained frequently that she considered herself to be black even if she was only half black, her father being a white Canadian. To most people she seemed Hispanic, which put her dander up. She knew nothing of things Spanish, having been born in the deep South. She had come north as a teenager and was proud of her black heritage.

She looked up suspiciously. It was near her lunch hour and she resented intrusions. She batted her blue eyes and hoped the doctor would go quietly away. Instead of moving on, he remained fixed in front of her desk.

"Yeah?" she said, waving her hands in the air to dry the polish.

"When Mills gets in I'd like to talk to him, Lee, okay?" Tim was aware of her sensitivities and always added "okay" at the end of each sentence.

She looked exasperated. She had worked in the medical examiner's office for fifteen years. She had seen them come and go. She viewed the bodies on slabs, watched while hearts and lungs were pulled out, saw the murdered, the suicides, the decapitated, the drug-abusers, the family assault ending in death. Cool as a cucumber, she was not impressed with medical examiners, paid or otherwise. They came and went, too. The only ones who remained were the pathologists, the people who did the actual disemboweling. These folks deserved her admiration.

"What is it?" she said, trying to conceal her annoyance. This one was clearly obsessed with murder. He seemed to wait breathlessly for a victim to show up. She wondered if he went out and looked for them. Behind his back she laughed with the other secretaries. What kind of a creep would get so turned on by a murder? Leona stared at the doctor. He was making a request that involved his most recent case. She was no dummy—she knew that someone had died and had been brought to the morgue for an autopsy. She knew the case was not closed.

Tim coughed politely. Leona was not responding to his order even though he had added "okay" at the end of the sentence.

"Well," he said nicely, "tell Mills I am thinking we ought to ask to exhume the bodies of the elder Schwartzes. Please tell him to write me a note on it, or call me at the other office. Okay?"

Leona's mouth was open. For someone who did not actually dig apart the bodies, he thought he possessed some overwhelming authority. Who did he imagine he was? Exhuming bodies? This was only done if there was clear evidence of foul play. Did he know something everyone else didn't?

Incredulous, she pushed up the sleeves of her sweater and looked him in the eye.

"He won't go for it," she said, "he won't dig it at all. You better tell him yourself, Doctor Levine."

Tim nodded. She dismissed him and flailed her hands in the air to dry her nails. He knew if he said anything further some kind of silly argument would ensue. She had seniority and guts. He dared not alienate her.

He walked back to his office. Perhaps she was right. Doctor Fenton should have looked into the case further. Maybe the responsibility should be passed to him.

He sat down at his desk thinking he should have become a police officer. Medicine was not exciting in the same way police work was. If he had not allowed himself to be pushed into medical school he would now be working as a policeman in a heavily congested urban area, perhaps even teaching criminal justice part-time at a university. He might have written a textbook on crime, or done some valuable research in forensic medicine. Was it too late or too absurd to make a career change now?

He checked his watch. He should go over to his other office and see what was going on. He pressed the intercom button.

"I'll be leaving now, Lee, okay?" he said.

"Okay," Leona called back, "me, too."

Tim got his briefcase together, loaded some papers into it and started for the door. The side door led to other offices and then onto the landing by the elevators. He did not notice Leona standing at the elevators, and when they both got in together, she did not speak. She watched him as the door opened and he walked away, unaware of her presence, absorbed in his own thoughts.

Tim got into his car. He drove off, thinking that before he went to his other office, where he had scheduled two patients for later in the day, he could stop at home for lunch. His mouth was watering for a peanut butter and jelly sandwich on whole wheat. He turned into the driveway of his parents' home. Peanut butter and jelly was definitely his favorite food. He felt too ridiculous to ever order it in a restaurant, but his mother didn't care. She would be busy with her students and he would make it himself, which was even better. She was always too light on the jelly, and he liked the peanut butter to be smothered in jelly.

His eating habits had been deemed unwholesome by Patti. That, as well as the fact that he still lived at home at the age of thirty-four, were the two battling points between them. She constantly berated him for living at home. But why shouldn't he? He had no wife, no one to cook for him —at least at home he had clean shirts. Everything was taken care of by his mother, who seemed to enjoy her role supremely. And it was not as if he could not come and go as he pleased. No one monitored his behavior except Patti. If he wanted to stay out overnight, he did. No one asked any questions. He did not have to report to anyone.

His mother was no fool. She knew what it was like to

want something else besides the role of housewife, so she tutored in French. Her students were mostly grade school kids from the private schools who needed help, or kids studying to get into a private school. His mother enjoyed the contrast between homemaker and professional. Somehow, he could never get across to Patti that a woman could do both.

There was no whole wheat bread in the refrigerator so he used pita. First he toasted it, then he slapped plenty of peanut butter and jelly in between the thin loaves. Within seconds it was gone. He made another and poured himself a glass of milk. He sat down at the kitchen table.

Hank Schwartz had died of natural causes, which was too bad. Tim desperately needed a good murder. He was dwelling too much on women, or the lack thereof. But why didn't he do anything about it? Sara and Susan were begging him to go out with their friends. His brother, Mike, was begging him. But his heart was not in it. Since he had seen that woman he wanted her, only her. It had all the makings of a first-class obsession.

"*Bonjour, cheri,*" his mother called, glancing into the kitchen. "*Ça va?*"

Tim looked up and smiled. His mother persisted in speaking French to him, knowing full well he would answer in English.

"How's dad?" he asked.

His mother drifted past the kitchen door and into the library where she taught her students. She closed the door without replying. He had not really expected a reply. If he wanted to find out about his father all he had to do was go upstairs. His father, having suffered a heart attack five years previously, never left the house. He operated his wholesale jewelry business from the bedroom. Once a day he came downstairs at dinnertime. Other than that he did little moving about, fearful this might bring on another attack. Tim had given up trying to convince him that exercise was good for maintaining the heart muscle. He had a good relationship with his father. They were buddies, friends, pals. Tim knew his father had mental problems, but had decided that it was okay. Everyone couldn't be completely sane.

Each day he spoke to him through the intercom system he had installed in their large but shabby home. His father always sounded cheerful. Sometimes, days went by and they did not see each other. If Tim was not home for dinner there was very little opportunity for them to meet, but every day at some point, even if it was late at night, Tim spoke through the intercom, if only to say hello.

Just before he left for his office, he buzzed his father.

"Yep?" his father shouted back.

"How's it going? Anything I can do? It's Tim," Tim said.

"Yep, Tim? Uh huh, so what do you want?"

"Nothing, Dad. Do you want anything?"

"Not me. A new heart, maybe."

He sounded cheerful as usual. Tim thought he might test him.

"Want to go out today, Dad?"

"Damn you," his father muttered, and clicked off.

Tim shut the front door and headed for his car. He suspected his father might be paranoid and that the heart business was simply an excuse. He felt safe in the house. So let him stay there, Tim thought.

He was opening the front door to his Monte Carlo when he heard his father yelling from the bedroom window. He glanced up. The old man, sun reflected in his glasses, was leaning out the window.

"Any good murders?" he yelled.

"Not today," Tim said, wishing he had not asked him if he wanted to go out. "You're better off up there," he called back from the sidewalk.

His father nodded. "I know, son. Have a good day. Have a good murder, son." He slammed down the window.

Tim stood on the sidewalk for a moment looking up at the window. If only his father knew the excitement he felt. . . . He got into his car and sat there for a moment trying to recapture that feeling he had experienced when he solved the Charles Pizowicky case. Charles Pizowicky had been murdered in Oakland County in 1979 and Tim had been sent as deputy medical examiner to investigate. The "Charley P." affair had made all the papers, and they even printed direct quotes from him. His parents had been pleased. The neighbors were still talking.

He revved the engine, suddenly feeling deflated. Now what was he doing? Going to his office to wait for the two patients he had scheduled for today. One had a liver problem caused by hepatitis, the other might be getting an ulcer. There was no comparison between their ailments and the excitement of a murder.

None whatsoever.

CHAPTER THIRTEEN

Jerry was Doc Matthews's first appointment of the day, having phoned during the night complaining of abdominal pain. Nothing thus far had been effective. Secretly, Jerry believed in the efficacy of prayer, but this time his prayers were not going to be answered. He was having a spate of bad luck, what with his card losses, the hijacked silver shipment, which had mysteriously disappeared in the Connecticut thin air, and now his aching stomach. He had considered seeing Rabbi Stone to ask him to pray for him. Of course, he had not got around to it, feeling too ashamed. What right did he have to ask anything of the rabbi when he gave *bupkes* to the building fund and only went to temple on Yom Kippur?

He was beginning to feel desperate. He could not concentrate properly on his work. He was spending more and more time playing cards at the club. Even his interest in women had declined.

He tried to rationalize that an ulcer was a disability of his profession, no doubt commonplace for a busy lawyer. My God, Melvin Belli, Judge Learned Hand, famous people could share the same problem. He was not alone. Writers, architects, even Nobel Prize winners could have ulcers. It wasn't such a stigma.

He picked up a magazine to distract himself and stared unseeingly at a picture. Jerry's head was in a whirl of anxiety. He tried to shift away from his body. He had a good mind, a fine education. Michigan undergraduate and Harvard Law School. He had been on law review. Great things were expected of him. He had graduated third in his class. So why was he such a lousy gin player? Why had he made such a mess of the silver shipment? He had trusted his go-betweens in the East and they had double-crossed him. The Connecticut police and the FBI were in on the case, but so far had got nowhere. Since gold had soared in 1979, and silver, too, was a valuable commodity, crimes had changed character. Criminals wanted anything gold, anything silver. Someone's grandmother's locket was suddenly worth a fortune. Just his luck.

His debts were increasing all the time. And when was Dodie going to find out about the silver shipment? Had Hank kept records? Jerry doubted that—the money Hank used to pay him was probably under-the-table money, income which had never been reported to the IRS.

Between his anxiety over impending discovery, the heavy work load which was not getting done, and his not feeling well he could not sleep a wink at night. He was constantly plucking at his mustache and rubbing his hands, and people were beginning to notice.

On his desk sat two wills, a divorce and a closing due for Friday. He should never have got into tax law. He was spreading himself too thin . . . Dodie would soon be arriving in his office ready for the will. He dreaded the encounter. He should have mailed her the will, but this would have appeared rude, and he did not want to alienate her any more than was necessary.

He put down the magazine. Perhaps after their encounter he would breathe more easily. He would at least find out what she knew about Hank's debts. Later in the afternoon he would have the relief of the men's card room at the club, the one stable factor in his life. He shut his eyes, hoping to conjure up the perfect gin hand . . . three threes, four tens, three nines would be nice, or seven, eight, nine, ten, three jacks, three fives would be nice, too . . . If he were dealt a gin hand soon he might recoup some of last week's losses. If this happened repeatedly he could get out of debt at least for the last week, but how about the month, the year, last year? . . .

He imagined Dickie David opposite him. They usually played together with a couple of others, sometimes Doc, sometimes Hank or Buddy. He felt relieved with the knowledge that Hank and Buddy would not be beating the pants off him anymore. . . .

"Oh God," Jerry said, unable to control the tears which sprang to his eyes. He was glad he was alone in the waiting room except for the nurse behind the glass window. His card losses, the hijacking—all had got him into serious trouble. He needed a miracle or he would go under. However, if Dodie were kept from finding out about the enormous doubt he owed the Schwartz family, he might just have a chance. She would not suspect he had anything to do with the early demise of the Schwartz family. But if she did find out exactly how much he owed, then she would surely begin to think that he was somehow involved. And how could he defend himself? . . .

"Morning," Doc said in a cheerful voice.

Jerry, glad of a diversion from his own morbid thoughts, glanced up.

"Hi, Doc, thanks for getting here early. I appreciate it."

"Having some pain?" He smiled at Jerry. Doc was one of the members of Crestwood who had fallen for the image Jerry had put about for so many years—Jerry as lover, Jerry as a great success with women. Jerry did seem to be an appealing, boyish creature, and lucky enough to be born with red hair, something Doc imagined women were mad for. He knew Jerry had been *shtuping* Bev David and was jealous. Bev seemed to have been *shtuped* by everyone at Crestwood who wanted her except for Doc. She ignored him totally although they had known each other for twenty-five years.

"Come with me," Doc said, secretly pleased that Jerry was not perfect.

"Got here as soon as I could," Jerry whined in a voice unlike him. He usually sounded distinct, controlled. Doc smiled, thinking that he must be scared.

He brought him into the examining room and pointed to the table.

"Get up there. But take everything off first, please."

"Everything?"

"I've got to look you over, Jerry. You need a complete physical—you know that."

Jerry glanced helplessly around the room. A trolley, pale yellow walls, a yellow wall phone, a basin, certificates on the wall in gold frames. The room really looked like a doctor's office. He felt as terrified by his surroundings as a child.

"Be back soon," Doc said, quietly closing the door, leaving Jerry alone with his fears.

He took off his jacket and trousers and placed them neatly over a chair. Then he unbuttoned his shirt and took off his tie. He lingered over his underwear, but eventually took off his undershirt and pants.

For a few minutes he walked back and forth, then he looked at a magazine. After a while he stole a look out the window. He called his secretary on the wall phone, but all he got was his answering machine—his secretary must be once again late for work. His thoughts could not settle on one thing. He paced the room, then used the phone again to call the Connecticut police. The silver shipment had been taken from the Greenwich area. He left word for Officer Gracey to call him at his office.

He moved back and forth in front of the mirror, plucking at his mustache and rubbing his hands. His thoughts drifted from his stomach to his card losses to Hank Schwartz, the very three things he did not wish to think about . . .

The day Hank died Jerry had gone to the Schwartz house to discuss the delay of the silver shipment. He knew they would be alone because Dodie had gone shopping. Hank had answered the door in his blue terry cloth bathrobe, the one he was later found in, his hands pushed into the pockets. They had gone into the library to discuss the deal. Jerry was tempted to tell him it had been hijacked, but before he could even get a word out Hank was screaming at him, accusing Jerry of screwing him on the two land contracts. He demanded his money back, but Jerry had none because of his card losses, and all his clients' fees were promised for the next two years. He owed everyone. Reasoning with Hank got him nowhere. They continued to argue. Hank could afford to wait, Jerry had said, he was sitting on a fortune. God, it was their friendship at stake. Didn't he remember all the things Jerry had done for him? Didn't Hank realize that Jerry knew enough about his crooked business dealings to put him away for a long, long time? But Hank would not listen. When money or gold was involved, this usually meek fellow, who did not get angry over cards like the others, turned into a *golem*. . . .

Jerry shook his head to get rid of the painful recollections of that afternoon. Doc had discovered Hank in the library just before Dodie returned home, and had claimed the front door was open, though Jerry was certain Hank had locked it. Jerry had left by the side door—at least he thought he had. He remembered rushing out to go home to feed the Dobermans.

"All set?"

Doc was standing in the doorway.

"Am I set? Sure," Jerry said, coughing, thinking of something to distract Doc from the business at hand.

"So how's it going at the club?" Jerry asked.

"Fine, why shouldn't it?" Doc said, looking embarrassed, wondering if Jerry knew that he had made no contribution to a charity in two years. Had word leaked out?

"I don't think that much of country clubs, do you, Jerry?"

"Who, me?" Jerry looked bewildered. All he could really think about was getting out of Doc's office.

"Of course," Doc said, "Crestwood Hills is a special place with special members. I hear it's second only to Hillcrest."

"Uhm," Jerry mumbled, "Los Angeles."

"Yes, L.A. I've been there a couple of times . . . with Sheryl. Her Uncle Moe belongs. It's ritzy, but it's not *that* ritzy—no more ritzy than Crestwood Hills. We can compete. Of course they've got their movie stars."

Jerry smiled, glad he could add his knowledge to what Doc seemed to know already.

"I hear Sinatra belongs," he said, pleased to be in the know and happy to distract Doc from the avowed purpose of the visit.

Doc looked doubtful.

"I never saw him there. He's not Jewish."

"An honorary Jew," Jerry suggested.

"Maybe," Doc said, "I guess if you're rich enough anyone can be Jewish."

"Or Gentile?"

"I don't think it works the other way, Jerry. Now, old boy."

Jerry stared at the instruments.

"You know," he began, "I feel much, much better. Really. It's funny how you feel rotten and when you get to the doctor's you suddenly feel fine again."

Doc turned and closed the door behind him.

"Up on the table," he said efficiently, "let's have a look."

"I'm in a hurry, Doc. I just found my secretary is not in the office. The mail's not even picked up yet. I'll have to get the mail. Got to go now."

He thought he saw Doc's hands shaking which further confirmed his urgency to leave.

"I don't think you should go, Jerry. I haven't examined you yet. We don't know exactly what's wrong, and I can't prescribe anything without knowing the problem. Come on, let's have a look."

"Don't worry, Doc, you don't have to prescribe a thing, I'll be better."

Doc smiled. "You're scared."

Jerry finished buttoning his shirt. "Not today," Jerry said, pulling on his trousers and zipping them up. He stood and put his Gucci belt in place.

"Maybe you just have gas pains," Doc said, "I'll have to send you a bill, however. Sorry, Jerry."

"Fine, I appreciate it. It's just gas, that's right. Thanks for your time, Doc."

"Buy some bran at a health food store," Doc called, "and I'm here if you need me."

Jerry was out of the office in a flash, down the street and quickly into his dark blue BMW. Dodie would be at his office waiting for him even if his secretary had not arrived. One day a week she did not show, but he hated to let her go. He hated change. He was used to her particular typing errors.

He had been lax about the jogging recently, he thought as he drove. Usually, he was up at six and on the streets of Palmer Woods by six-fifteen. He had met two good-looking, sexy wives and a divorcée this way. He was going to have to force himself to start running again.

He parked his car in the lot and bounded up the four flights to his office. His thoughts had made him forget about Dodie, and he was taken aback to see her standing at the closed door to his office. Jerry felt like turning and running away. A curiously vacant expression covered Dodie's face as if she were in shock. She turned but did not smile.

"What are you doing?"

"I was wondering the same thing about you, Dodie," Jerry said, advancing. He found the office key, inserted it into the lock and opened the door.

"There's so much typing today and Alana didn't get here. She's so incompetent."

Dodie followed him into the dark office.

"Your telephone's been ringing."

"Probably. The answering machine picks up, though, if Alana isn't here. God, I wish I understood that woman."

Dodie smiled nervously. She switched on the light and glanced straight into his blue eyes.

"Do you have any coffee?"

"I just got here, Dodie, or didn't you notice?" Jerry snapped. He walked into his inner office and opened the drapes, flooding the room with winter sunlight. "I don't make the coffee, *she* does, and *she* didn't get here yet. I just told you that, Dodie."

Dodie nodded and threw her gray mink over the chair. She took off her cashmere cardigan and threw it on top of the coat. Then she unfastened the top two buttons of her silk blouse, revealing a cleavage Jerry did not know she had. For a second he stared at her in a new light. She was pretty —sexy, even. And, she was free. If he played his cards right she could release him from the silver shipment debt. On the other hand she might never find out. And as far as the cash Hank had advanced him for his card problems, this had been taken care of in the will, along with the two land contracts Jerry had welshed on.

The pains in his stomach became sharper. He plucked at his mustache.

"I'm a little hungry," Dodie said.

"There isn't much to eat. Some hard candy, that's all."

"Thanks anyway."

"Why don't you sit down, Dodie?"

He felt better when she sat—now he could stand tall. Dodie was almost his height, he noticed, and did not like the feeling. He leaned against his desk and eyed her.

"I've got the will for you to read. I'll get it in a moment. Is there anything troubling you, Dodie?"

She blushed, the color moving down into her cleavage. Dodie felt embarrassed in his office. Embarrassed, but excited too. The will was within her grasp.

"May I see it now?"

Jerry moved reluctantly to his desk, opened the top drawer and brought out a sheaf of papers bound in light blue. He handed her the will. Then he sat down to wait. There would be a reaction, hopefully a quiet one. He did not like loud noises, but then again, neither did the skittish Dodie.

Dodie looked at the will. As she began to read, her eyes bore no expression. A couple of times she grimaced so that her dimples showed.

"This is amazing," she said calmly.

He had fully expected her to cry, perhaps even to shout out in frustration.

"He's cut me out."

She put down the will and stared across the desk to Jerry who was pushing a candy into his mouth. He did not know what to do. Her dark eyes were cold, and he began to sweat.

"Please, Dodie."

"No, I am not pleased."

"It was Hank's wish. I tried to dissuade him."

"Listen to this," Dodie replied, and then went on to read part of the will.

"I leave my entire estate to my brother Ben, who was mistreated and misunderstood by my parents. I leave nothing to my wife, whom I suspect of helping my parents to an early grave."

She glanced up at Jerry and blinked the tears from her her eyes.

"This isn't fair and it's a damned lie," she said.

"It may not be as you wish, Dodie, but by Michigan law you are entitled to one-sixth anyway. You'll get it. You're still young, attractive; you'll find another rich husband."

He shrugged and avoided her eyes.

"My father was right about lawyers. Can't be trusted. Ben is a psycho. He wouldn't know what to do with thirty million."

Forty-six, to be exact," Jerry said, hoping she would leave quietly. He had phone calls to make.

Dodie's eyes, more and more furious, swept his face with contempt.

"I think you're in cahoots," she said. "You and Ben. How about it? You had a debt to Hank—"

"What debt?"

"The land contracts . . ." Dodie began to stammer. She loathed confrontation.

"If you turn that page, you'll see that Hank has excused the land contracts."

Dodie turned the page and stared down at it.

"Yes, I see," she said, the doubt clear in her tone.

The phone mercifully rang and Jerry picked up.

"Excuse me, it's Alana making her usual dumb excuses." He thought Dodie might smile, but she did not. She was standing now, staring in disbelief at the will. When he hung up with his secretary, Dodie was ripping up the will and scattering it across the rug like confetti.

"I'll get another lawyer. You won't get away with this. I'll fight it," Dodie said in a low voice. "I'll start a will contest. And don't think I don't know what *that* is. I know more than you give me credit for, Jerry. You'll see."

It was then that Jerry noticed her neck. Funny he had

not noticed it before. She had a good neck for wringing and if he would ever do that sort of thing he would surely wring hers first.

"That's up to you, Dodie. I'm sorry."

Dodie's angry eyes bored into his. Then she began to cry, the tears trickling down her tawny cheeks.

"A will contest might bring this entire case to the attention of the authorities. You don't want that, Dodie. Wasn't it enough that poor Hank had to have a postmortem? If we don't keep very quiet there will be an enormous inheritance tax to pay. The authorities could become interested in how the other Schwartzes died. You don't want that, surely?"

"I don't like your implication," Dodie stammered. "I have nothing to be ashamed of, nothing. But I do think that there was some collusion here. Something is wrong. I know that Hank wouldn't cut me out . . . Hank loved me!"

With that she grabbed her gray mink coat and flounced from the office.

"You'll be hearing from my lawyer," she cried from the hallway, "and don't forget it."

She intended to call Myles Rush, the well-known Wasp litigator. A sixth of the estate was obscene, and Dodie was tired of obscenity.

CHAPTER FOURTEEN

"I've been up since six this morning," Beverly whispered in Ben's ear as they lay side-by-side in Ben's double bed.

"Out jogging with Fryman?" Ben giggled and rolled away from her. He loved her in the morning, or at night, and he delighted in afterplay, but Beverly was sometimes a glutton. He wanted to get away from her, get out of her grip. The edge of the bed felt cool and refreshing after being locked for so long in her arms. He glanced at her to see if she felt hurt by his movement. But Beverly was gazing at her nude body in the mirror she had had installed over his bed.

"You like my breasts, Ben?"

"Love them," he said, but he did not reach out to touch her. Her breasts stood straight out like those of a young girl. Beverly was a lucky lady to be born with such a body. Her skin was smooth and soft. Still, at times he did not want to touch her. This morning he felt especially tired.

Beverly looked at him and smiled, pushing her wheat-colored hair out of her eyes.

"You're going to be a mighty rich boy. Where shall we go first?"

Ben shrugged and covered his nakedness with the flowered sheet Beverly had brought with her one evening. Before he went anywhere with Beverly she would have to tell her husband, maybe even ask for a divorce. He did not like the idea of going around openly with a married lady. There was no point in seeking notoriety.

"Go and get your divorce," he suggested.

He got out of bed and wrapped a towel around his waist. There were other things he had to do today other than make love to Beverly, although next to killing animals humanely this was far and away his most favorite activity. However, now that he was going to be very rich he had to see his lawyer. There were many matters to discuss and things to get under way. He would need more accountants, financial advisors, maybe even a business manager.

"Yes," Beverly agreed. "I'm glad that's what you want, darling, of course I will. I'll tell Dickie soon, maybe tonight. I'll tell him I'm going to file. I think it's time. Or should I file and then tell him. Should I use Jerry?"

"No," Ben said, "better get someone else. It's too incestuous."

Beverly stretched out her long, slim legs on the bed and regarded Ben's hairy chest. He had a vague look of Buddy about him but was light years younger and thinner. Buddy was actually a better lay, though she was not going to tell this to Ben. No, the male ego was too fragile, could not take it. She would go to her grave with the intimate knowledge of the Schwartz family's sexual prowess. Even at sixty-two, Buddy was definitely the best. Hank was the worst and Ben was in between somewhere. Beverly smiled to herself. There were few women who could claim to have had sex with all the male members of one family. Certainly no one else at Crestwood Hills had this distinction.

"What did you think of the Ford divorce?" she asked, idly

123

stroking her stomach. Ben peered into the mirror over the dresser, wondering if he ought to grow a beard. He had always wanted to look like Nat Hentoff, one of the journalists he most admired.

"Ford who?"

"Henry Ford."

Ben looked at Beverly in the mirror.

"Nothing. Should I think something of it? What is there to think?"

"Do you think she got a fair settlement, that's all?"

"What did she get?" Ben asked. He was not familiar with the Ford divorce and did not care.

"Over ten million, perhaps. The papers said, 'an undisclosed amount.' I remember reading that and longing to know how much Cristina got."

"Who was she?"

Beverly sat up straight in bed, her perfect, eighteen-year-old breasts catching his eyes. He turned to look more closely at her body.

"You never heard of Cristina Ford?"

"You don't think I would really know, do you, Beverly? I'm not into society, or gossip, or any of that crap, you know I'm not."

"That's what I love about you, darling; come here."

Ben went obediently to the bedside.

"I've got to go and dress and get over to Fryman's office, Beverly," he said. "Should I shave, or grow a beard?"

Beverly gazed into Ben's nut-brown eyes and thought how remarkably like his mother's they were.

"Poor Rose," she said.

Ben stepped back. His mother's name was not exactly what he had expected to hear from her.

"Poor Buddy," Beverly said, "I saw him the night before he died. I want you to know the truth, darling. Let's not have secrets, I want to tell you everything."

Before the words were out Beverly realized she had made a dreadful mistake.

"I don't want to hear," Ben snapped, moving away from her, grabbing the towel and wrapping it around his waist again. "Whatever it is, keep it to yourself, babe."

He went into the bathroom and shut the door. Beverly got up quickly and marched to the bathroom door. She knocked twice, then tried the handle. The door was locked.

"Let me in, sweetheart, let me explain, it's okay, it really is fine."

"No," Ben shouted through the door. "No way, lady."

"But you always let me in. Come on, don't be silly."

"Go and call Fryman," Ben said firmly, "tell him I'm on my way up, please."

Beverly shrugged and went to the telephone. Maybe it was just as well. Ben might not be able to handle the fact that she had made it with his father the night before he died. The news might lead to a rift between them.

When she rang Jerry's office she got a taped recording of his voice asking that messages be left.

"Not there," she called to Ben who had opened the bathroom door and was standing in the bikini underwear she had bought him at Frederick's of Hollywood.

"He won't be gone for long, probably just went to the bathroom," she said.

"Where's the secretary?"

"Not there, apparently. Maybe they went to the bathroom together."

Ben laughed, picked up his jeans from the floor and pulled them on.

"Is it cold out? What should I wear?"

"Your yellow sweater."

Ben slipped into his old yellow sweater and grinned at her.

"You can take me shopping soon, Bev. Buy me anything

you want—a suit even—what the hell."

"Hey," Beverly said, "as long as he isn't in his office and maybe he's gone out for a while, why don't you take me to lunch at the club?"

"The club? Are you crazy?"

"Absolutely. Who cares? I can have lunch with my friend's son. I don't care what anyone thinks anyway, not now."

"Don't be too sure of yourself, babe. *I* happen to care."

"I bet Jerry's gone to the club," she persisted, "let's go over and see if he's there. The three of us can lunch together. There's nothing wrong with that. And if he isn't there we can find a dozen others we can eat with. We can mix in with the crowd, sweetie."

She stared at Ben with her bewitching cat-eyes until he said yes. Tired or not, he just couldn't resist those eyes. . . .

CHAPTER FIFTEEN

Murder had been on Doc's mind all morning, especially now as he wandered down the hallway toward the Schiawasee Room where he hoped to meet Dickie David for lunch. He had felt obliged to call Doctor Fenton to Hank's house and Doctor Fenton in turn had felt obliged to remove the body to the morgue for a further evaluation. Nothing was detected during the postmortem, which seemed peculiar. As far as Doc was concerned, he was off the hook. Hank had died of natural causes—mainly an embolism to the heart. No one could blame anything on Doc. He was free and clear.

This was an enormous relief. He would be an accomplice if it were thought—even suspected—that he had falsified the death certificate. But no one would think this when even a medical examiner had found nothing out of the ordinary. Of course, if the medical examiner got wind of the death of Hank's parents, interest could be aroused. And then what? Doc did not want to think of any possible ramifications.

He stopped in the hallway for a lingering look at the

framed, tinted photographs of the past presidents of Crestwood Hills. None of them looked like murderers. He squinted his eyes. None looked as if they had ever committed even a white-collar crime. They were pristine, pure. He imagined his face up there on the wall, his face without bags, lines, wrinkles or any sign of age. He imagined his own much younger face, the way he had looked in his twenties before his hair fell out and the look of a basset hound befell him.

Doc laughed. He knew he would never become president of a country club—he was not important enough. He was not rich or influential. No one kissed *his* ass. Yet each time he passed those photographs he could not help but fantasize about himself as president.

Doc was about to be kicked out of the club because his dues had not been paid in nearly six months. People laughed at him behind his back, and except for a handful of the members who remained his patients, most believed he was a quack.

He glanced down the hallway making sure he was absolutely alone. Nobody was walking toward him. Suddenly he spat at one of the photographs. Fred Morton Tannenbaum would have been shocked if he knew that Doc had spat in his face, the face that had hung for a decade in the hallowed halls of Crestwood Hills.

After furtively looking around to make sure he was still alone, he spat across two more pictures. Smiling with pleasure, he continued his walk down the hallway.

What would the president of the entertainment committee say if she saw what he had done? Mrs. Bernard Stein was a proper person, although Doc suspected she resented her conventional role in life. She was the one who had ordered invitations to her husband's fiftieth birthday that looked like the cover of *Time* magazine with Bernie in the center. Nevertheless, she had confessed to Doc's ex-wife Sheryl that she did not have the courage to divorce Bernie even though she hated his guts.

What would Charles Tauber think? Charles had been organizing the Pro-Am charity events and took his work seriously. He owned shopping centers, weighed three hundred pounds, smoked obnoxious cigars and was rumored to have a beautiful mistress stashed away at the St. Moritz in New York. He would certainly be on the committee to blackball Doc. Charles had been president in 1976–77 and considered himself a very important person. He drove around in a Mark V Lincoln Continental which had fur carpets on the floor, a telephone and a refrigerator stuffed with Twinkies and fudge ripple ice cream.

Doc felt much better, almost wonderful, as soon as he had spit in these faces. A sudden elation arose in him. Who would be the first to notice his unscrupulous attack? Might Harold Newman, the pompous stockbroker-cum-nursing home financier-cum-show business entrepreneur go mincing past those photographs, then stop in horror at the desecration of the portrait? He must remember to get Harold's father's photograph at the next opportunity, Doc thought.

This combat with the pictures gave Doc a feeling of control. He felt optimistic, thoughts of murder having been crowded out of his head by the adventure. Dickie would lend him the money he needed. Dickie owed him. Doc had straightened out his ailing back, cured him of sudden violent rashes around his ankles, and given him excellent exercises to avoid impotence. And then if Dickie let him down there was Dodie, who promised to help when she got her inheritance. Did she mean it? Would she really lend him the generous amount she offered? Between Dickie and Dodie he could extend lines of credit throughout the Crestwood Hills-Birmingham area. He could remain in the club and pay off the bastards who were cruelly shutting him out.

He stopped. Up ahead was Rabbi Stone, escorted by Beverly and Ben Schwartz. Doc had seen Ben at Hank's funeral party, and did not relish running into him so soon again. What the hell was *he* doing at the club, anyway?

"Good morning," Doc said. "Dickie inside?"

"Hi," Beverly said coolly. "I didn't see him. You know that Dickie sometimes sleeps late in the morning. He's an afternoon person. By ten at night he's asleep."

"I spoke to him early this morning. He did sound sleepy," Doc admitted, glancing at Ben who looked scruffy despite his clean-shaven face.

"And how are you today?" the rabbi said, making an effort to be friendly.

"Fine," Doc said, thinking that any one of them, or all of them together, might notice what had happened to the pictures when they got to the other end of the hall. What would they think? Would they accuse him?

Rabbi Stone gazed at Doc, knowing that he would not be a contributor to the temple this year.

"Where were you three going?" Doc said, remarking to himself that they were an odd threesome, a clique he had not noticed before.

"We're going to the temple with Rabbi Stone," Ben explained. "I'm giving a donation to the building fund."

Doc's mouth fell open in surprise.

"You?" A terrible thought came to mind. He glanced at Beverly whose look of disdain made him want to spit in her face, too.

"You obviously don't know," she said.

Doc shifted his weight from one foot to the other as anxiety filled him. If his intuition was correct some bad news was about to be thrown his way, something ghastly which would leave Doc out in the cold.

How did Beverly know everything so quickly? She seemed to know the most intimate details of people's lives. He peered at Ben. It could be that Dodie was not in the will, a possibility that Doc had never considered, especially after Hank had assured him that Dodie was specifically mentioned in his will. If Dodie were cut out she would still be entitled to whatever a widow got in Michigan. But it would not be enough to lend Doc the generous amount promised.

"I think we better go," Rabbi Stone said gently. Conversations about money disturbed him unless they were indications of donations to the temple.

"Ben is the heir to the Schwartz fortune," Beverly stated in a hard, cold voice.

Doc stood motionless, his heart sinking into his stomach. He felt sick. The last vestiges of power and courage were vanishing rapidly.

"Dodie is *out,*" Beverly said. "And now, gentlemen, let's get over to the temple before you, darling, change your mind." She flicked Ben's arm with her sharp, brightly painted fingernails.

Rabbi Stone avoided looking at Doc. He allowed Beverly to guide him toward the entrance although her sharp nails could be felt through his suit jacket. She was insisting that Ben make a substantial contribution to the building fund. Her reasons were unclear, but it didn't matter. He only hoped and prayed that this wasn't some sort of overture to him. Beverly had openly flirted with the rabbi ever since he could remember, causing him much anxiety and discomfort.

" 'Bye," Doc called. In a second they were out of sight, having passed the photographs without noticing anything.

Doc tucked his shirt into his trousers. He had to pull himself together. Dodie might be out of her husband's will, but she could still inherit a substantial portion of it. All was not lost. He had to make a triumph out of a disaster, somehow. He walked directly to the dining room.

Lunch was bustling, and nearly all the tables were taken. But Dickie was not to be seen. Doc found the nearest empty table and sat down, trying not to feel the stares of animosity from other tables. He had as much right to be here as they did.

Many of the members in the room had witnessed his thwarted attempts to strangle Sheryl in the women's locker room. It had only been fifteen months and no one had yet forgotten. . . .

He and Sheryl had been golfing together, their first mistake. Doc loathed her outfit, which fit snugly over her behind and gained unwarranted attention from the other men. After nine holes Doc refused to play, and they had retired to the locker rooms. While showering, Doc overheard a conversation between Charles Tauber and Hank, who was giggling like a mindless idiot. Doc began to listen in earnest when he realized they were babbling about Sheryl. For some time Doc had suspected thae Sheryl was having an affair with the cardiologist. She was never at home—she *had* to be meeting someone. He discovered right there and then that everyone in the club knew it was Doctor Max Shine.

Dressing quickly, he'd gone to wait outside the women's locker room. His frustration turned to rage before Sheryl could appear and he had rushed into the locker room and began strangling Sheryl in her slip. Her wild shrieks brought everyone running. He was yanked off her and tossed unceremoniously into a shower. Their divorce followed shortly thereafter. Nat Kanterman, the president of Crestwood, intervened in his behalf and saved him from being blackballed. . . .

Doc stared into his empty water glass, moodily reflecting on this frightful experience. In an effort to rid himself of such painful memories he glanced around the room to look at the women. They got themselves all dolled up for a simple lunch. Today the Bernstein woman was wearing purple silk slacks and a shell pink blouse with unexpected short sleeves, odd for the autumn weather. The blouse was beaded and embroidered, or whatever that was called. Women, mysterious beings, had a word for everything. His eye moved to Mimi Cross, one of the few *shikses* in the club. She had Jean Harlowesque white-blond hair and baby blue eyes. She tended to wear white and turquoise, and her outfits were very fashionable. He had heard she shopped in New York because the Midwest did not have the clothes she desired. Today an expensive diamond watch clung to her tiny wrist.

He felt a surge of envy mixed with pride. Her husband was rich, very rich, having made his money in wholesale meat. There had been talk of a prison sentence for bribing an inspector, but since Doc saw him regularly in the men's card room he doubted whether he was really going to jail.

Doc wondered what Sheryl was wearing. One of the ensembles paid for by the rich doctor?

Doc suddenly felt a hand on his shoulder. Twisting around, half expecting to see the cardiologist, he was instead pleased to see Dodie.

"Sit down," he said.

He got up immediately and helped her into a chair.

"You don't look good, Dodie," he murmured.

"I feel lousy. I've been taking diet pills."

Doc sat down across from her.

"Diet pills. You're so skinny. Careful, girl, don't fool around with that stuff. What is it? Dexamil?"

Dodie shrugged.

"Don't know, found them around the house. Hank was taking them to lose weight."

"Maybe you better eat something. You know better than that, you should never take another person's medication. Never."

"I'm not hungry. Besides, I'm supposed to have lunch with Dickie."

"Dickie? Are you sure?"

Dodie looked across the table at Doc with her liquid brown eyes and smiled.

"Of course I'm sure. He called me early this morning. He said he had to see me. I don't know what it's about. It sounded urgent. I said yes, naturally. But frankly, I feel kind of sick and I have a lawyer's appointment at one. I won't have much time."

"I heard the bad news, Dodie," Doc said, wondering why Dickie had made two lunch dates unless he had not meant to keep the one with him.

"Hank cut me out," Dodie said sadly, tears springing up in her large eyes.

"Want a tissue?" Doc said, reaching into his pocket. He was surprised at what Dodie had just said. This could mean that the money he expected from her, the money he so desperately needed, the money he would do anything to get, might not be coming his way at all. He had put himself out on a line for her, hoping and praying and most of all believing that she would be good for a large sum of money.

Dodie waved her lace handkerchief at him.

"I'll have to change that lawyer's appointment. I'm too upset to go today. Tomorrow I'll be more rational. I'm using Myles Rush, know him?"

"I've heard of him."

"I'm suing Ben. And Jerry, too. I don't know if suing is the right word. It's a will contest. I am going to challenge that will. I know Hank loved me in his own way."

Doc gazed at Dodie's face as she talked. Her dark hair was trimmed with a large gold clip, and she was wearing gray suede pants and a soft-looking cashmere. She looked prettier than ever. She was a beautiful woman, but so naïve . . . Or was she?

"You can't give me the money then, can you?"

"Sorry, Doc, not now. No."

Dodie looked around the crowded room to see who she

134

knew. There was Joanne Beitner and her two children. There was Sandy Lippman, her sometimes golf companion. She had not seen Sandy since Buddy's funeral. Sandy was a tall beauty with red hair.

"Undue influence," she said, glancing back at Doc who was trying to get the waiter's eye with no success.

Dodie yawned. "It's those diet pills."

"Diet pills do the opposite," Doc said, waving his hand anxiously at the waiter.

Dodie got up and removed her mink from the chair. She wanted to lose four more pounds by Friday night when she intended going to temple to flirt with Rabbi Stone, whom she had just before seen at the entrance of the club. He had looked so incredibly attractive that she had resolved to make an effort to go to temple.

"I'm going to the ladies' room," she said.

Doc watched her as she moved out of the room. Why did she take her coat? Did she imagine he might steal it? He sat at the table feeling miserable for nearly twenty minutes when he admitted to himself that Dodie was not returning. She had left and Dickie had not arrived. Quietly, he left the table, hoping no hostile eyes were upon him. He slipped out the side entrance where a boy waited to fetch cars for the members.

Doc took out fifty cents, but noticing that no one was around, quickly changed it to a quarter.

CHAPTER SIXTEEN

"Dodie, Dodie," Rabbi Stone called through the car window, trying to stifle a giggle, Mrs. Schwartz's name sometimes made him laugh. After all, a dodie was a fool, a *nebbish*.

He had left his own humble Chevrolet in front of her home and had not immediately noticed that she was slumped behind the wheel of her car. He had gone up to the front door, rang the bell and patiently waited. When a few minutes passed and no one came he decided to leave. He would have to abandon his condolence call. After seeing Dodie at Crestwood Hills he had decided to visit her as soon as he was finished with Beverly David and Ben. It did not take much time to get Ben's written commitment to the temple, which prompted the rabbi to drop any proceedings he might have made against the elder Schwartz's estate. One good turn definitely deserved another. Especially since the good turn Ben had done the building fund was far greater than the pittance the rabbi might have collected from the estate of Buddy Schwartz.

The rabbi turned to go back to his car, and it was then he noticed Dodie.

He rapped on the car window again, feeling a touch of impatience. If the woman did not wake up shortly he would be late for his other appointments today. Rabbi Stone looked at his watch. He had little time, and he was beginning to feel cold. He turned away. To his consternation he saw Doc Matthews coming around the side of the house, panting, his face flushed.

"Oh, what are you doing here?" Doc asked, equally surprised.

"Paying a condolence call," the rabbi said, regretting Doc's sudden appearance. Now he would certainly be late.

"I rang the bell," Doc explained, "then I went around to the back and banged on the door."

"Right there," Rabbi Stone nodded in the direction of the Cadillac. Doc looked at the car parked in the driveway.

"I think she's asleep," the rabbi said, "the strain, you know."

The rabbi pushed his hat back over his thick hair. It was actually good fortune to have run into Doc because now he had a witness to his condolence call, just in case Dodie was not sleeping in there but had passed away, like the rest of her family.

"It's not like our girl to sleep at the wheel of her car," Doc mused. "Let's have a look."

The rabbi's heart did a flip-flop when again he glanced at his watch.

He followed Doc back to the car.

"I think she's dead," Doc said nervously. "I don't see her breathing, do you?" His face was white.

"I don't know," Rabbi Stone mumbled, gazing in at Dodie's black hair. Had he loved her the way a rabbi ought to love a member of his flock? He had been aware of faintly antagonistic feelings towards her for some time. . . .

"I've an appointment," the rabbi said. "Let her sleep."

"No, I think she's dead! We better call for the police, rabbi."

"Do you really think she is dead in there?"

The two men stared at each other in eerie silence. The rabbi was about to say something when from out of the house next door flew a tall, white-haired lady, her fur coat flung carelessly across her trembling shoulders.

"*Oy,*" she called, "I was looking out the window. I've seen you. I heard him say she's dead. *Oy vey.*"

To his horror the rabbi could see very clearly that the woman was wearing a diaphanous nightgown and nothing else under her fur coat. The face seemed familiar. Maybe she was a member of Crestwood Hills?

"I'm Ida Kunnerwitz, I live next door," she said hysterically. "Do something!"

"Go and call the police," Doc urged, "meantime we'll try to pry the car door open. I've a hanger in my car."

The woman fled back to her house. In five minutes the Emergency Medical Service, a fire engine and a police car arrived. A policeman immediately took the hanger from Doc and began to pry open the car door. Once opened, the medics pulled the silenced Dodie from the car.

The rabbi stood aside for them to lie her in the snow to begin cardiopulmonary resuscitation. There was a great rush and clatter around her. Oxygen was dragged from the ambulance, she was hoisted onto a trolley and glucose was administered. Someone pushed him out of the way.

"Dear God," he mumbled, thinking about himself. He felt guilty that he was unable to help her in these final moments.

Ida pushed her wrinkled face into his.

"*Oy,* this is a miracle, rabbi."

Rabbi Stone, tears in his eyes, turned toward the dead woman. Dodie Schwartz, risen from the dead, was standing on the sidewalk barely three feet away. She looked ghastly.

The rabbi, suddenly remembering who he was, ran over to her and gripped her arm.

"What happened? We thought you were dead. Are you okay?"

Dodie attempted a feeble smile.

"Don't talk," a medic ordered. "We'll get you into the house first. She refuses to go to the hospital, what can we do?" The young medic was staring at the rabbi for a response.

"I'm her rabbi," he said. "I can help her."

"I want to go inside," Dodie whispered weakly, "and throw up."

"It's the diet pills," Doc said, taking her other arm and steering her toward the front door. "Give me the key."

"I must cancel Myles Rush," Dodie said. "Got to go inside and throw up."

She turned and faced the little crowd that had gathered in front of her house.

"Thank you all very much. I am grateful. I just passed out in my car, that's all. I'll be fine. Thank you all very much." She looked from the police to the firemen to the ambulance people.

"I'll call you tomorrow, Doc. I'm all right. The rabbi will help me, won't you, rabbi?"

The rabbi nodded reluctantly. He was already twenty minutes late for his appointment.

Dodie went inside the house, the rabbi following. She shut the door in Doc Matthews's startled face.

"Excuse me," she said, quickly disappearing from the living room. The rabbi sat down on a pale pink chair and examined his surroundings. The room was large, well-decorated and in excellent taste. The room was the sort his mother would appreciate. She always loved pretty things. When he was little she had dressed him in lovely old-fashioned clothes.

Suddenly there was Dodie, looking quite pale and weak.

"Feel better? Maybe you had better rest, get into bed."
Dodie smiled directly into his eyes, causing fear to sweep through the rabbi's entire body.

"Have you ever seen the master bedroom?" she asked.

"I'm sure I have," he said. What possible reason could there be to see the master bedroom? "It's quite attractive, I'm told. You have a wonderful home. You must have had a very fine decorator."

Dodie grimaced at the recollection of the woman who inflicted her pink and red velvet taste on her.

"Come, I'll show you the bedroom. I have a terrific closet. The closet is the way I wanted it even if nothing else in the house is. I am going to do the house all again if I don't sell it. Really, the closet is remarkable."

Obediently, he followed Dodie into the bedroom. She did not turn on the light switch right away. They stood there a moment, and she marched into the closet. The closet was enormous and completely mirrored.

"Oh my," he said admiringly. There were floor-to-ceiling shelves which contained all Dodie's new clothes: the sweaters, the skirts, shoes, bags. One section was for clothes which hung to the floor, and then there were the furs.

"And behind the clothes is my surprise," Dodie said.

"Really?" the rabbi asked, bracing himself. The woman had a sudden flirtatious look about her, the same look Beverly David had cast his way too many times recently. He felt instantly threatened. He began to perspire under his heavy clothes. He was afraid to look where she was pointing. He had glimpsed a large bathroom behind the mirrored closet.

She did not believe the lies everyone told about him. He couldn't be queer. Whoever heard of a queer rabbi? She stared into the rabbi's large green eyes, marvelling at them. He had the look of a poet.

"My marble tub is what I love the best," she murmured. "Come," she said, grasping his arm, "let me show you."

Dodie, consumed with the idea that she might prove the members of Crestwood Hills wrong, dragged him into the bathroom. Bathrooms were such intimate places, she reasoned, that this experience might put him into a romantic mood.

"Look, isn't it lovely?"

"Uh," Rabbi Stone said reluctantly, wishing she would stop touching him. What was she up to? Her face had a peculiar look on it as if she were going into a trance. She was beginning to breathe heavily. He'd better call the paramedics back.

"There is another part to this fabulous closet," Dodie said, "I keep my summer clothes in there. Come, let me show you."

She led him through the bathroom to the door on the other side. The rabbi glanced in, wishing he had not decided to pay a call on her. It had been a terrible mistake.

Dodie stood in the darkened closet, waving at her summer clothes which seemed to be entirely wrapped in plastic bags.

"Why don't you turn on the light?" Rabbi Stone said, trying to humor her. He moved slightly, and then felt himself falling over something.

"My God," he screamed. He had fallen over a chair and was lying face down on the closet floor.

Rabbi Stone continued to scream. Dodie reached down toward him and tried to pull him to his feet.

"Stop, stop," she said, "what's wrong? What's the matter? What are you screaming about?"

"Look!" he shrieked.

She peered into the darkness, then got the rabbi by his ankles and began pulling him out of the closet. She had seen the reason for the rabbi's screams.

In the dim light of the closet Rabbi Stone had perceived the battered, lifeless form of Po Lee slumped on the closet floor, a magenta and brown Geoffrey Beene shoved between her teeth, hands tied viciously behind her back with what looked unmistakably like a black, two-piece Halston.

"*Oy vey is mir,*" the rabbi moaned, "the Schwartzes' *shvartze!*"

The police returned to the Schwartz home, confirmed that the maid was dead, cordoned off the closet and sent for a medical examiner.

"No one is to touch anything, particularly the body," Officer Gracey ordered. He had called the identification unit which arrived promptly for fingerprinting and taking pictures.

Dodie sat stupefied in the large red velvet chair. Rabbi Stone sat on the couch, wishing he were elsewhere, thinking that he could be linked to this hideous crime. The contributions to the building fund would certainly diminish. His job might even be at stake. He tried to suppress the image of Po Lee; the bloody body wrapped in stained clothes. The whole thing was too awful for words.

"The entire background surrounding the death has yet to be determined," Officer Gracey said. "She was wearing your clothes, ma'am? Is that what you said?"

"I think so," Dodie replied vaguely, her face so cryptic that the rabbi wondered what she was thinking. She looked almost unconscious.

"In her mouth," the rabbi said.

"What?" The tall policeman gave the rabbi a quizzical look.

"She was wearing her clothes," the rabbi explained, but they were in her mouth, too. Gagged. Yes, she was gagged."

"No," Dodie said, the blankness of her face giving way to an expression of hysteria.

"She often wore my clothes. I mean I let her. I gave her my old clothes . . . but they were like new . . ." she began to cry quietly.

"I'm sure they looked like new," Rabbi Stone comforted, "don't cry."

But Dodie could not reply. The tears welled up in her eyes and streamed down her pale cheeks. In a moment she was sobbing.

"She's hysterical," Officer Gracey said.

"She's been through too much. What with the death of her husband, her in-laws, all just the other day . . ." Rabbi Stone noticed the officer staring at him.

"The medical examiner will be here shortly. You'll have to come down to the station for questioning. Just routine. And anyone else you know who could have seen this woman before her death. Her husband and so on . . ."

"She wasn't married," Dodie sobbed, aware that the rabbi had told the policeman about Hank and Buddy and Rose. Now they would be questioned further.

"She lived with us here. Didn't even have a boyfriend."

"What does the medical examiner do?" Rabbi Stone asked, hoping to get the subject off Po Lee. He was having enough trouble getting her out of his head without Dodie constantly bringing up the whole bloody subject.

Officer Gracey took a deep breath and began to explain.

"If there is anything suspicious," he said with a penetrating glance which sent shock waves of guilt through the rabbi, "if the death has not been from natural causes —say suicide, or anything that looks like murder—a doctor from the medical examiner's officer investigates. He ought to get here any minute. Anyway, this guy makes his own investigation independent of the police. He takes his own photos and all that stuff. The body actually becomes his property."

Dodie stopped crying. She sniffled back the last tear.

"I think that must be contrary to the Jewish religion," she offered timidly.

Officer Gracey grimaced.

"I doubt if Po Lee was a Jew," he said.

"No," Dodie quickly replied, "I was just saying that for your information."

"An autopsy," the rabbi said, trying to recall what he had learned from Doc Matthews. "That's what you mean, isn't it? They cut out the vital organs and examine them."

"Yes, but there's more to it. There's an inquest."

Dodie began to whisper in a strained voice.

"I hope they find the animal who did this. She was such a sweetie, so loyal. God, it's horrible."

"Yes, ma'am," the officer murmured.

"What about the inquest?" the rabbi asked, praying he would not have to be part of it.

"The inquest," Officer Gracey said quickly, pleased with the opportunity to explain all that he knew. There were not that many murders in the Crestwood Hills-Franklin-Birmingham area. How often did he get to tell people?

"It's a study of the circumstances surrounding the death. Everyone will be questioned."

He looked at Dodie for a response.

"Everyone who saw, or was with the woman before her death—anyone who knows anything at all will be investigated," he added.

"But there were hundreds at the funeral, maybe a hundred at the party," Dodie protested.

"Then there will be hundreds at the inquest," Officer Gracey assured her. He scooted across the room to answer the doorbell. He opened the door and greeted the medical examiner.

"This way, sir."

The man looked familiar to Dodie. He looked like her high school heartthrob, Sydney Bergman, the Dutch guy everyone was after. But no, it was that man from the furrier's. He was remarkably good-looking with thick blond hair that curled over his collar. He was about her age, perhaps a little older, slim and tall.

"I'm Mrs. Schwartz," she said, rising, wishing she

could use her maiden name, Margolis. She felt suddenly young, nubile. Staring into his romantic face she noticed his eyes were a strange violet-blue color, his nose straight as a Roman soldier's and his chin possessed of an adorable cleft.

"I'm Doctor Levine," Tim said nervously, extending his hand, unable to wait a second longer to touch her. He tried to get everything into perspective. This was the lovely lady he had seen at Somerset Mall, only she was now thinner. He had spent enough time thinking about her to recognize her in a minute. She had that same ingenuous look on her face as before.

"Hello," Dodie said, pressing his hand.

He stared at her, then glanced around. He was here for a purpose and it was not to admire his fantasy lady.

"Where is the body?" he asked the officer, who was impatiently waiting in the doorway.

"I'll be back to talk to you folks," Tim said, taking in the room, his eyes trying to focus on something other than Dodie. The man sitting on the couch had a peculiar look about him; he had not even bothered to get up, which struck Tim as strange. Now that the initial shock of meeting "Madame X" was wearing off, he would try to put his energies to sorting out the situation.

He walked out of the room, feeling suddenly elated as he approached the bedroom. This was the first murder in the Crestwood Hills area in over a year. The last one was committed on a quiet, tree lined street inside an upper-middle-class home. A husband had killed his wife of twenty-nine years. As he walked through the master bedroom and the mirrored closet, Tim wondered if this would be a brutal murder or a neat little job. He enjoyed the challenge which a difficult, possibly bizarre case posed.

His heart leaped in excitement as he glanced at Po Lee's body for a quick look. There was no question here of brutal murder. Had she also been raped? He bent down, but did not touch her. She was trussed up like a turkey—what sort of odd person would wrap her up like this? She had probably choked on the fabric in her mouth.

"Okay, Gracey, bring in my gear, please. I'm ready to begin, and I'm not leaving here until I get everything. Tell those folks to stay out."

He stared at Po Lee's beaten face. She was an Oriental woman of medium height, attractive, around twenty-seven, with long dark hair which was partly pinned on the top of her head. In a case like this there could be plenty of forensic evidence; a nail clipping, a strand of hair, even a shred of the clothing the murderer was wearing. He would bring the clues back to the crime lab and study them. They would be analyzed and compared with the samples in the reference collection. Yes, this looked good. There had been a struggle. She may have recognized her assailant and tried to flee.

Tim glanced around the immediate area. There could be fingerprints. All sorts of substances could stick to the fingertips and when the hand touched a clean surface a fingerprint could show up.

"Damn," Tim said in disgust. He had failed to notice whether the man seated on the couch had clean hands. He should have shaken hands with him. He must be careful not to be too preoccupied with Mrs. Schwartz. Doing a good job as medical examiner was uppermost. She could wait, or rather, his thoughts about her could wait.

"Any prints?" he asked Officer Gracey who had brought his equipment into the tiny closet.

"Plenty," the officer said, "but they're probably the people who live in the house, and maybe the rabbi's."

"The guy on the couch?"

"He says he's a rabbi," Officer Gracey said, shaking his head.

Tim turned his attention to Po Lee.

146

"You know, Gracey, this looks like the work of an amateur, don't you agree? I mean a hit man would not stuff clothing into the victim's mouth. Looks like a personal vendetta of some kind."

"Yes, seems so."

"Well," Tim said, "this will take about an hour, then we can put the body in the ambulance. Your I.D. finished completely?"

"Yes, sir."

"Then you can go now. Thanks."

"Sure thing."

The officer went into the living room where Dodie was placing a large silver tray loaded with coffee cups and a silver pitcher on a table. She turned and unexpectedly smiled.

"You're welcome to coffee, or would you rather have tea?" she asked softly.

"Coffee," Officer Gracey grunted, embarrassed at the unexpected courtesy which somehow seemed inappropriate. How could she recover so quickly from her tears? He poured himself a cup and drank. Maybe women were more flexible than men.

The rabbi was sitting on the couch as if in a trance, staring at the wall.

"Can I take some to my partner, ma'am?"

"Oh, yes."

Gracey left the living room, balancing a cup of coffee in one hand, hoping he was not going to spill it on what looked to be an expensive carpet.

"Coffee, rabbi?"

"No," Rabbi Stone answered. "I wouldn't mind a small glass of whiskey, though," he said. "I need it."

Dodie went over to the bar to find the scotch. The rabbi had been through a lot with her and for such a sensitive soul the situation must be extremely trying. In a way they

147

had grown closer because of Po Lee's death. She poured a generous amount of whiskey into a water glass, threw in several ice cubes and a little water and returned to present it to him.

Within the hour Tim Levine had finished his preliminary investigation. The body was removed.

"I'm sorry, but you people will have to go down to the station for questioning and more fingerprinting," Officer Gracey announced.

Dodie sank back into a chair, her face weary. She had helped herself to the whiskey and she was not used to alcohol.

"I'm exhausted," she said. "Can't I go down to the station tomorrow? I don't feel well. Please."

The officer regarded her with skepticism.

"I think you had better go along with us, Mrs. Schwartz."

"Hey, I'll take the responsibility," Tim interrupted, "just take the rabbi with you. I'll see that Mrs. Schwartz gets there tomorrow. She isn't running away, are you?"

Dodie attempted a feeble smile.

"You, then," the officer pointed to the rabbi and before he could protest, ushered him to the door. Rabbi Stone waved helplessly at Dodie, the person who had got him into all this. Or was it Hank—but for Hank's death he would not have been at the Schwartz house at all.

The door closed, and Dodie and Tim were left together. Dodie felt instant panic at being alone with the handsome doctor, terrified her lusty thoughts would overwhelm her. She tried to look respectful.

Tim stood in the living room wondering why he had been so impulsive, yet he could not help but be entranced by her. He felt some kind of vibrating warmth emanating from her which roused his curiosity. This was nearly as stimulating as a murder.

"Is it day?" Dodie asked, blotting out anything sexy for

a stab at what was real at the moment.

"It's daytime, yes, Mrs. Schwartz. Shouldn't you phone your husband? Is he at work?"

"I always thought murders happened at night," she said somewhat vaguely.

Fascinated by her tone, Tim found he was staring at her. "At night reality recedes," he carefully explained, "our fears come to us willy-nilly. In the day everything appears normal again. The light makes it seem unthreatening."

Dodie sighed deeply and shut her eyes. Here was a person who was as intellectual as he was good-looking *and* his name was Levine.

"Where is your husband—at work?" Tim persisted.

"Dead," she answered, looking directly at him. She wanted to check out his curious violet-blue eyes once again.

"Dead? Oh?"

Why hadn't he thought about this before? This must be Hank Schwartz's widow. She had just lost her in-laws, too—clearly, she needed protection. The poor girl looked drained, as if she could barely keep her eyes open. Yes, the look of grief was apparent in her undernourished frame.

"Maybe you ought to go to bed?" he suggested. "Shall I take you up to your room?"

Dodie's eyes flew open, her cheeks quickly filled with color as if they had been crayoned in. She sat up in the chair, wondering if he noticed she was trembling.

"Uhm . . ." she murmured.

"I mean you look tired, maybe I ought to leave," Tim said, immediately embarrassed.

He paced up and down the room. He did not want to lose sight of his work which, after all, was the reason for being here.

He suddenly looked at her. She was a suspect.

"Did Po Lee have any enemies?"

"No, I don't think so."

"Did she get along with your husband?"

"Yes."

"No . . . ah . . . fraternization?"

"Oh, no, well, I'm not really certain."

"Did your husband have enemies?"

"Everyone seemed to like Hank," she said thoughtfully. "I don't really know about all his business associates, though. He was owed large sums of money."

Tim looked interested. He took out a pad and pencil and began taking notes.

"Do you know who owed him?"

"Yes. I do his accounting work, well, recently. His books are in a terrible mess. I've been reorganizing them."

"Tell me about those debts."

Dodie obligingly recounted what she knew. She spoke without pause for nearly an hour, only stopping for Tim to catch up on his writing.

"These are helpful details, Mrs. Schwartz."

"Please, call me Dodie, won't you? Mrs. Schwartz is my mother-in-law."

"Was, you mean?"

Dodie nodded and smiled into his eyes, making Tim want to put his arms around her, protect her from all the misery, the pain that life offered. She looked so fragile, alone, and now with her entire family wiped out she really was truly alone.

"You seem to be, I'd guess, approximately the same size as your maid. What size do you wear?"

"Size six," Dodie said, wondering if he had a girlfriend and who she was. Dodie did not like to compete, always feeling that she would be the one to lose out. The feelings of insecurity which Hank had instilled in her had never disappeared. Deep within she still felt somewhat inadequate, not believing that anyone handsome or important would find her attractive. The doctor was certainly being nice to her, but perhaps he was just a kind person.

"She was wearing your clothes," he said.

"Oh, goodness," Dodie said, the tears springing to her eyes, "do you mean she could have been mistaken for me?"

"Exactly."

Their eyes met and locked.

"I'm scared," she said, "scared and lonely."

"I'm sorry," he said, coming and sitting next to her on the couch. He could smell her perfume, something delicious and feminine.

"She was in my closet," Dodie whispered. "Do you think the murderer put her in there, or do you think he murdered her while she was doing something in my closet? She might have been putting clothes away."

"My own personal view is that she was standing in the dark and he thought it was you . . . ah . . . *you*, Dodie."

"Who would want to murder me?" Dodie said, the fear evident in her voice.

Gently, he touched her shoulder, then took her hand in his. Her skin was soft.

"You mentioned a Ben Schwartz?"

"No, I didn't," Dodie said, the terror subsiding. She moved closer to Tim until they were touching arm to arm.

"He went to Cranbrook, I believe, with me. Perhaps he was younger."

"Yes," she said. "He hates me. I'm suing him. I missed my appointment today with the lawyer, but I'll go tomorrow."

She felt dizzy from the alcohol and the diet pills she had taken in the morning. She leaned her head against his shoulder and shut her eyes.

"I'm suing him because I was cut out of my husband's will, can you imagine?"

"A widow is entitled to one-half of her husband's estate," Tim said helpfully, stroking her hand, then moved his fingers up her arm to her face. The skin on her cheek was amazingly smooth and soft.

"The new probate code," he said, remembering Patti telling him about it.

"I want it all," Dodie said weakly.

Tim stroked her eyelids, thinking she was a lovely creature sent from God. . . .

CHAPTER SEVENTEEN

"I must tell you about the pornography," Dodie said gently.

Dodie's revelations about her relationship to her father-in-law fascinated Tim. Family relationships were important and when a man lusted after his daughter-in-law that could almost be considered incest. At first Tim found Dodie's story difficult to swallow, but in the end her sincerity convinced him it must be true.

"Come to the bedroom," she said, beckoning him.

Tim was aware of her shapely body, the perfumed scent that came recklessly from her body. She had beautiful large breasts. He was definitely aroused, but confused whether to follow her into the bedroom.

"I think I ought to show you the pornography . . . ah . . . as evidence, of course . . ." Dodie said, her dark eyes lighting up from within. "I've thrown most of it away but there's some left. I want you to see it, Doctor."

Tim followed her obediently into the dim bedroom, lit only by a soft lamp next to her king-size bed. He took his briefcase along with him so he would not feel intimidated.

He tried repressing his sudden desire for her but her perfume wafted toward him. Her voice was gentle as she displayed the pornography.

"Look," she whispered, handing him some eighty-by-ten glossies.

The pictures were graphic and detailed. Tim felt excited. He plopped down on the edge of the bed, glad they were in the semi-darkness which would hide his unwelcome erection. He didn't want to embarrass her—or himself.

"They're devastating," he said.

He averted his eyes from the terrible pictures. The combination of Dodie's presence and the rank sexuality of the photographs had overcome him. He felt ridiculous.

"Yes, devastating," she said in her breathless voice, and sat next to him on the bed. He glanced up and stared into her face, realizing that his face was just an inch from hers. Their eyes met.

Involuntarily, Tim pressed his lips against hers. She returned his kiss with unexpected fervor and in a moment they were feverishly undressing each other.

Their clothes were strewn around the room and he was holding her and fondling her breasts with one hand while he stroked her smooth buttocks with the other. She was wet, ready.

"Forgive me," he said, unable to stop.

As soon as he penetrated her, she climaxed, her cries stimulating his own animal reaction. They climaxed together on top of the bedspread, moving ensemble as if some pagan god had made them for each other.

"Oh," Tim said afterwards, "I'm sorry. I'm really sorry. I took advantage of you. You poor thing."

He held her and rocked her as she cried quietly into his arms. She did not speak for some time but after a while she looked up at his guilty, bewildered face.

"Let's do it again," she said, an intense light coming into her eyes again. She knelt down and with her warm

lips, stroked him with her tongue until he was hard once
more . . .

Later Tim returned to his lab to go over possible evidence. Now that he had found this lovely girl who was in
the center of a strange case, he wished more than ever to
solve the case as quickly as possible and relieve her of the
burden of suspicion.

There were a few strands of hair on Po Lee's clothes and
a comb had been found under her body. This struck him
as odd. Why would she be combing her hair in the closet?
Or had she been murdered and then placed in the closet?

While he sifted through what he had collected, the pathologists were working on the postmortem. The results
would not be in for at least a day. Po Lee's death apparently
was from strangulation or suffocation. In addition she had
bruise marks on her arm, shoulders and face, as if there had
been a terrible struggle.

Despite this morbid assemblage of facts, Tim felt amazingly happy. He had found a murder and fallen in love the
same day.

He walked into his outer office to speak to Leona, who
was typing up some notes for him.

"You look happy," she remarked, noticing his smile.

"Yes," he agreed. Even if she was touchy at times, he did
enjoy working with Leona.

"Doc," she said, "I forgot to give you this message."

She handed him a piece of paper which he could not
decipher.

"I wish you would type your messages, Lee," he said,
"your handwriting is as bad as a doctor's."

"I should have been a doctor," she said.

He studied the message, all of a sudden realizing it said
that Patricia O'Malley had called. The sudden remem-
brance of Patti filled his mind. He had a fleeting image of

her in her burgundy and mustard kilt, her long legs in boots, her dark hair covered by a beret. He thought about the sprinkle of freckles across her nose and how they deepened in the summertime. He felt good knowing he still felt warm towards her, even now that this other woman loomed on his horizon.

"She didn't want to leave much of a message," Lee said, wanting to get on with her report. She hoped he wasn't going to ask her for any details because she didn't remember any.

"What time did she call?"

"About one o'clock, you weren't here," Leona said, dismissing him with a gesture. Her hands raced across the keys of her typewriter. In finishing quickly, she could go early and avoid the rush hour.

"Did she leave a number? Should I call her back?"

Leona shrugged. So far as she was concerned, the conversation had ended. She would appreciate it if the good doctor would leave so she could get home in time for her poker game.

Tim stood hesitantly at the door. He wanted to question her further, but he could see by the look on her face that the touchy syndrome was about to begin. He closed the door gently. He could call Patti's parents; she was probably staying with them.

When he got home he ignored his mother's usual greeting of *bon soir* and went to the kitchen telephone. He dialed the O'Malley home, but instead of getting the cheery voice of Patti's mother he got an answering service that informed him the O'Malley's were in Palm Beach West for the rest of the winter.

"Would you like a peanut butter and jelly sandwich?" his mother asked in English when he put the phone down. Tim smiled at her. She was wearing her at-home teaching outfit, a pair of old red corduroys and a red sweater. Her gray hair was tucked up under a red scarf.

"Oui, maman," he answered, wondering where Patti was and why she had called.

"A good day?" his mother inquired while she made his sandwich.

"Excellent."

"Oh ho ho," his mother said, turning to look at her handsome son. "I know what *that* means. *Oui?*"

"Yes."

"Anyone I know?"

Tim shook his blond head and bit into the sandwich.

"No," he said, "but you may know the employer. You knew some members of Crestwood Hills, didn't you?"

"Well," she said doubtfully, "I used to, yes, a million years ago. Not any more."

"Didn't you know the Schwartz family? Buddy Schwartz—his younger boy went to Cranbrook, too."

"Don't know," his mother answered, wiping some peanut butter off the bread. "A Jewish person?" she asked, alarmed.

"Yes."

"A murdered Jewish person, that's odd. Jews don't usually get involved with murder."

"And we don't drink and we aren't homosexuals," Tim laughed. "Mom, we're just like everyone else, just as good, just as bad."

She clucked her tongue.

"Not as bad."

"The victim is Chinese," he said.

"A Chinese Jew, hmmm?"

"A Chinese Chinese from what I can gather. There may be others who have been murdered who are Jewish, if that makes you feel better."

His mother frowned. "That's not nice, son."

"Yes, well, they may have been murdered, too. Right now there is probably an autopsy going on. The elder Schwartzes were just dug up."

"I don't want to know about Jews being murdered," his mother said, covering her ears with her hands. *"Quelle problème!"*

"Mother," Tim said in a loud voice, "it may be that Jewish persons murdered those Jewish folks."

Mrs. Levine put her hands down and stared incredulously at her son. Having eaten the last bite of his peanut butter and jelly sandwich, Tim rose to go back to the lab to continue his investigations.

"What do the police say?" Mrs. Levine asked, breathless, still reeling from the meaning of her son's words.

"We'll be getting together later for a conference to compare notes, basically to see if they've come across anything we haven't. But I doubt it. We do a good job, mom."

"I'm sure you do, son," his mother quickly answered.

Tim sat down again.

"Patti's back."

"Did you speak to her?"

"Yes, I did. She called this morning. I gave her your office number."

"Well, she knows my office number."

"Don't be irritable, son."

"Sorry. Is she on vacation?"

"She's not alone," Mrs. Levine said, "I think she brought someone back with her. That's what she said."

She watched her son for a reaction. For some time she had been aware of his sufferings over this girl who had tormented her Tim for several years to no purpose. She had seen him drift into a pattern of being hurt by her and she could do nothing about it. Since his breakup with Patti, Mrs. Levine had frequently wondered about the level of intelligence and maturity her son had achieved. In the end she decided that he had not grown up at all.

"Who?" Tim said blandly, not allowing any disappointment to show. The last thing he wanted was for his mother to know his feelings; he preferred to keep his personal affairs private.

"She didn't say," Mrs. Levine answered.

"Uhm, okay, mom."

"Come to think of it," his mother said, changing the subject altogether, "I do know someone at Crestwood Hills Country Club. Beverly David. Yes, Beverly and I went to high school together. I ran into her shopping a couple of months ago, and she recognized me. I didn't know who she was—when she introduced herself I thought she was Beverly David's daughter."

"How is that possible?"

"Well, she has hardly aged. I mean the woman must be my age, more or less. I'm fifty-three at least."

"Everyone at Crestwood will have to be questioned," Tim said, trying to push away thoughts of Patti. He still felt hurt and abandoned. Yet he was curious about her life on the commune. Had she brought one of those dreadful women with her as a slap in his face? By now she must certainly be a lesbian. She had always evinced an interest in her own sex . . .

"How can you question everyone?" his mother was saying.

"We will," he said, "we can Xerox a questionnaire and pass it around. Every member who's still in town will have to answer. We've the power to do this."

"It's unorthodox."

"So is murder," Tim said flatly, glancing at his mother. She had that look which said she wanted him to stay to talk.

"Got to go now, mom," he said, giving her a quick peck on the cheek. " 'Bye, Dad," he called up the stairway.

Driving away from the family home, he waved at the window where his father was usually stationed.

"Tim, wait a minute," his mother shouted. He looked up just as he was pulling away from the curb. She was waving something. He stopped short, the car lurched forward and he cranked down the window. "What is it, mom?"

His mother stood at the curb waving a brown paper bag. "The rest of your sandwich, son, you left so quickly."

Tim knew he had finished the sandwich. She must have made him a new one. He took the bag and smiled.

CHAPTER EIGHTEEN

Beverly could barely contain herself at the card table. Her hand was lousy; a good suit had not come her way for an hour. Mignon Teedberg was talking endless rubbish about her sex life. Who cared? Since the call from Jerry, Beverly could think of nothing else. She was to be at the medical examiner's office at four o'clock, when she and Dickie were to be questioned along with the others. What a humiliation! Simply because Dodie Schwartz's maid was murdered.

Glancing around the table at the other girls, she wondered if any of them knew what was going on. Jerry assured her that anyone who had seen Po Lee in the previous days would be suspect, but so far no one at the table had uttered a word about the death. Maybe they did not know? It was possible that none of them went to Hank's funeral, nor to the Schwartz home for condolences, nor to the club to sit *shiva*. Not all Crestwood members knew one another; within the club there were little cliques and private groups. In fact no one could deny that it was a snobbish hierarchy. People who were members back in the old days felt superior to new members. The richer the member, of course, the more elevated, and those who were masterful at a sport were courted by everyone.

There was one exception to this otherwise iron-clad rule. Dodie Schwartz. Although she was excellent at golf and a terrific tennis player, she had never been classed as a so-called "desirable." There was something about her behavior, her whole attitude, which put people off. She was known as a little *meshuggeh*, and no one could quite figure her out.

"These hands are dreadful, darlings," Beverly moaned. "Frankly, they stink."

Sarah Jane Friedman looked at her and smiled. "Hon, you're not paying attention. Should we deal you out?"

"Yes," Beverly smiled, putting her cards on the table. "Forgive me, girls. Dickie is picking me up pretty soon. I can't concentrate, you're right. I think I'll go now and powder my nose."

"Such a patrician nose," Mignon purred.

Beverly did not bother to reply. Mignon was on a perennial diet and was probably jealous of Beverly's trim body. Most women were.

Beverly went to the powder room and took out her lip pencil, drawing a red line around her lips, then filling in with another color. She drew a comb through her freshly coiffed hair and stood back for a look. She was pleased, she looked the picture of a respectable, upper-middle-class housewife. No one would dream she was having a wild affair with young Ben Schwartz.

Before she had finished primping, Mignon came into the powder room.

"You owe me fifty bucks, remember, Bev?"

Beverly turned. She hated being called Bev. Stifling an impulse to stick out her tongue like a child, she fished out her wallet, removed the money and handed it to her without a word.

"Thanks," Mignon said.

Beverly smiled sedately. She would like to stuff the money between Mignon's puffy lips. Instead, she walked out of the powder room in a ladylike fashion, without a backward glance, and proceeded to the entrance of the club where she was to meet her husband. She had not yet told Dickie that she wanted a divorce, saving this little tidbit for the right moment. She had to be careful—she did not wish any punitive action on Dickie's part. He had to feel he was to blame—guilt would make him generous.

Outside, ever-faithful Dickie was waiting in his new Lincoln Mark V, the smaller model, for which he had paid straight cash.

"Hi, dear," Beverly said, presenting her cheek to be kissed.

"Hello," Dickie responded, automatically kissing her.

"Have a good day?" Beverly asked, falling into their usual, predictable conversation. Dickie was no fun, hadn't been in years. He was boring, dull, conventional, never changing from year to year. At times she had wished he would go out and find himself a woman. This might brighten him up a little.

"Not really," he said, pulling away from the curb.

"That's nice," Beverly said, not quite listening, sinking into her trench coat as she leaned back in the seat.

"Play cards?"

"Uhm. Spite and Malice. I really hate that game, it's too vicious. Those girls are vicious."

She lapsed into an uneasy silence, preparing herself for the little speech she was going to utter in the next few minutes. She had an intuition that the time was right, and a glance at his profile reinforced her view. She had twenty minutes before they arrived at the medical examiner's. She could rehearse, then begin, saving the pièce de résistance for moments before they got there. He would have no time to question or to object. He would sit pathetically at the medical examiner's thinking of ways to be good to her. She assumed that a generous financial settlement would be what he came up with. It was a calculated risk—he might go to the opposite tack and become angry. She was gambling on what she had known about him for over twenty-five years.

He skidded around a car, jolting her upright. Relax, she told herself, sit back, relax, this is not the time to criticize his miserable driving. They both agreed he was erratic behind the wheel of a car, where his usually controlled aggressions emerged. Beverly held this against him, but today was not the day to discuss this problem.

Today was important. Nothing but civility and respect must issue forth from her mouth, the mouth which had all too often spewed insult and invective his way. He had become adept at avoiding open conflagrations. His own background, which was high German, dictated that people did not shout at each other, nor tear each other to shreds as a usual means of communication. He tended to be low-key, civilized, even on those rare occasions when he told her off. Dickie was not what she considered a man of passion, and this failing had driven her to the beds of others. So she believed.

"I bet if I put my hand on your knee and got sexy, you'd be surprised," she said. The stunned look on his face was her answer. She laughed. Beverly liked shocking her husband, each time hoping there would be an unpredictable reaction. There never was.

"Never mind, forget it," she said pleasantly, not wanting any casual remark to lead to provocation. She wanted an amicable divorce.

Settling into the seat again, she tried to plan in her mind the opening words of what she dubbed her "divorce speech."

"I won't be able to go with you to Paris in April," Dickie said quietly.

"Oh, I forgot all about Paris. That's too bad, Dickie."

"I've got to take some business trips. The motels aren't doing well. The recession's killing us."

Beverly felt relieved. He was mentioning a separation all by himself, saving her part of the problem. She had thought to bring up the Paris trip as a prelude to her "divorce speech."

"This is a bad year, tax-wise. Money is hard to come by," Dickie said, speeding up and jerking the car so that Beverly's neck began to ache. She took the seat belt and fastened it around herself.

"We had hopes that a new president would improve conditions. Looks just as bad as ever. I'm sorry about the trip, Beverly."

"Okay," she said agreeably.

He was confused by her unexpected softness. Glancing into the rearview mirror to make sure there were no police behind him, he speeded up to eighty-five.

"Uhm," Beverly murmured, observing fearfully the way he was driving. She was beginning to feel frightened. How could she bring up divorce when he was about to kill them both?

Bickering was the stuff of their relationship. Whenever they happened to agree about something, their conversation would come to a halt. Since neither could tolerate silence, arguments had become a necessary part of their existence. Right now, Beverly wished to avoid their usual routine, but couldn't help herself as Dickie careened past two cars ahead of them.

"Please slow down," she said irritably.

"No!" he snapped in a voice new to her. She instantly became quiet.

"Say something," he said, annoyed, his bright eyes flashing in her direction. Beverly remained silent, trying to think of a way of talking without arguing.

"It's that driving," she said reluctantly, realizing that

any mention of a divorce would have to be saved for another time. Maybe in bed?

"This is good driving," he said.

"You almost smashed into that guy."

Dickie looked at her. She had to say something, no matter what. And when she really wanted to punish him she was dead silent. Either way he couldn't win—he was at her mercy.

"Maybe you should learn to be quiet when it's important and to talk when you have something *nice* to say," he suggested, unable to bring forth the urgent, hard words he had in his mind.

Beverly sat up, her best intentions slipping away. She was alert, ready for the fray. Dickie speeded up, swerving around a car that was in his way, which caused Beverly to whack her head on the seat.

"Hey," she cried, rubbing her neck, "what are you doing? You don't know how the hell to drive."

Her eyes opened wide in fear as he accelerated, passing cars until he was on an open stretch of expressway.

"Slow down, slow down," Beverly urged. "Isn't that Dodie's car?"

Dickie slowed to sixty to see where his wife was pointing.

"Honk her," Beverly said.

"No."

"Right there, wise guy. You nearly hit her, almost smashed right into her with your wonderful driving ability."

"I'm an excellent driver."

"Is she wearing the new mink?"

"How would I know? I suppose she's wearing some kind of fur. It's winter and she's not a communist."

"Ah, we've got Steve Martin in the car," Beverly trilled.

Dickie could not really tell who was in the car ahead of him. The car did look like Dodie's, but he thought she was

166

now driving Buddy's custom-made Rolls.

"You should have honked," Beverly said.

"I don't honk on command."

Beverly chose not to respond, knowing that this would irritate him more than anything. To refuse to play the game was outside the rules, and at a moment like this, extremely irritating.

She glanced at him. His face was clouded with rage. She knew he was waiting for her to say something vicious so that he could retaliate with sarcasm.

Biting at her fingernail she wondered if Dickie had ever realized that she had lovers. Did he know about Buddy? Ben? The others? Hank's death made her feel especially guilty. She and Ben had jokingly discussed Hank's death countless times. With big brother gone, Ben would be a millionaire. When Jerry had told them that the elder Schwartzes had cut Ben out, and that the entire estate was going to Hank with the exception of a stipend to Dodie, they were furious at the injustice. Even Jerry had agreed with them. He had tried to convince Hank to put his poor baby brother back into his will . . .

Beverly sighed. If Ben did not kill his parents, his brother and the maid, then who did? Who had a motive? A lot of people—maybe even Dickie. If she thought about it long enough she knew she could concoct a damned good reason why Dickie might want to get rid of the Schwartz family. And how about Dodie? Beverly quickly dismissed the thought. The girl seemed unable to swat a fly, much les plot a murder . . .

In a sense Beverly herself had a motive. With the Schwartzes out of the way her lover would be a truly rich man. Of course, Dodie was standing in the way, too. She was to have been an heiress and must have known it . . . But wasn't Doc, who owed everyone large sums of money, also a suspect? . . . Jerry, too. He was a known loser at the card table. . . .

167

Damn Dickie. The unfriendly atmosphere in the car had curtailed any mention of a divorce. Damn men. They were always in her way, keeping her from getting what she really wanted.

"Speak," Dickie said. "Speak, woman."

Beverly ignored him.

"Why aren't you saying anything?" Dickie demanded.

Beverly was silent, her thoughts still fixed on the Schwartz deaths . . . It was not as if Hank did not deserve to die. He was a jerk, a man without values, or consideration for women. It gave her great pleasure to dump him after using him for her own needs. After all, she only did to him what he and other men did to women on a regular basis. They deserved it. They all deserved it. Even Buddy.

She recalled Hank's "seduction." He had come up to her at the club and stage whispered, "I'd like to pinch that *tuches.*" He was not unlike his father in the subtlety of his approach. But when she had batted her eyelashes at him, Hank had just stood there.

The next afternoon she called him for a matinee at the Sheraton Hotel in Southfield. He was not a great lover. Even worse were his stupid knock-knock jokes.

"Knock, knock."

"Who's there?" she said.

"Harris."

"Harris who?"

He had giggled and pinched her left nipple until it hurt.

"Harris nice to have on top of your head."

Beverly had not laughed. He was much more interested in conversation than in screwing.

"How about this one?" he said, taking a drink off the bedside table. "Knock, knock."

"Who's there?" she asked indulgently, hoping her attitude might make him a better lover.

"Abie."

"Abie who?"

Before he replied he mounted her.

"Abie, Abie stung me on the nose."

"I don't get it," Beverly said, wriggling beneath him. He was crushing her with his weight.

"A bee, dummy, a bee."

They finished quickly, and he rushed off to the bathroom. . . .

Beverly glanced at Dickie, his hands gripping the steering wheel.

"You're going to kill us," Beverly said to goad him. She knew he expected her to say this.

"I want a divorce," Dickie said. "And I want it immediately."

Beverly smiled. This was a new one in their endless soap opera.

"Did you hear me, woman?"

"I heard you, man."

"I mean it, Beverly," Dickie said, without a trace of venom in his voice. "I want a divorce."

"That's ridiculous."

"Yes, perhaps it is."

"What the hell are you talking about, Dickie?"

Beverly refused to believe what she was hearing, though Dickie did sound serious. Or was this another ruse, a way of getting her involved in the debate?

"I've trailed you around many times," Dickie said. "I've known for years what you've been up to. You thought you were fooling me, but you weren't. I trailed you in your Mercedes, the one I paid for. You're the original Jewish Princess, you know. We're getting divorced, dear, so tell your friends. I'll write to Lori. There's no-fault here, and I've already worked out the property settlement. Because of your numerous and well-known indiscretions you will get less than you imagine. You'll get the house, the car, some cash—and you won't belong to the club anymore."

"That isn't fair," Beverly murmured. She felt herself

reduced to a meekness she had not experienced before.

Dickie had slowed to within the speed limit. There was no reason to speed any longer.

"Why are you driving so slow?" Beverly whined, hoping that their exchange had just been an ordinary argument. Perhaps keeping it up would get it back on an ordinary footing.

"I don't have to kill you," Dickie mused. "I can divorce you."

"You want a divorce just because I allegedly slept with another man," Beverly said, crocodile tears in her eyes. She might as well play it to the fullest, she thought, using Dickie's declaration of her infidelity to her own advantage. She would play the victim.

"You never paid any attention to me, Dickie," she said. "What was I to do?"

"Tell that to the judge, dear."

"There must be another woman," Beverly said, accusation glowing in her cat-eyes. She realized this was impossible; he was a faithful old dog. She knew this the first night she seduced him in the back seat of her father's Zephyr.

Dickie nodded. He had not wanted to tell her this so soon, knowing she could use it against him. To hell with it, he thought, let her try to prove it.

"Yes, there is another woman. I love her."

Beverly looked at him suspiciously, not certain whether he meant it or whether it was part of the game.

"I love her enough to kill for her," he said flatly, and speeded the car up, screeching down the freeway. . . .

CHAPTER NINETEEN

When Ben heard Jerry's harried, anxious voice over the telephone saying that the medical examiner wanted him for questioning, his first thought was skip town. Then he thought better of it.

"I'll be there," he assured Jerry. "Don't want them coming over here, man."

"You know Dodie's going to Myles Rush. I did tell you, didn't I?" Jerry whispered.

"You did," Ben whispered back, "but let's rap later. I've got to get dressed and get over there, right?"

"She was married to Hank, after all," Jerry said.

"A will is a will," Ben replied quickly, "or what's the point of making one if it can be put aside?"

"A will is not *always* a will," Jerry continued. "She has more than a fighting chance. Wills are overturned all the time."

"A jury could say she murdered her poor husband. Then she couldn't inherit—we all know that." He raised his voice as if he were addressing a judge.

"You don't know what juries might do," Jerry said and hung up.

Ben headed for the bathroom, glancing in the mirror on the way. He would have to shave close and wear a tie. At this moment he looked like something left over from the sixties, an errant flower child. This was the mistake his brother Hank and his dull friends made over and over. Ben desired money as much as anyone. He had more taste, more feeling for life than Hank's philistine friends, who thought playing cards at a dreary country club was exciting. He knew more about life at his age than poor dumb Hank knew at forty. Hank had wasted his life.

Ben knew he was creative, but did not know in what manner. It didn't really matter, he thought—it would come to him. What was important was that now he would have the necessary capital . . . he could easily take up painting in France, or poetry in Italy, or whatever he damn well pleased.

He began to shave, wincing as he caught himself on the chin. Hank lived a silly life, he mused. Marriage to Dodie could not have been much fun. She was such a flake, and as much a gold digger as anyone. He had known this all along, and the tacit understanding had passed between them for years now. . . .

Ben finished shaving and began to get dressed. He selected the one new suit he possessed and took out a Countess Mara tie he had taken from the house in Wabeek, no doubt a present from his mother to his father. It was ugly but suited the occasion. He arranged his clothes on the bed and regarded them. He would present the picture of a conservative gentleman to the medical examiner and company.

He glanced down at his body and thought of Hank. As a child Hank had played diligently at sports, even though he was no good, in a vain attempt to be macho. Hank had been a decent brother when Ben was little, taking him everywhere, protecting him. But when Hank had joined Crestwood Hills, they had a parting of the ways which was never mended. Ben hated country clubs. They were so smug.

Ben stood deep in thought in the middle of his bedroom as the time ticked on, his thoughts focused on poor Hank and the inheritance. Eventually he got dressed, combed his thick, curly hair, and then went into the living room to smoke some dope. He sat down on the couch, cleaned the seeds away, then rolled a reasonable amount between the papers. He puffed away vigorously for a minute thinking about his summer plans. First Europe, maybe Germany and Austria for the summer music festivals and the museums, too—the Maeght in the south of France, the Léger. After Europe there was China, India, Russia, South America. He and Beverly would have a world tour, and he would teach her things. She had once visited him at his job and watched while he showed her how to inject the dogs. She was not at all squeamish. She had guts.

Yes, they would stay at the best hotels, the way she liked. He wanted to give her an elegant view of the world.

His parents disliked traveling—unless it was to Palm Beach or La Costa. They did not want to spend money on "foreigners," forgetting that they themselves were only a few generations away from being foreign. Nevertheless, they shunned anyone with an accent.

Ben forced himself to leave the house. Stopping twice en route to the medical examiner's office to smoke a joint, he was late, and a secretary quickly ushered him into a waiting room where she said the others were waiting. In the room he found a dispirited Beverly, Dickie, Jerry, Doc, and his cousins, Del and Danto. No one spoke when he came in, but he saw Beverly acknowledge his well-groomed appearance with a slight nod and a wink.

"Hi," Ben said to the twins. He disliked his cousins, whom he thought had no class and were silly besides; they

173

lived in Flint and sometimes talked in unison. That especially made him want to throw up.

Doc was plopped down on the couch, avoiding all eye contact. Ben sat down next to him.

"What's up, Doc?" he grinned.

Doc did not wish to identify himself with any of the suspects, particularly Ben. He owed nothing to Ben and did not have to be nice to him. He gazed sadly around the room. Jerry Fryman was tweaking his mustache and staring disapprovingly at him.

"What's wrong?" Doc asked.

"Nothing," Jerry answered, "I'm looking at Ben—feel okay, Ben?"

"Just dandy," Ben replied, trying to sit up so as to impress everyone with his unusually sharp demeanor.

"Fine," Jerry said, and coughed to prepare his little speech for the entire room.

"This is only routine, folks. They want us all for questioning, even me, and I was nowhere near the Schwartz house. But let's try to cooperate. Po Lee is dead and that's why we're here."

"Where's Dodie?" Ben asked.

"Don't know," Jerry answered.

"I don't like this one little bit. I didn't go into the house. I already told them that. I don't see why the medical examiner has to butt into this. I've got enough problems," said Doc.

Before anyone had a chance to reply, the door opened and a lovely blond woman entered. She was wearing a white coat and looked professional to Ben. He rose for the occasion.

"Good afternoon, I'm Annabelle Goldman," she said. "Doctor Goldman. I'm an assistant medical examiner. Please make yourselves comfortable because Doctor Levine is tied up for a little while longer. If anyone wants coffee, Leona is making it in the other room." She spread her dazzling smile around the room and turned to leave.

"That's perfectly said," Ben mumbled, "perfect. Did you have to rehearse?"

"You don't have to keep standing, sir," she snapped and went out.

"Sit down," Beverly said, alarmed at the flirtation which had just taken place between an upstart doctor and her lover—possibly her future husband.

"I wonder if that's Doctor Goldman's daughter, the psychiatrist." She glanced at Dickie for an answer. He was the doctor *maven.*

"Yes, I think it is," Jerry offered, wanting to let everyone know he was well-informed.

"I don't think so," Dickie said.

"How do you know? Is *he* a member of the club?" Ben sniped.

"There are few psychiatrists in the club," Doc said. "They don't want to join."

Ben slipped back to the couch. Beverly, who had been shaken to the quick by Dickie's recent declaration, and who was now being further threatened by Ben's attraction to another woman, arranged herself in a sexy position on the chair. She crossed her legs, then uncrossed them to get Ben's attention, then, in a desperation move, she pulled up her navy blue skirt and hoped he might be able to see clear up her skirt and notice she wasn't wearing any panties.

"You shouldn't do that," Danto said. At first she thought he was addressing her, but then she saw him look at Ben, who had slumped down on the couch, loosened his tie, and seemed to be smoking what any fool could see was marijuana.

"Look, Del, he's smoking pot, we'll get arrested!" Danto's voice was filled with excitement.

"Put it out." Del ordered, "Jesus, right here, I don't believe it."

Ben gazed blankly up at the twins.

175

"Get rid of it," Del urged.

Ben just smiled.

"My God, there's a time and a place," Jerry said, his face twitching.

"What does that mean?" Dickie asked. "Does that mean that you would endorse drugs at some other time, Jerry?"

Ben broke up in a fit of laughter.

"Please," Beverly begged, "you'll get us into trouble."

Ben just howled.

"Quiet down," Jerry said kindly, not knowing what to do.

"I can't afford these *tsuris,*" Doc said, getting up. He opened the door to leave, but was greeted by Leona.

"The Davids, please," she said efficiently. "The doctor will see them now."

Doc stepped aside to let Beverly and Dickie out of the room.

"And you," Leona said, her light eyes riveting Doc to the spot, "you stay in there."

She closed the door.

"*Shnooks,*" Ben muttered, "You're all a bunch of *shnooks!*" With that, he promptly fell asleep.

CHAPTER TWENTY

Dodie sped along Jefferson Avenue in the general direction of Grosse Point, where she was to meet Myles Rush for a drink at Hillview, his country club. Used to manipulating the Rolls at high speeds, she was not aware that she was doing nearly eighty.

She was grateful to Tim for allowing her to keep her appointment with the lawyer and then to drop over to the medical examiner's for further "routine" questioning. Tim was such a sweet soul, she mused.

She reached across the seat and picked up a half-eaten Twinkie. Since Tim had told her she was thin enough, she felt it better to give up the diet pills. There was no reason to be too skinny—it wasn't seductive. Men seemed to like women with a little flesh on them, anyway.

Dodie's heated liaison with the medical examiner had shifted her thoughts from murder to love. She wondered if she could fall in love with him, and the thought made her happy. She did not seem to notice that even after their fateful encounter in bed, he was still preoccupied with the murder of Po Lee.

"Rabbi Stone is a definite suspect," he had said. "He was hanging around your house when Po Lee was killed, wasn't he? So was Matthews."

The police officer had filled him in on the events immediately surrounding the discovery of Po Lee's body in the closet.

Swallowing the last of the Twinkie and switching the car radio to a station which played romantic ballads, Dodie wished the whole miserable mess to be over with already. She wanted to get on with the business of love with Tim Levine. Her anxiety about going to bed with him again was great, greater even than her anxiety about the fact that the bodies of the elder Schwartzes had been exhumed. The whole horrible event would be prolonged, the entire community would be shocked and horrified, and there surely would be a chain reaction of paranoia that traveled from member to member of the club. Yet Tim's explanation for this ghastly business had been so logical that she could only congratulate him on his instinct for foul play. She could see that he was clearly devoted to his work. Could he be as devoted to her? Thus far he had been entirely kind, questioning her in the most delicate manner and letting her give answers that at superficial glance made no sense. He himself had clarified them, writing *his* interpretations down for her answers. He had stretched points and added what he thought was wise. Eventually everything was to be fed into a computer. He had comandeered the computer and a small task force to probe what he called "the crime of the century in Oakland County."

Dodie expected that by tomorrow, the *Detroit Free Press*, the *Oakland Press*, all the newspapers and the media would be full of the story. There was no way he could keep it quiet, he told her. She cried when he said the media would be involved. Some people might want pictures, mostly of her and Ben, as they were the surviving Schwartzes. She had to prepare herself for the worst—reporters and cameramen circling her house, begging for interviews. Tim had asked her to say nothing to them until after the results of the autopsies. He felt that soon the computer and the task force would narrow the suspects down and he could make an arrest. It was just a matter of time. . . .

Dodie pulled the Rolls into the parking lot at Hillview, not remembering to leave it with the valet at the entrance. She wrapped her gray mink tight against the still bitter winter wind, and proceeded toward the club, not unlike Crestwood Hills in atmosphere.

Myles Rush said he would meet her at the bar, which unnerved Dodie, not used to bars. Nor to the long stares from other drinkers.

A large man in a neat three-piece suit confronted her and took her by the arm.

"Now then, honey, I'm Myles Rush, give me your coat."

He guided her to a table and sat her down, placing her coat on an empty chair.

"You look a little like your mother used to look, honey. She worked for the family back in the early fifties before she met your dad. I hear she's ailing."

Dodie nodded, embarrassed. The man was overbearing, large, perhaps six foot four with broad shoulders, a square face and black, bushy eyebrows. His hair was snow-white and worn in an eccentric shag style. He did not look like the country club type.

"A nice glass of white wine for you," Myles said with assurance, summoning a waiter.

Dodie mentally put herself into his big hands. Here was a man who seemed to know what he was doing.

"I think you have an excellent case," he said, patting her on the shoulder. He gazed at her luxuriant abundance of dark hair, her olive skin, her eyes and thought she was an exotic beauty, actually far more beautiful than her mother.

"I have to get the facts together, of course," he said, still beguiled by her looks. "I'll call you Dodie, honey, may I?"

Dodie nodded, trying to throw off a fantasy which was coming on. Now was not the time. She wanted to listen to Myles Rush without distraction. He was an old man, anyway . . .

Dodie began to blush. Her cheeks felt hot. She was grateful the bar was dimly lit. Though Myles Rush could not possibly be aware of what was going on in her mind, she still knew she must try to listen to what he was saying. If only she could stop these thoughts . . .

"Oh," she gasped.

"What's wrong?" Myles asked.

"Nothing, nothing," Dodie replied, quickly taking a sip of wine.

"As I was saying," Myles continued, wondering what was bothering this lovely young thing. Her cheeks were flaming and she looked extremely uncomfortable. Perhaps it was the discussion of money? Money made people edgy, especially if there were large sums at stake as there were in this case. She was going to be a very rich widow, and when he got through with the case she would be indebted to him.

Dodie sighed. The sexual fantasy, or whatever it was that had taken possession of her, had disappeared as rapidly as it arrived. She felt perfectly normal now. Her eyes brightened, focused. She smiled enouragingly at Myles and tried to respond to what he was saying.

"My fee is one-third, I'm afraid. This is how I conduct my business."

The light faded from Dodie's eyes. She had thought a non-Jewish lawyer would be less expensive. Otherwise, she would have gone to Leon Freed, who would have done a good job for her. She must not get like Hank, who liked to save the odd sum whenever possible, and then would turn around and spend senselessly on his girlfriends. She knew; she had seen the charge account bills pouring in.

"One-third?"

"You can well afford it," Myles said with confidence and finished the last of his double vodka martini.

At that moment a woman expensively dressed in a raspberry-colored suit and black silk blouse came over to them.

"Myles, angel," she said effusively, throwing her arms up and around his neck. She eyed Dodie.

"I'll be damned, it's Mary Burton, haven't see you since yesterday at the bar."

Mary Burton laughed, then turned to face Dodie.

"How do you do," Dodie said.

Mary Burton put out a polite hand. "So this is Myles's new girl, huh?"

"A client, just a client," Myles said quickly and hurried Dodie towards the pool.

"She looks Jewish," Dodie said.

"Jewish?" Myles commented, "Well, she *is* Jewish."

"There are Jews in this club?"

"She's married to one of the members. We don't think of her as Jewish especially, just a member's wife, that's all."

"You don't have Jewish men, though?"

"No, I don't think so," Myles said. "Does Crestwood Hills accept Christians or Hindus?" He laughed again. "Okay, splendid, now let's take a little tour. I want to show you around the club." He did not wait for her to finish her wine although she had taken only two sips. He took her by the arm and helped her out of the chair.

"What would you like to see first?"

"I don't know," Dodie said, thinking she would like to see the inside of her car and be on her way to the medical examiner's office. She wanted to see Tim again. She also wanted to find out if he had found out anything about Buddy and Rose and Hank and Po Lee.

"I'll show you our indoor pool," Myles suggested.

"How long will this will contest take?" Dodie asked.

Myles opened his mouth wide and let out a big laugh

which seemed to emanate directly from his solar plexus. He was the sort of larger-than-life man who would make a great Santa Claus.

"A matter of a few months, that's all, Dodie. By spring you'll be all set. I'll get right to it when I get back to the office. I'm going to give Jerry Fryman a call. See what I can come up with. I know how to deal with him."

"He's stubborn," Dodie warned.

"Me, too."

"He's very stubborn."

"Me, too."

Myles took her on a guided tour of the club, then delivered her to her car. She felt a little dizzy from the two sips of the wine, but drove carefully and arrived at the medical examiner's office ten minutes before her appointment.

Tim Levine's secretary told her to wait. She sat down on a small couch and looked at a magazine. Before long Tim came to the door and beckoned her into his office.

"I have some news for you," he said.

She gazed at him for a moment, wondering if any sexual feeling would return. It did—but not in the mental images to which she was prone. Instead, she felt a warm excitement pushing its way through her body.

He took some papers off his desk and began to read.

"Although there is no obvious indication on Rose Schwartz's body that she was murdered, there is also no conclusive indication that she died a natural death."

His eyes scanned the rest of the report.

"The same is true for Buddy Schwartz but I suspect there may be traces of something. And it's worth going on. There are lots more tests we can do on their organs," he said.

"Traces of something?" Dodie sat down and faced him squarely. "Traces of what?"

Tim paced back and forth in front of her.

"Well, say they were poisoned. If they drank poison

there would be some trace of it."

"Oh, I see," Dodie said.

"Apparently they were not drowned, nor knifed. They weren't shot to death, beaten, strangled. What is left but a lethal injection?"

"Death by natural causes, of course," Dodie said.

Tim shook his head. "Don't worry, we'll get to the cause, the source. I promise we will. Now, I must see your husband's accounting books. You can bring them here. Or shall I pick them up? Whichever is more convenient for you."

"I'll bring them."

He smiled at her. She was so very cooperative.

"I hate to ask you to fill out more forms, but it's vital to fill out this questionnaire in detail. I'm feeding everything into the computer to see what we can come up with."

"How about a psychic?"

"Maybe," Tim said, thinking she was beautiful.

"I admire the way you are handling it," she said, their eyes locking together. She suddenly felt a violent attraction to him.

"What's wrong?"

"Nothing," she said, moving into his arms.

"I should not be doing this," Tim said, captivated by her. "Not here." He took her in his arms and bent to kiss her. Her lips were soft, smooth; he felt her tongue pressing into his mouth. Returning her embrace, he felt her pulling him hard against her body, her breasts upon his chest, the smallness of her waist, the pressure of her legs against his. He reached to fondle her breast and he heard her sigh. They were unaware of the minutes passing, only of what was happening between them . . . Before he realized what he was doing he had slipped her cashmere sweater over her head and was unzipping her Jaeger skirt. All the time he was undressing her he was stroking and kissing her while she murmured soft words of acquiescence.

Somewhere in the back of his mind the word *work* was trying to make itself heard. One thought dismissed it—there was no written document saying that a medical examiner ought not to kiss a woman in his office—or make love to her, either. This was a matter for *him* to decide.

Slowly, gently, he backed her toward his desk. Dodie had other ideas, and guided him to the floor, lying down on the woven rug.

"Take off your clothes," she said breathlessly.

She helped him by putting her hand down his trousers and finding his swollen penis, gently unzipping his fly and bending, placed her soft lips around him. And it did not seem pornographic in the least—not when you were doing it. All her pent-up excitement had focused in her mouth. She wanted to give him pleasure more than anything else.

"Wait," he pleaded, "I'll come, don't."

He pushed her head away, and getting quickly out of his clothes placed her gently on the rug. They were both entirely naked now, her voluptuous figure a wonderful counterpart of his masculine, athletic form. She trembled at the sight of him.

She moaned with joy and let him spread her legs. There was no time for the romantic buildup she had always imagined. That would have to be saved for some other time. He entered her quickly, his hardness filling her completely. They moved together in short, rapid strokes while his hands held her underneath so they were as close as could be.

She climaxed and climaxed again, and at last, with a cry of amazement, she came with him. When it was over he buried his face in her hair, which smelled of lilac. He kissed her earlobe, her neck, her face. She stared up at him with soft eyes.

"Your back must ache," he said. "Would you like to get up?"

"What if someone had come in?" she asked, letting him

help her to her feet. She felt suddenly embarrassed to be standing naked in his office. She looked at his body. He still had an erection. They could do it again.

He saw her looking and bent and kissed her breasts. He moved her against his desk and pushed himself inside her. The position was awkward, so he moved a little ways off and picking her up, held her while he penetrated her. She was not heavy and he felt he could remain in that position forever. They came together in a shudder which left their legs weak and trembling.

"You're a passionate little thing," he murmured, holding her in his arms.

"I think we'd better dress," she said. "Don't you want me to answer that questionnaire?"

He was surprised by her businesslike tone.

"You were good," she said, smiling, "very good, wonderful."

"So were you," he said.

"Goodness," she said, dressing, "I hope I wasn't too aggressive."

"You were great," he said reassuringly. "And thanks for wanting to fill out the questionnaire. We need them from everyone as soon as we can get them. I want you cleared, you know that."

Dodie obediently dressed and then went into the other room. There was a wet, warm feeling between her legs—the memory of their pleasure. They would have to try that again soon . . .

She glanced at the questionnaire. Mostly the questions were obvious ones, such as where she was the day Po Lee was murdered, the day Hank died, her in-laws, and so on. She sat down at a desk to address herself to them.

When she finished she got Tim from his office.

"Did you know that your husband charged usurious rates of interest on loans?" he asked.

"No."

"This is against the law." he said, "Did you know that Jerry Fryman owed four hundred thousand to your husband and father-in-law?"

"No."

"He told me himself. He was the broker on a shipment of silver that was hijacked. We ran a computer check and the incident is correct. We would have found this information even if he did not tell us."

"How?"

"Anything known to Interpol, whether nationally, internationally or locally, is all put on a computer that we now have access to."

"Wow!" Dodie said, "I didn't know that. Four hundred thousand? Must be a record of it somewhere. I just haven't come across it yet."

"Keep looking, it's important, if you see what I'm getting at."

"Goodness, that in itself could be a motive for murder. I mean, if you were a murderer. A murderer must be a certain kind of person, right?"

"Right," Tim said, pacing back and forth.

"You don't suppose, you don't *imagine* that he—uh, the murderer—would want to hurt me?" Dodie's voice trembled. "Is that why you're telling me all this? Are you warning me?" she asked.

"We've decided to give you police protection until we've got a handle on the case. It's for your own good."

"I'll be in police custody?"

"Sort of," Tim explained. "A police officer will be following you around, staying outside your home at all times. I'm sorry for the lack of privacy but it's better for you."

"For us?" she asked nervously.

"My sweet," he said, reaching for her, holding her, caressing her. "We'll work it out."

"I'm so grateful to you," Dodie said with affection, putting up her mouth to be kissed.

He kissed her, thinking that he would want to protect her even if he had not just made love to her, but now that he had there was all the more reason. He was pleased with the decision to provide a police escort. Whoever was out there killing people could try it again.

"Would you excuse me while I answer my phone, Dodie? It's strange that it's ringing at this hour." He left her in the outer office and picked up the receiver.

"Doctor Levine here." he said.

"*Putz!*"

"What?"

Tim was not sure of what he thought he heard.

"*Putz!*" the voice repeated, and then was gone.

Puzzled, Tim put the phone down. While he was thinking about who it could have been, the phone rang again. He picked it up and the same voice greeted him.

"*Schlemiel,* you think you're such a great, big *putz* 'cause you're a doctor. Man, keep that fat nose out of the Schwartz case!"

"Who is this?" Tim asked. His reply was the dial tone.

His hand shook as he put down the receiver. If this nut could kill four people he could manage five. This was a near-epidemic of murder, certainly nothing to be taken lightly. Whoever it was had nothing to lose in killing one more. Five life sentences were the same as four.

The phone rang again. Quickly, he grasped the receiver in both hands.

"Who the hell is it?" he demanded.

"Is that Tim?" a female voice asked.

"Who are you?" Tim said, thinking that the murderer could be using a woman as a decoy.

"Patti O'Malley. May I please speak to Doctor Levine? Have I got the right number?"

"My God, it's you—Patti."

"Whatever are you swearing about?"

"I'm sorry, Patti. Well, how are you? I've been trying to call you."

He felt peculiarly guilty . . . However, she could not see through the telephone wires that he had just made love to another woman. Besides, his life was no longer her business. Still, he felt awkward. She had been an important part of his existence for a long time and he wouldn't get over it that quickly, no matter who else he encountered.

"I'm fine," she said. "When can I see you?"

"Whenever you want, okay?"

"Okay. Can I bring a friend?"

"If I can bring a friend, too," he laughed, wondering what she meant. Why would she want to bring a friend?

He played with some papers on his desk. Doctor Mills must have put them on his desk while he was out. He looked closer. His eyes took in the words "pinprick on upper left thigh, possibility of needle mark, but uncertain." It was the latest pathology report on Buddy Schwartz.

"Patti," Tim said, trying to sound casual, "if you're with a woman I'd rather not know. I'd like to remember you as a heterosexual."

Patti roared into the phone.

"God," she said, "I consider you my best friend and I want you to meet Lyn. I want your approval, I guess."

"I'm right."

"Lyn happens to be a guy and I'm going to marry him but we wanted to see you first. Don't ask me why. The heart has its own reasons."

"Yes," Tim agreed, wondering why she needed approval. "Married," he barked, "are you kidding?"

"Well, he's just eighteen," she said.

Tim was silent, thinking of something suitable to say.

"You've got to be kidding," he repeated finally.

"I've got love fever," she said, "and streaked hair. I look like a California girl."

CHAPTER TWENTY-ONE

The telegram that Rabbi Stone received from the medical examiner's office came as complete a shock to him as it did to the other members of Crestwood Hills:

Please report to Crestwood Hills at 10 A.M. Thursday, November 3, for group questioning.

Dr. Timothy Levine
Medical Examiner

The rabbi was scared. Was he now a suspect? He had only minimal contact with the maid—were they all *meshuggeh?* He could be fired from the temple. And then what? Where could he go?

Driving up Crestwood Drive he saw numerous cars parked at the side of the road. What was going on? It looked like a street fair or a parade. He instantly noticed the crowd of reporters and television cameramen at the entrance to the club, and in an effort to avoid them left his car in the lot and tried to get in a side door.

"Sir, excuse me, sir," someone screamed in his ear. He looked around to find several men and two women.

"Rabbi," one of the women said and snapped his picture. In a moment he was besieged by reporters and photographers crowding around him, pushing him up against the mock-Tudor façade of the club.

"Can you make a statement, sir?"

Rabbi Stone opened his mouth to speak but nothing came out.

"Anything at all," someone yelled.

The rabbi began to pray to himself. Never had he been in such a terrible situation. Despite all his dealings with groups of people he had never experienced this feeling of hopelessness. He looked helplessly around, praying for a familiar face, someone, anyone, to rescue him from these *golems*. In the back of the group he saw the ugly osteopath and the lawyer Fryman sneaking around the side of the building.

"Help," he shouted. Over the din of the crowd, he could not be heard.

"Sir," a young man said, scribbling in a pad, "is it possible that *all* the members of this club are suspects?"

Everyone laughed. Then a hawk-faced man came forward.

"Don't be silly, Ralph," he said. "The police are doing their job, that's all. Many of the members saw the murder victim."

"It's prejudice," the rabbi said, suddenly finding his voice. "I mean, it's prejudice to think that three hundred nice people could be connected to this heinous crime."

There was a momentary hush in the crowd of reporters and photographers. Rabbi Stone looked around. He felt excited now, in the limelight, so to speak.

"And around Passover," he said boldly, considering that here was an opportunity to be famous. *"Tch, tch."* He shook his head dramatically.

There was an immediate babble of interested voices.

"Are you leading them to the promised land?" someone asked.

"They don't need me for that," he said. "These are all good people, though I think the police may be using them as scapegoats. Time will tell. Frankly," he paused and looked through the crowd, "frankly, I don't believe anyone at Crestwood Hills would ever *murder* anyone."

"We understand they have exhumed the bodies," a reporter yelled.

The rabbi shrugged.

"Three bodies," a woman said, scribbling in her pad.

"Ask the medical examiner," the rabbi said haughtily. "Now, please, please excuse me. I've got business here."

His moment of panic had completely gone and had been replaced with a feeling of confidence, if not triumph. Everything he said would be in the *Detroit News,* the *Free Press,* the *Oakland Press,* and the *Birmingham Eccentric.* His picture would be included. It might even make the front page.

People parted like waves for him to pass. He walked briskly around to the entrance and went inside.

The first person he saw was Dodie, who linked her arm through his as if for protection. He wanted to extricate himself but found he was unable to elude her grip gracefully. He would just have to put up with it.

"We'll sit together, rabbi."

Rabbi Stone smiled, recalling that he was, after all, supposed to be some sort of leader. People looked up to him for guidance.

"I'm sorry about all this," Dodie said, looking into the rabbi's aquamarine eyes. "It's possibly my fault in a way," she said. "You were visiting me and if you hadn't been there you would not now be a prime suspect."

The rabbi froze.

"Me? I'm a prime suspect? Me?"

Dodie looked embarrassed.

191

"Well, you did see Po Lee a number of times before she died. And you did see Buddy and Rose and Hank."

Nervously, Dodie twisted the pearl buttons on her handknit sweater which she had bought for five hundred dollars—on sale. She had bought four of them in different colors and considered them a steal. What with the recession, the depression, they were a kind of investment. She gazed wistfully at the rabbi who today appeared particularly attractive to her, even if his eyes were slightly bloodshot. But then no man was perfect, not even a rabbi.

"I don't believe I could be a suspect, not to mention prime," the rabbi said defensively. Whatever was the woman mewing about? Where had she got her information? This just proved his point—that people were being made scapegoats. Someone ought to put an end to it.

"Hmmmm," Dodie said.

The rabbi glanced around the room to see who was being considered. Many members were still down south for the winter.

"The reporters told me three bodies were exhumed, goodness," he said, wondering where Dodie got her information. Perhaps she knew something he didn't.

"I can't think how they could find anything at this point," Dodie whispered confidentially. "The bodies will be disintegrated, you know, decayed, won't they?"

"Uhm, decomposed. I do hope they find something, though, that would prove that none of us was involved. *I* had nothing to do with this mess."

"Yes, rabbi, dear," Dodie said in a comforting voice, and led him across the room to an empty table. The dining room tables had been removed and replaced with long tables crowded together. The questionnaires were lying out on the table for the members.

"Why don't we sit next to Doc?" Dodie suggested, taking him through the crowd of noisy people.

She changed her mind when she saw that Jerry Fryman,

Ben and Beverly were together with Doc. She glanced around to find that Dickie David was sitting with the Teedmans and pretty Sandy Lippman, her tennis and sometime golf friend. She steered the rabbi across the room to the other side, but before she got to Sandy Lippman's table some people she did not know usurped the remaining places.

"Why don't we just sit at the first empty table?" the rabbi asked, puzzled. "Let's get this over with; it's not a social occasion, it's painful. Imagine what the papers will say about this—"

"Okay," Dodie agreed, "it's just that I thought we could sit with people and copy the answers if we had to."

"It's not a college test," Rabbi Stone said, "come on."

In order to get her moving, the rabbi was forced to take Dodie by the hand and guide her to the nearest table. They sat down and began to read the questionnaire. It was just what the rabbi thought it would be: questions of time and place. He busied himself with the questions for several minutes then began to write his answers.

Dodie watched him as he wrote. She had regarded him as handsome until she met Tim, and although she no longer thought the rabbi was a Rex Reed lookalike, she could still feel herself lapsing into a reverie whenever he was around . . .

"What's the matter, Dodie," the rabbi asked. The girl looked sick. Her cheeks were flushed and her eyes wild. Was she going to pass out the way she had done in the car?

"Did you take a diet pill today?"

The word *diet* erased Dodie's fantasy. She blinked twice. "Are you sick?"

"Sick?" she murmured, "No, why do you ask?"

"Well," the rabbi said, "you were staring at me in such a bizarre way I thought you might be sick, or having a petit mal or something."

Dodie smiled.

"Petit mal? I doubt it."

"Maybe you ought to see a doctor."

"Maybe I should," Dodie said.

"I'd like to help you," the rabbi offered.

"I'd like to help you, too," Dodie replied, flashing a diamond ring at him which she had recently purchased. "I know you have nothing to do with Po Lee's death, rabbi," Dodie said, "you're a gentle man. This whole thing is silly. They should try to eliminate the obvious non-murderers, like you, like me. I think I'll tell Tim."

"Tim?"

"The medical examiner," she said.

Rabbi Stone stared uncomprehendingly at Dodie. At times she made no sense. Maybe he had correctly stumbled onto something. Maybe she did have petit mal and did not know it. He did have difficulties often understanding what she was saying . . .

"Tell him," he said placatingly, "and if at any time you want to come to the temple for solace or advice, please do so. Whenever."

"I have to see my lawyer today, but how about tomorrow?"

"Tomorrow?" the rabbi asked, watching Dickie David coming towards them. Dickie was one of the nicest people at the club and he gave generously to the temple. The rabbi felt relieved. He could finish the questionnaire and turn Dodie over to Dickie.

"Is tomorrow okay?"

"Yes, certainly," Rabbi Stone answered.

Dickie stood over them, his bright blue eyes looking anxiously at Dodie.

He and the rabbi exchanged nods.

"Good to see you," the rabbi said, rising, preparing to go.

"Oh, don't go," Dickie said, actually pleased the rabbi was departing. This was better than he had hoped.

"Go ahead, Dick," the rabbi encouraged, "sit down, have

194

a little chat with Mrs. Schwartz. Cheer her up. She's had a lot of *tsuris* lately. I think she's feeling forlorn—right, Dodie?"

"Oh, yes."

"Sit down," the rabbi begged, trying to get away.

"Can I ask a favor?" Dodie said.

"Yes, of course, I said so." Rabbi Stone hovered at the table, establishing his graciousness in the tone of voice of the ever-concerned shepherd of his flock.

"I wonder if you could go with me to my mother's tomorrow. She's in a nursing home, not far, about forty miles from Ann Arbor. I hate to go alone. The poor thing is really ill."

"Poor thing," the rabbi repeated.

"I hope I'll be able to go in your place," Dickie said.

"No, oh, no, the rabbi must go. Mommy must see a rabbi," Dodie insisted.

"Call me tomorrow," the rabbi said, drifting away.

Rabbi Stone moved away from Dodie and Dickie. He looked for the table where he had first seen the lawyer Jerry Fryman. He might be a good person to consult about his legal rights.

"May I sit?" Dickie asked.

Dodie nodded at Dickie.

"I have barely written anything," she said.

"Must be terrible for you," Dickie said in a soothing voice. "You're so young to have all this happen to you. I wish I could protect you."

"You do?" Dodie gave him a sidelong glance. He was a sweet person. He would never harm her, nor anyone else.

"If the rabbi won't go with me to Ann Arbor, could you?" she asked in her breathless little girl's voice.

Dickie's cheeks went red.

"I'd like that very much, *very much,*" he said, glancing at her, almost afraid to look in her eyes. "I might combine it with a trip to the University. My daughter is there, and I want to talk to her. I'm getting a divorce. Have you heard?"

Dodie looked surprised. "No," she said, "but I don't hear much sitting at home waiting."

"Waiting?"

"Waiting for this mess to be over. The medical examiner said it might take a few weeks, maybe longer."

"Oh? Listen, Dodie, I want to tell you something. Something important."

"Sure, what?"

At the front of the room Dodie recognized a few people from the medical examiner's office along with the Crestwood Hills police.

"Wait a sec, Dickie, he's trying to get our attention."

She saw that Tim was fanning a newspaper to try to get the attention of the group. She could not hear what he was saying because of the noise in the room.

"Could you have lunch with me tomorrow, well, one day this week maybe," Dickie asked. "There's something important I want to discuss with you, Dodie." Just saying her name caused excitement to course through his body.

"Shhh, Dickie," Dodie said, "the medical examiner is trying to speak."

Tim banged the newspaper down on a table, clapped his hands and shouted for silence, but the tumult in the room continued. Few had heard him or were even aware he was trying to address them. He then said something to one of the police officers, who immediately took out his service revolver.

"Silence," Tim yelled to no avail.

He nodded at the police officer and Dodie ducked under the table thinking he was going to shoot the gun. She heard no shot, and peeped out to see the officer simply walking around the room waving his gun. This was enough to bring quiet into every corner of the dining room.

"Thank you for your attention," Tim said in a business-like voice. "I'd like to apologize for this group questionnaire which is unprecedented in Oakland County or the annals of police work in general. Nevertheless, we decided this was the easiest route to take; you can appreciate the problems we face with such a large number of people having been in contact with all of the deceased prior to their deaths."

Puzzled looks and grim glances were exchanged around the room. No one was pleased to be there to begin with.

"This is, perhaps," Tim began, then paused for effect, "the worst case of suspected murder in Michigan history."

There was a gasp from the group when they realized what he was saying.

"You will hear it on the six o'clock news and I want to be the first to set the record straight. We believe that whoever killed the maid, Po Lee, also killed the Schwartzes. Remember you heard it first from the medical examiner."

Everyone looked at each other with shocked expressions.

"We are working night and day to bring this case to a close," Tim added. "We do not have a specific motive yet but when we do we will have the murderer. At this point there are a number of suspects and all, I repeat, all are under careful investigation."

Dodie moved restlessly on the bench, crossing one leg and then the other.

"I've got to get out of here soon," she said to Dickie, who patted her on the shoulder.

"Yes," he said, "you will. Be patient, my dear."

Dodie nodded . . . Dickie reminded her of her father, only Dickie was more accessible. Though she had worshipped her father, he had always been hidden behind a newspaper or a magazine. He had thought he was a failure because he was a pharmacist instead of a doctor. He had been brought up to be a doctor but hadn't made the grade, and after his illness he could only work part-time. Instead of devoting himself to his family, he just read more books, magazines and newspapers. He had not been aware that his daughter suffered because of him—he did not seem to think much about his family . . .

"Well, when could you have lunch then?" Dickie asked in a timid voice. He looked lovingly at her face, which he longed to touch. For a split second she gazed at him and their eyes met. Then, abruptly, Dodie's eyes closed.

"Open your eyes, my darling, you can't get away from me."

Obediently, she opened her eyes. He was a sweet old thing but why were they playing games? Of course, he would not have the remotest inkling she was about to have one of her delicious waking dreams. Her eyes seemed to watch him but they were focused inward . . .

"We must swim again," Dodie giggled.

Dickie smiled. Since he had informed his wife that he intended to seek a divorce, he felt liberated, self-confident. He would begin again—with Dodie, if she would have him. Only now he realized he could not afford to scare her away by being too direct. He would have to build up to it; she was not the sort of girl you pushed into things. She was such a mysterious soul. He would tread softly but with determination. Lunch was the first step. If only he could get a commitment from her, yet this was beginning to seem impossible.

"Dodie, dear Dodie," he said reaching for her hand, which was smooth and wonderful to touch. He glanced around to see if Beverly was in the vicinity. She was not. The coast was clear, and he stroked Dodie's hand. She did not seem to notice.

"Mrs. Schwartz, Mrs. Schwartz," Tim was calling.

"Dodie," Dickie whispered, "you had better answer. Everyone is looking at us."

He had discreetly let go of her hand when he realized the entire room was looking their way. Dodie suddenly snapped out of her reverie. Tim was standing at the front of the room talking to her.

"I thought you might like to comment, Mrs. Schwartz."

"Oh, yes," Dodie stuttered and got to her feet, feeling quite intimidated by the attention.

"I want to thank everyone," she continued to stutter, "thank you. And . . . I am sorry . . . sorry . . . for all of this . . . sorry that you had to be here."

"Sit down now, it's okay," Dickie said and gently took her arm, guiding her back to the bench.

The babble started up again. No one was looking at them. Their private moment had returned.

"Lunch," Dickie demanded again. "When? Now that I have you I am not going to let you go."

"Have me?" Dodie asked, bewildered.

"Tomorrow for lunch. Noon is fine," Dickie said. "I'll be expecting you. I'll take you to Jacques's. Do you like it?"

"Jacques's? Yes, I think I do."

"Well, that's settled," Dickie said.

"Yes."

Tim ended his little speech. "It is not the role or the place of the medical examiner to slant the case in favor of the prosecution or the defense. We only want to get our facts and information straight in order to help apprehend whoever committed these terrible crimes."

He was staring over at Dodie, thinking that even at this distance she looked incredibly beautiful . . . He would take her back to the lab and show her why he was fascinated with his work. He wanted to show her everything. There was something exciting about a modern-day crime lab he wished to share with her; the instruments, for example, the gas chromatographs, the spectographs, the ultraviolet and infrared spectrophotometers, as well as the paper and thin-layer chromatography equipment. Wouldn't she be amazed? And the lectures on forensic medicine he sometimes gave at colleges and country clubs he would give for her.

"I hope for all your sakes, for the sake of the community,

that we get this case solved. Thank you very much."

He flashed Dodie a smile and departed. They were to meet at the entrance; meantime, he was going to have a drink at the bar with Ben Schwartz, the man he privately considered his prime suspect. He gave Dodie one final look, wondering if she thought the same . . .

Tim was surprised to see Ben with Jerry Fryman. They were drinking champagne.

"That could be lethal," he said, nodding at the bucket of ice containing the best Taittinger.

"I don't think we'll be poisoned," Ben grunted. He was wearing his new suit and a tie. He felt just as good as anyone at the club—shortly he would be a lot richer.

"You are his lawyer?" Tim inquired, ordering a Coke.

"Uh huh," Jerry said, feeling uneasy. He had already been interrogated three times by the Crestwood Hills police and had been down to the police station twice. One of the medical examiners had visited his office. He had even filled out their questionnaire twice. What more did they want? Let them prove he did it, he thought.

Sipping at the glass of champagne, he felt a wave of contempt come across him but he pushed it away. Jerry did not like to hate anyone. Saving his energy for jogging was far more constructive. He was now trying to adopt a casual attitude toward all his recent problems: the mounting gambling debts, the loss of the Schwartz money on the silver shipment, the fact that his law practice was not doing particularly well. He was counting too much on Ben to bail him out and he knew this was not wise. Still, what could he do? He knew he should try to relax.

"I want you guys to be aware of something," Tim said firmly. "We have exfoliated epithelial cells found under Po Lee's fingernails. She was probably trying to scratch the hell out of the killer."

Ben glanced at Jerry for a reaction. Jerry's face was blank. He said nothing.

"Ex–what?" Ben looked at Tim for an explanation.

"Microscopic shreds of tissue, human tissue. We found bits of hair in her hands, too. Someone, some guy out there is missing a little hair. We want you to journey down to the lab for an examination, Ben."

Ben nodded obligingly.

"That's outrageous, Quincy," he said jokingly. "I just had a hair cut but of course I'll do it, right, Jerry?"

"Yes," Jerry said, nervously rubbing his hands.

Tim was looking at Ben's head, which did look different from yesterday. This could get in the way of an examination. Perhaps it was too late to do hair tests, but, no, he could eliminate him as a suspect if his hair did not positively match the samples they had taken from the maid's body.

"How can you tell anything by the hair?" Ben asked.

"They can," Jerry assured him, tweaking his mustache.

He had spent two hours being questioned by the medical examiner. The guy looked like a nice fellow but Jerry felt he was too much the do-gooder for comfort. Jerry had readily admitted to him that he owed the Schwartz family the silver shipment money, although, he pointed out, it was not his fault that the money went astray–legally, he was probably safe . . . Maybe he might be able to make some deal with Dodie, or was that just wishful thinking? Now that Dodie knew she was inheriting half the estate at the very least, she seemed to have adopted an attitude he had not thought she was capable of. Suddenly, from a little know-nothing, she was now involved with interest rates and contracts. She seemed to know more about the Michigan probate code than he did . . .

"We can determine whether the hair is Oriental, Caucasian, Negroid, or Indian," Tim said, "we can determine the age, sex and just about everything else. We have fantastic equipment. You ought to see our lab."

He realized his invitation sounded silly, but he had forgotten that he was talking to two of the suspects.

"Hair from a victim could have splintered shafts. We want to examine your shafts."

"Sounds weird," Ben said, "anyway, how about Jerry's hair, why just mine?"

"Shhhh," Jerry hissed, "calm down."

"I'll be glad to have an examination, Quincy," Ben said. "I wouldn't hurt a flea. If you ask down at the Humane Society, they'll tell you I'm kind to dumb animals."

"We have already asked and I agree that you are kind to animals," Tim said. "And my name's Levine."

There was a quality of sneakiness about Ben he did not like, his way of making light of serious things. And Jerry was a nervous man—the sort of controlled person who might suddenly break out and do something violent . . .

"Okay, okay, Doc."

"But how are you to humans?" Tim asked.

Ben could not think of a suitable reply to convince Tim of his basic humanity. And before he could make any comment at all, Beverly had wiggled her way over to the bar in her black pleated skirt and silk blouse. She looked striking and impressive, her blond hair gleaming. Ben smiled at her.

Beverly attempted to smile back. She was worried.

"Buying drinks?" she asked Ben.

"What'll you have?"

"A Seven-Up, please."

Ben did a double-take. Beverly's newly acquired manner of meekness upset him. He had always admired her balls, but since her husband told her *he* wanted a divorce she had seemed to change. Ben hoped it was an act . . .

Tim suddenly became authoritarian again.

"Sorry, guys, time to go. We're all due back at the lab. Mrs. Schwartz is going along with me. I have some matters to discuss with her. You're all expected."

He glanced at Beverly who was looking at him with incredulous eyes.

"You, too."

"Me? Why me?"

"Why not you?" Tim said. "I'm afraid you're one of the suspects. We've got four dead people here and you knew all of them well and saw all of them. In fact, according to our investigations, you seem to be, ah, let us say, ubiquitous."

"Oh no, not anymore," she said.

"Well, maybe ubiquitous is the wrong word," Tim admitted. "I don't mean to be unkind; only you do seem to . . ."

"Get around," Ben smiled mawkishly.

Beverly did not seem to appreciate the comment. She shrugged, hoping a casual attitude would garner Ben's respect. Since she got the word from Dickie, her ego had done a reverse. She did not feel confident any longer, and had begun to lean on Ben. This seemed to turn him off completely.

"Well," Tim said, "let's go, we've got unfinished business."

He went to find Dodie, who was waiting for him, looking gorgeous wrapped in her gray mink. He felt a sudden surge of passion when he saw her, and then a fleeting image of Patti came into mind . . . California had changed her from an intelligent bluestocking into a blond in hippie clothes. Her boyfriend had a gold stud earring through his right ear.

As he talked to Dodie his thoughts kept returning to Patti. She had run into his arms when she saw him, only to bring forth the boy for an introduction. If Patti liked this guy how could she ever have liked him?

Patti had taken the three of them to a dark coffee shop around the Renaissance Center and then insisted on paying the bill. She seemed to want Tim's approval, so he gave his blessing and sent them home . . .

Tim smiled into Dodie's mysterious eyes. Other than the images of Patti, something else was bothering him . . . Dodie . . . She was, after all, still a suspect—he could not erase that from the record. He would feel much freer to love her and care for her once the case ended. Meantime, he had better keep his feelings for her in perspective. He might not actually consider her a suspect himself, but Doctor Mills and Doctor Fenton, who had performed poor Hank Schwartz's postmortem, did.

"Oh, Tim, I do apologize but I don't feel well and want to go home. Officer Wiggs is outside waiting for me. He'll go home with me. I'll be all right. Anyway, you said the other suspects are going to be questioned again. They'll all be together."

Tim nodded agreement.

"We assume that the killer of these four persons is among a small group, but we could be wrong, Dodie. Don't be so sure that the killer is in the group I named. We don't know yet, not really. If we did, the case would be solved. It's not going to be that easy, not with poison."

"Oh? You're certain it's poison? Not with Po Lee, of course."

"She may have been poisoned too, we're not certain yet."

"Po Lee poisoned?" Tears came into Dodie's dark eyes.

"Oh, don't cry, Dodie, please."

"I can't help it."

Tim gave her a sympathetic glance. She did look tired. "Go home, rest; I'll call you later. Dinner?"

"Yes."

She drifted out the door and got into Officer Wiggs's patrol car. She leaned her head against the back of the seat, but after a moment turned to Officer Wiggs, who was waiting attentively for her directions.

"I want to go to the temple," she said, "I need to see the

rabbi. I need something spiritual after that ordeal . . . I definitely need guidance."

"Yes, ma'am, just point the way."

Dodie looked at his profile, wondering what it would be like to sleep with a cop. Were cops more macho than other men? That Officer Gracey seemed sexy.

When was she ever going to have the nerve to make her dreams come true? She was already thirty years old and the only men she had known were Hank and Tim. Of course, she worshipped Tim and she enjoyed making love with him, but time was running out and two men in a lifetime just were not enough.

"It's Twelve Mile and Lahser," she said, smiling brightly at the officer as he turned for the directions.

CHAPTER TWENTY-TWO

Tim looked at his notes. Doc Matthews's taped responses were interesting, although sometimes confusing. For example, once he said he hated his ex-wife and then a few minutes later he said he loved her. He continuously seemed to contradict himself.

"Excuse me," Leona said, standing in the doorway, a glass of water in her hand and some little white pills in the other.

"It's about twelve o'clock, doctor, don't you have your usual headache?"

Tim smiled.

"No, I haven't had any headaches recently. I thought I told you."

"You did. I guess I didn't believe it. Oh, well."

Leona turned and left in a huff. Tim returned to Doc Matthews's taped interrogation. The cassette played on.

"It's true I would know how to inject. It's true I know something about poison; well, a little. Any doctor knows a little about it. Not like you toxicologists."

There was garbled laughter on the tape, then Doc went on.

"I could easily steal some poison from a hospital where I have privileges. But I didn't do any of that. I had no motive. What would my motive be?"

Tim turned off the tape. His thoughts were drifting once more to Dodie Schwartz. There was a romantic quality about her he needed and loved, something Patti lacked. Patti was too independent for him.

He turned the tape recorder back on and listened while Doc talked on. He had fed all pertinent information into the computer, but thus far the computer had not come up with anything vaguely exciting.

The police chemist and the medical examiner's office had each found hair samples as well as fibers and threads all over Po Lee. The next step was to search the suspects' premises for articles of clothing to match the samples. It was not easy to solve the murder of the maid in terms of incriminating evidence. Not easy to solve the Schwartz case, either. To Tim it seemed the modus operandi was different in the Po Lee murder. There was no shred of evidence that Po Lee was poisoned, which was too bad because he would have preferred a more obvious connection between the four murders. It appeared as if at least two people had committed the murders. Someone had injected the Schwartzes but perhaps someone else suffocated Po Lee. Why?

Tim tapped the desk. Were there two killers? It seemed ridiculous. The Schwartzes had been obvious victims of premeditated murder. Whoever wanted them to die had thought long and clear about it, had gone to the trouble of selecting a suitable poison, one that would leave little or no trace. The poison had to be obtained, either stolen or bought. The needle was carefully prepared and the death was executed by plan. There was nothing haphazard there.

Po Lee's death, on the other hand, seemed spontaneous, messy, with a multitude of clues left at the scene. Entirely unprofessional. There certainly was no mystery to the manner of killing here.

He pondered the idea: If anything connected all four deaths it was Po Lee's mistaken identity. Someone wanted all the Schwartzes killed. If this was so, wouldn't Ben be the next logical victim?

Perhaps it was better to stick to the idea of one murderer who might have gone to the house for some purpose other than to murder Dodie, but once there had shaped the notion and gone ahead with it. Yes, the difference in the method of killing would just have to remain unsolved for a while. He had no doubt that the truth would ultimately come to light.

He had known, or sensed, all along that the Schwartzes had been poisoned. Now he must prove it. The most difficult part was deciding which poison had been injected and running the correct tests on the remaining organs. Many poison tests had already been attempted but nothing had shown up thus far. As there were over fifteen hundred different kinds of poison, it would be a long, tedious haul to find the right one. Nevertheless, he would persevere with the help of the crime lab chemists.

All of Michigan was waiting for results. After finding the needle marks on Henry's left thigh, Tim had ordered full-scale toxicological analysis which was still underway. Michigan would have to wait a little longer.

Tim suddenly thought of something. It was surely possible that Hank Schwartz had written another will, one that predated the will the lawyer had presented. If so, he would have to see it. This other will might shed light on Schwartz's real intentions. The document could prove invaluable in the investigation.

He wrote out a note for his secretary to carry to Jerry

Fryman, who was now waiting in another room for questioning.

Tim felt confident that he would soon have a grip on the mystery.

When Jerry Fryman read the note from Doctor Levine, a feeling of panic descended. He stared through the dirty window at the winter's day. The sun was shining and the weather was pleasant. Not a bad day for jogging. He would just slip into his jogging gear after he left the medical examiner's office. A good jog would clear his head . . .

The first will that Hank had made left money to Dodie and Ben, with Dodie getting the lion's share. This will had been written some years before the elder Schwartzes died, and when Hank still cared for Dodie. The second will left everything to Dodie—Hank had had a falling out with Ben at that point. A third will left the major part to Dodie and a generous amount to some girl named Charlotte whom Hank was putting through college. The fourth will cut out Charlotte entirely and again divided the estate between Dodie and Ben. The fifth will put everything in trust for Dodie. The sixth will reversed that and left the money to her outright. Jerry could not remember the seventh one only that he knew there had been one. The eighth will was so complicated he needed the advice of another lawyer. He could not remember the details of the following wills. One of the wills left money to the twins, Del and Danto Tannenbaum, but he couldn't remember which will that was. It had been undone anyway, he thought, but was not certain.

He would have to dredge up these wills and show them to the medical examiner and the police or be considered as harboring evidence. He loathed being a criminal. White-collar crime, which looked easy in the beginning, was now a noose around his neck.

Jerry twisted on the chair, feeling a sharp pain in his stomach. He got up, glanced furtively around, saw that no one was about to enter the room and went out, gently closing the door behind him. He marched to the elevator, rang, waited impatiently and darted in as soon as the elevator doors opened. He'd call the medical examiner later, tell him he had an emergency. They could do their tests on him tomorrow. He was in no rush for them. He needed a break. Instead of jogging he would take a leisurely drive to the Art Institute and see what was doing. Sometimes, especially during the week, there were girls down there. He needed consolation, had not had any for a long, long time, not since that lovely, dark-haired gal, Elaine Shapiro, had spoken to him in the cafeteria. However, she did reject him when it got to the hint of seduction, claiming she loved her husband.

Driving down the expressway, he began to feel more relaxed. The farther from the medical examiner's office the better he felt. He could jog around the museum, get all the knots of tension out of his body.

Jerry allowed his thoughts to drift. The office couch badly needed recovering. There was something depressing about his office which did not suit a Harvard-trained lawyer. Ben had agreed to advance him the money to paint and to hang pictures, not just any old thing but originals from the Hilberry Gallery. He wanted contemporary art, nothing obscure. With his muddled knowledge of art he had to be careful. He could be easily led.

He played with his mustache. The police knew about the silver shipment, the FBI knew and the medical examiner's office knew. Everyone knew except Ben, who would never have given him his power of attorney—the right to invest the Schwartz monies where he saw fit—had he known. Still, Jerry felt his own guilt was questionable. It was not *his* fault the silver shipment was hijacked. He was guilty of many things but not that escapade; it had nothing to do with him at all. In a way he wished it had—why hadn't he been shrewd enough to hijack the shipment himself? He could have sold everything to the Hunts in Texas, perhaps would even have forestalled the silver crisis. He could have been a hero now instead of a *shmuck*.

He tried thinking about Elaine Shapiro, her raven-black hair, her high I.Q., her knowledge of modern poetry. She was married to a stockbroker who liked novels, he remembered. Her children were all bright. Her life was a success.

A feeling of anxiety came over him as he thought again about Hank's numerous wills. He would have to produce them, and that would throw into dispute the present will. It would be fuel for Dodie's case . . .

Parking near the museum he went inside and to the cafeteria where he once had luck picking up a girl. The cafeteria was crowded at this hour. He could not tell which girls were alone—he would have to wait and see who walked off by herself. He decided instead to wander around for a look at Baron Thyssen's collection. He had read about it in the newspapers and was intrigued. He might even meet someone that way.

The word *newspaper* brought back a feeling of panic . . . The newspapers were having a field day over the Schwartz and Po Lee murders. For the last three days they had been overflowing with not just information but comments and lewd speculations. Thank God he was not considered a suspect by the press, or he would have been inundated by phone calls. The medical examiner had released his name only as a lawyer involved in the case. He was grateful, although it was evident that he was a suspect. Doctor Levine had already told him point-blank he was considered a suspect in the murders of all three Schwartzes. He had a motive and a good one—money. With the Schwartzes out of the way he would never have to return the enormous sum he owed them. Furthermore, his friend and client, Ben Schwartz, would then inherit the family fortune, putting him in a more favorable position to get his hands on the money.

As Doctor Levine explained this theory to him, Jerry felt like throwing up. He had controlled himself, however, and had even sounded confident when he told Levine he was wrong. Levine could not prove anything, could he? It was then the doctor had told him he would be needed for further questioning, for a hair examination and for more fingerprinting. Jerry had not objected. Objecting might make the doctor think he *was* guilty, or indeed had some major role to play in the murders of the Schwartzes. But how about Po Lee? The doctor had not mentioned her. Doctor Levine had told him they were going to search his house and he had given permission. By his watch, it was now two o'clock and they were there right this moment searching the premises, sorting through his drawers, going through his clothes, taking samples from this and that. He did not care. He had nothing to hide at home. Anything incriminating was in his office and had been put away in his safe to which he alone had the key. He found a pay phone and called the medical examiner's office.

"Doctor Levine, please."

A soft voice asked who was calling. Was this the Puerto Rican woman with the blue eyes? She was sort of attractive.

"Winston Churchill," he said.

"Winston Churchill?" She clicked off and in a moment the doctor was on the phone, speaking in an annoyed way.

"Who is this?"

"Jerry Fryman. I was called away. An emergency."

"*This* is an emergency, the only emergency. Where are you?"

"The Detroit Art Institute. I've heard the exhibition is excellent."

"I'm going to say this just once: return here in the next

ten minutes. Understand? This is a serious matter."

"No," Jerry said, "I'm busy. It can't wait. I didn't do anything to those people, and I won't be demeaned in this way."

"Either you return immediately or we'll send someone down for you," Tim said, hanging up.

"No," Jerry replied stubbornly.

He hung up, thinking that he would feel much better if he could find a pretty girl to talk to. He saw one walking ahead of him and followed her toward the Thyssen collection, then changed his mind and went to look at the Rivera murals. They were comforting relics of childhood when his class made yearly pilgrimages to the art museum.

Jerry made the right choice. There was a pretty girl with blond streaks in her hair. Maybe this would be his lucky day. Jerry stood nearby looking at her legs. They were slender, shapely. He was observing her minutely when she turned, saw him, and smiled expansively. He did not smile back, too startled by the sudden eye-to-eye contact.

"Hi, there," she called to him.

"Oh, hello."

He moved closer to make sure she was actually speaking to him. He glanced around to see if she was possibly talking to someone behind him. They were alone in the great hall with only Henry Ford, Senior staring down at them from the Rivera murals.

"Aren't they fabulous?" she said.

"What?"

"These, naturally," she laughed, throwing out her arm at the murals.

"You're an art lover?"

"Absolutely," she said, "next to life, it's the best thing."

She had blue eyes and a lovely smile. He felt apprehensive; but this could be the test of his mettle: was he a man, or wasn't he? Now was the time to act. Either he could get quickly to the matter at hand, or he might as well turn himself in. Jerry was alarmed at his recent lack of confidence in himself.

"Listen," he said plaintively, "I don't have much time. Can I get to the bottom line?"

"What's that?" She looked interested.

"Would you come somewhere else with me?"

"Like where?"

"Well, we could go to my house, or a hotel, or your house."

She smiled. "I live in an apartment."

"That's good enough."

She nodded and without further ado they turned and started walking towards the museum entrance.

"Uh oh," Jerry said, stopping dead in his tracks.

"What's going on?" the girl asked.

Up ahead near the postcard counter were four policemen, two of whom had their guns drawn. The girl froze.

"Oh, God, maybe they think we're someone else."

"I think they know who they want," Jerry said. "Sorry."

He looked around for a quick way out. There wasn't any.

"I guess I've been a bad boy," he whispered confidentially.

"Some kind of nut," she said, slipping to the floor in a dead faint.

"Give her the smelling salts," one of the policemen ordered as he advanced on Jerry and clamped handcuffs on him.

"Give her my sincere apologies," Jerry requested.

"Yeah, sure. And I'll give her a big kiss, too," the policeman replied, pushing him toward the front.

"Get moving, art lover," he growled into his ear, "and don't give us any trouble or we'll take you to *our* precinct in the inner city and beat the crap out of you."

A crowd was following behind them and outside another little crowd was waiting. If he had been smarter, this would not be happening to him. Levine was overenthusiastic, wanting to make a name for himself, even if he had to humiliate others to do so. There was no real reason to have gone this far. He must have known that Jerry was not running anywhere, that he would be around for further questioning.

"You've got the wrong guy," he said.

He looked behind him as he was pushed through the revolving door and saw the pretty girl being helped to her feet. She was awake. She had been willing. He could have been listening to music and making love to her in his bed, his Dobermans at the foot of it. Instead, he was being shoved into a Detroit police car.

CHAPTER TWENTY-THREE

Dodie turned on her favorite radio station, and listening to the romantic music, gazed at Tim as he undressed. He had broad shoulders, muscular arms, an amazingly small waist and long, lean legs. He suited her perfectly. She loved him because he had freed her of all inhibitions. Never had she felt so liberated and so desirable.

She watched him fondly as he threw his clothes on the floor, as Hank had done, as all men did. They seemed to be sure there would be someone there to pick up the clothes for them—a woman, of course. She did not really like to be put in the position of maid, but was resigned to it. She bent and scooped up his pants and shirt and tucked them over the brocaded chair in Rose Schwartz's dimly lit massive master bedroom.

They looked at each other and were in each other's arms instantly. He threw himself over her nakedness, kissing her neck, her shoulders, with a wild passion. His tongue pushed its way inside her mouth . . . Then, all of a sudden, he released her and went over to the window.

"Oh," he said, "I forgot to tell you that we've arrested Jerry Fryman."

Dodie giggled nervously. "Really? What for?"

"He was told to get down to our office and didn't. Once he produces the writ of habeus corpus I don't think we can keep him. Frankly, I believe he is Ben's accomplice in the murder of your family and in the murder of your maid."

Tears sprang to Dodie's eyes. Here was her darling Tim doing his best to protect her. She glanced at his strong body, his erect penis and then embraced him. He led her to Rose's huge bed.

"We're getting together a tight case," Tim said, placing her on top of the quilt, gently stroking her stomach.

"Let's get inside," Dodie said, pulling off the bedspread.

"The real problem is your in-laws. They're badly decomposed. We even tested the earth around the coffins to eliminate arsenic, but we have not come up with the correct poison. And there is something else I have to tell you."

He leaned across her and buried his head in her breasts. He began to rock back and forth in a rhythmical motion.

"Ben injects animals at his job. He would know how to wield a needle. He has access to poison. But so does Doc. Even Beverly David could inject something lethal. With practice anyone can learn to inject without leaving a mess."

"Yes, my Timmy," Dodie said, stroking his hair, "but not everyone can do it properly."

"Uhm," Tim moaned as she touched him.

"I think this is all so unpleasant," she said. "Did you know Dickie David told his wife he would kill for the woman he loves?"

Tim looked up at her. Her eyes were closed, her face flushed.

"How do you know?"

"He told me," she said, placing his hand down between her legs.

"There's something else," Tim said, "the hairs from Po Lee's fingernails don't exactly match Ben's. It's not exactly that they do or don't—we're uncertain. We need more tests."

Dodie sighed. With all the evidence around she had hoped for a quick resolution. If Ben were arrested, there would be no will contest. The entire affair would drop from the front pages and be only a vague memory in the minds of the club members.

"Then there's something else," Tim added, hating to tell her anything that might further upset her. The poor girl had been through too much already.

"What is it, sweetheart?" Dodie murmured as she drew herself over and onto Tim's body.

"The department has not eliminated you as a suspect, my darling, not yet. Uhm, I'd like to, believe me. I want the whole sordid thing to come to an end. But we haven't got the goods on anyone, not yet. I would hate this to be a circumstantial case. We want a definite conviction."

Dodie groaned with pleasure. A sudden image of herself wearing a bridal gown, walking down the aisle in front of two thousand people, came to mind. There would be no *chuppah* this time like the one Hank had insisted on. A famous judge would marry them . . .

"You need a confession," she mumbled, "yes, oh, yes, a confession."

She saw Tim beneath her, his face illuminated with desire for her. He was so handsome. He would make a wonderful husband . . . She had always wanted to be married to a doctor. You got better tables at restaurants, and good seats on the aisle at the theatre. People treated you with respect. She might even be able to get him into Crestwood Hills, although once she married him *she* was automatically out—he would have to be the member. She could donate a large sum to his favorite charity, perhaps to medical research, and pay the initiation fee and this would get him in.

They would be *the* couple in the club. At last her mother would be proud of her . . .

"How do we get a confession?" Tim said, opening his eyes.

"I love you," Dodie said, and turned on her side to face him. Their eyes locked as she slowly, gently, drew him inside her. The sensation of their finally connecting was overwhelming, a feeling akin to a giant sigh of relief. Tim's hands, lost in her mass of raven hair, drew her face close to his own.

"We'll solve this, Dodie, somehow . . . " Tim moaned as he moved above her.

Dodie just smiled.

CHAPTER TWENTY-FOUR

Dodie put the telephone down. She had lost her nerve when Ben had answered on the second ring. For twenty minutes she paced, a glass of sherry in one hand, the telephone in the other, before she finally decided to dial his number again.

"Yeah, who is it?" Ben yelled into the receiver.

"It's Dodie," she said timidly, wondering if he would hang up on her.

"Who? Speak louder. I can't hear you."

"It's Dodie; I'd like to see you."

"See me? What for?"

"I'd like to talk to you, Ben. It's for your own benefit, believe me."

"Well, babe," Ben rasped, the interest clear in his voice, "go ahead."

"I want this to be confidential until I speak to my lawyer; is that okay with you?"

"Confidential? Yeah. What's this all about, anyway?"

"I have to speak privately, not on the telephone," Dodie said.

"Well, come over sometime. But aren't you scared?"

"Scared?" Dodie asked, "of what?"

"I'm a homocidal maniac. Supposed to have killed my family, remember?"

Dodie felt awkward. She was supposed to be scared but she wasn't. The only things which frightened her were her night terrors, her daydreams, her constant sexual fantasizing—all of which were increasing all the time . . .

"Yes," she lied, "I'm scared, but I have to see you. Alone."

"Okay, so?"

"Right now. Tonight."

"Can't it wait until morning?"

"I might change my mind and it's important for you."

"Okay, get over here, then," he said, hanging up.

Dodie hurried through her house to peek out the living room windows. Officer Wiggs, on duty for the night, was sitting in his car, his hat off, his head against the seat. He looked asleep as far as she could tell in the dim light.

He ought to be, she thought. In fact, he ought to be out for the next three hours if what she had slipped into his coffee was working properly. Nothing that would harm him, however; just a little something to help her accomplish her mission, which would hopefully bring the whole case to rest. She felt she was helping along justice, which sometimes needed a little push.

She took her coat and slipped out the side entrance to the Cadillac. She turned on the ignition and waited to see if the sound of the engine woke up Officer Wiggs. He did not move a hair. Looking at the clock she figured it would take her at least twenty minutes to get down to Ben's apartment. Getting to the point might take another fifteen and getting home a further twenty. She had enough time if everything went as planned. She was still allowing herself some leeway in case the officer woke up prematurely.

Everything had to go smoothly, perfectly. There could

be no mistakes because a mistake would be costly, even deadly. Her fate rested on this night.

Tomorrow she would visit her mother at the nursing home and try to explain everything. On the phone her mother did not seem to understand that the Schwartzes had gone to an early grave. Maybe in person she would be able to better understand.

Dodie had never had an easy time communicating with her mother, but at the same time had not given up, assuming that the fault lay with herself. Somehow her mother would have to understand her. . . .

She looked into the rearview mirror half expecting a police escort, but no one was behind her. She smiled. The officer was sleeping like a baby. With a new sense of self-confidence, she revved the motor and began her journey to Ben's neighborhood. It took her less time than anticipated. She parked at some distance from his building and proceeded on foot to where she knew he lived, walking the two blocks quickly, making sure no one saw her hovering near his building. She opened the unlocked entrance door and took the stairs to the second floor. She tiptoed down the hall to the end apartment, then stood outside listening. She wanted no witnesses to her visit.

As she stood in the hall, she heard Beverly's hoarse voice.

"I'm telling you he says he's in love with her; I'm *not* making it up, Ben."

Beverly slammed her hand down on a table and retreated into her own disturbing thoughts. Since Dickie had given her the news about the divorce her steadfast self-confidence seemed to have disappeared. She was in a state of shock, never having realized until now how dependent she was on her husband. Yet she did not want Ben to know her fears. What he liked about her—*out* of bed—was her cold-bloodedness, her steely nerves. He did not want an insecure, vulnerable woman. Men were all the same, without conscience, heartless.

Ben looked at her with doubtful eyes.

"I think you and Dickie have some scheme going, babe, why don't you admit it already? I can dig it."

Beverly got up and began to pace the living room.

"So you get a divorce and then you marry me. Dickie marries Dodie. Either way you collect, you and Dickie."

"What does that mean?" She turned and stared at him. He was slouched across the couch wearing the yellow sweater she hated.

"Well," he said, his voice hard, "if you two've got some master scheme going and you marry me and he marries Dodie, you can't lose. I mean we don't know who really is going to collect the fifty or sixty million, do we? A judge or jury decides. I'll get something and she'll get something, but one of us will get a lot more than the other, or maybe all. Then, whoever doesn't collect the big amount gets dumped. In fact, we both get dumped. Then you and Dickie get back together again that much richer."

"He doesn't need your money," Beverly snapped. As soon as the words were out of her mouth, she regretted them. She couldn't afford to make him angry.

"Let's not fight, honey," she said. "Let's go to bed." She had had her hair done, a peducure, a facial, a manicure and bought two pairs of new shoes, but it did not make any difference. She felt awful; ugly, old, and unwanted. Ben had been subtly trying to get rid of her for the last half hour. She was no fool.

"No," Ben said, sneering.

"Why not?"

"Don't beg, Beverly. What happened to your balls?"

"They're still there, want to see?"

"No, go home. We'll see each other tomorrow."

"I don't want to go home."

Beverly tried to look sexy. She tried to smile, wondering if perhaps it would be wiser to leave.

"Let's make love, Ben," she said.

Ben regarded her skeptically, then he smiled.

"Well, that might be nice, but not now. Maybe tomorrow. Come back in the morning."

"Sure," Beverly said, going to the closet for her trench coat.

"But don't be abject," Ben warned.

Beverly looked puzzled.

"You don't know what the word means, do you, babe?"

"Certainly, sweetheart, I invented it."

He patted her on the behind and helped her into her coat.

Beverly put her shaking hands into the pockets of her coat. She did not want him to know the level of her anxiety. He might totally reject her if he knew. He could easily find someone else, someone younger, more ballsy than she really was. She no longer felt she could depend on his devotion. He had grown perceptibly colder toward her, and now that he was a suspect in the four murders his disposition had become completely miserable. And nothing helped.

"I love you," she said. One couldn't be too careful.

"Love you too," he said breezily, holding open the door.

"What's that noise?" Beverly said as she peered out into the dim hall.

"Someone walking upstairs, I think," Ben said. "I'm not the only tenant, you know."

"It's creepy. That might be a nut out there."

"Go ahead, you don't need me. If there are any rapists out there, enjoy it—you can handle it. You're parked near the front door, anyway. Just run to the car, babe."

He gave her a little shove and closed the door, then walked to the kitchen and let the two puppies he had brought home from the Humane Society into the living room.

Dodie crept back to his door and listened—he was in his apartment alone now except for an animal. She knew he collected various stray cats and dogs. He was talking to an animal now, or to himself.

She knocked shyly on the door, then louder when he didn't answer. Ben came to the door and yanked it open. When he saw her standing there he felt strangely unsettled. He had known she was coming, but the reality came as a sort of shock. There she was standing before him, her lustrous black hair hanging to her shoulders, her dark, soulful eyes looking directly at him. Her skin seemed pale and she looked a little sick.

"Come in," he said.

His eyes followed her hips, clothed in tight suede pants, into the room. She had taken off her coat in the hallway and was carrying it over her arm. As much as he hated to, Ben had to confess there was something more attractive, more provocative about Dodie since Hank died, even though she still wasn't terribly clever. But here she was in his apartment, the lamb entering the lion's den.

"Does anyone know you're here?" he said, looking into the hall to see if she was accompanied.

"No, no one."

"How can I believe that?"

Dodie shrugged.

He eyed her for a sign of lying—nothing, her face was guileless. He suddenly smiled brightly, thinking he could do anything with her he wished and no one would know —he could even waste her. Of course, that was out of the question now that he was suspect *numero uno.* He wanted no more trouble with the police. They had come to his apartment, turned it upside down, taken samples from his clothes, his furniture, even his food. They had even searched his garbage. And now they had probably sent Dodie as some kind of trap.

"Let me tell you," Dodie said, sitting down carefully on the dilapidated couch.

"Yes, I'm listening."

He watched her, sensing that whatever she was about to tell him would prove disastrous for him. Why else was she here? It could not be good news she was bringing. Nothing that had ever transpired between them had been good.

"Well, what the hell is it?" he said impatiently. "Tell me, or get out."

Dodie felt intimidated by his tone but remained impassive.

"Calm down," she suggested mildly. "I'm getting to it. I'm just trying to think of the best way of saying it."

"Say it any old way, just spit it out, Dodie."

"It's just that I think you and I could do much better if we were not at odds with each other. I'm actually willing to drop the will contest if you will agree to do the same."

Ben looked at her for a further explanation. There had to be a catch here. No one gave anything away for free.

"We'll each have plenty," she went on.

"Why would you want to do that when so much money is at stake? You could have much more."

"I'm not greedy," Dodie said, "my wants and needs are not that great. I've only myself to support, and my mother. I have no kids, no relatives to speak of except for her. So what do I need it all for?"

"But why would you want to do this? What's the reason?" Ben suddenly felt on guard. People did not do for others unless they gained themselves; the entire world was proof of this.

"Because," Dodie said carefully, "the will contest only focuses attention on us. The media is making a third world war out of it. Don't you see, it's the wrong kind of attention. They are making *money* the motive for killing Hank . . . "

"And Buddy and Rose," Ben finished, "but how about Po Lee?"

226

"Po Lee was my stand-in. Whoever killed her wanted to kill me."

Dodie studied his face for a reaction. For some odd reason he seemed to be embarrassed.

"What's in it for you?" he asked bluntly.

"The limelight will shine on someone else, can't you see that?"

Ben sat down next to her on the couch. He gazed at her mysterious eyes, hoping to find something other than the blankness he now saw.

"They'll think we were accessories. They'll think we planned everything together," he suggested.

"I hadn't thought of that. But I don't really see why," Dodie said, taking his hand. "You know I don't dislike you. I admire your intelligence . . . and the work you do with animals. Think about it, Ben," she said, "and while you're thinking can you get us a little drink?"

Startled, Ben got up. He did not know she drank—this was a new woman. What she was saying sounded interesting, and anything to get the heat off would be helpful. He was feeling the pressure from the medical examiner's office, the police, the media. It wasn't fair. He was facing a possible arrest for multiple murder.

"I'll see what's in the kitchen. I've got some wine."

Dodie got up.

"Where is it? Let me get it, Ben. Got glasses?"

"On the shelf. I don't know if they're clean," he said, enjoying the idea that Dodie was waiting on him.

Dodie walked off to the kitchen, stepping out of the path of the puppies who had suddenly become aware of her as a possible source of food.

"Can you put them in the closet?" she asked.

"The closet?" Ben asked, horrified. "No."

"Well, somewhere, please."

He pushed them into the bedroom and shut the door.

They whined for several moments, then were quiet.

"Well, Ben," Dodie said, toasting him with her glass, "here's to our new relationship."

Ben glared at her. He did not trust her, though he could not figure out why. If he dropped the will contest, it would make him look like the hero.

"To our new relationship," he said.

They lapsed into silence, each occupied with his own thoughts. Eventually Dodie poured him another glass, then a third. He was beginning to feel sleepy. He much preferred grass to booze. Alcohol never did much for him.

"Why don't you show me the rest of your apartment?" Dodie said in a seductive voice.

"There's not much to see. A dirty bedroom, a crumbling bathroom."

"You could get a maid—you've got the money. You could afford anything now," Dodie said, walking towards the bedroom. She opened the door and the puppies rushed out. She turned to avoid them.

"I'll put them in the kitchen," Ben suggested.

"That would be nice."

He hustled them into the kitchen and shut the door.

"I suppose there's dog hair all over your bed?"

"I suppose," Ben said, looking with renewed interest at Dodie. She entered his bedroom and seemed to be looking around. What was she looking for? He followed her into the room.

"It's a mess," he said, "but frankly, I don't give a damn."

"Why don't you lie down, rest," she said.

"I *am* sleepy," he admitted.

"You look very sleepy," she said. "Lie down and I'll stroke your back. Would you like that?"

Ben lay down on his flowered sheets. She had a mesmerizing effect on him that was uncanny. Had she cast a spell—was she some kind of a witch?

"I've wondered about you all these years," she said.

"Why don't you take off that warm sweater? Aren't you hot? I'd rather touch your skin than your sweater."

Ben scrambled around and flung off his sweater. He looked at her hard to make sure he wasn't hallucinating.

"Now just lie there and relax. I'm excellent at massage. My father taught me."

"I thought your father was a drugstore clerk," he muttered.

Dodie felt her cheeks go momentarily red, but she quickly got control of herself.

"My father worked in a drugstore, that's right. He was a pharmacist, a very good one, in the army, and when he came out he worked in a drug store. That was the only job he could get. He worked overtime to support my mother's illnesses."

Ben did not reply. He was no longer listening. He had drifted into a twilight zone. All he was aware of were Dodie's skillful fingers moving across his back.

"Are you asleep?" she whispered.

She waited a moment until she was certain, then quietly got up from his bed. Glancing around the room, she did not see at once what she was looking for. She opened the top drawer of his dresser and looked inside—nothing but a stack of unpaid bills, some paper clips and two dollars in change. She searched through the other drawers, but did not find what she wanted. She went into the bathroom. Why hadn't she thought of that to begin with?

"Good," she breathed to herself.

Ben's hairbrush was lying on the sink. It looked as if it had never been cleaned. She took a generous amount of hair in her hand and pulled it out of the brush, placing it in a tissue which she put back into her handbag. She noticed some of the hairs were silvery. He must be pulling out the gray hairs, just the way Hank had. What vanity! She then took fresh tissues and went around the apartment to wipe each place or thing that she had touched. She wiped the wine glasses carefully and after wiping the wine bottle put it back where she had found it. She brushed off her coat to make sure there were no dog hairs.

Before leaving she took a last look at Ben who was fast asleep. He would awake feeling groggy and might not even recall her visit—if she was lucky.

She sped away from the area and was home within twenty minutes. She went immediately inside and got undressed, pulling on her turquoise silk dressing gown, then changed her mind. The job was best done naked. She took off the dressing gown. Opening her handbag, she brought out the hair. She would not need all of it, just a little, and she would flush the rest down the toilet. She walked into her mirrored closet. Po Lee's body had been discovered on the other side of the closet behind the bidet and toilet. She opened the door. Getting down on her hands and knees she carefully spread a few of the hairs over the carpet. With the aid of a hairpin she embedded them in the carpet pile. Next, she draped a few hairs randomly over the clothes in the closet, across two fur coats and a raincoat. It was conceivable that the medical examiner's office and the police could have missed these valuable clues.

She stood up to regard her work, feeling satisfied the job was expertly done. Po Lee had grasped Ben's hair in the struggle to the death. So hairs would naturally be spread around the closet. Dodie smiled. There was now enough evidence to burn him.

She walked out of the little room and into the bathroom where she surveyed her naked body in the mirror. Her body looked so attractive. She felt aroused. Sitting on the bidet she turned on the hot water, adjusted it so she would not be scalded and sat back to relax and enjoy the flow of water against her.

When she had enough she returned to her bedroom and got into bed. She felt sexy, excited. She reached for the telephone and called Tim.

In a moment Tim's low voice greeted her. He sounded a little sleepy.

"I can't sleep," Dodie said. "Can you come over?"

"Thought you wanted an early evening," Tim said.

"I do . . . with you," she said.

"Oh?"

"I feel jumpy, nervous," she added. "Please come over. I don't want to bother you but if you don't come I'll have to take a Valium. I don't want to impose, but I'm really nervous tonight, just a wreck thinking about everything."

"I'll be there, sit tight," he said reassuringly.

"'Bye," she purred.

She lay naked under the sheet stroking herself. Here she was, a grown-up woman waiting for her lover. At last. She did not wish to end up like her sexless mother . . . Her father's eyes bore the silent implication when he talked to her about her mother. He compensated by having an occasional affair. He tried to include Dodie in his double-life by inviting her out for sodas and movies with whomever his girlfriend at the moment happened to be. This lasted only until her mother discovered what was going on and forbade Dodie to go with her father unless she went too. They were forever fighting about this. Her father felt he had too little time with Dodie and kept trying to persuade his wife to see his logic. She never cooperated, however, and ultimately turned relentlessly bitter toward her husband, an unpleasant yet never-changing fact which the whole family had to live with for years.

Dodie's father never actually abandoned her mother. He was basically a gentle man with a sense of obligation to his family. Maybe her mother managed to finally henpeck him out of the house in order to bring about a certain stability. Dodie was always caught in the middle, while her parents maneuvered to attain the kind of life they thought they deserved.

But it wasn't only this emotional tug of war in which

Dodie found herself year after year. Her parents were also at constant odds about money. This was the central conflict. Whatever her father earned was never enough for her mother. She wanted more.

Their relationship was finally resolved when her father died . . . Dodie suspected that it might have been suicide . . . After he died, her mother appeared with a boyfriend she claimed she had known for years. He moved right in and together they spent the insurance her husband had left. When the money was gone, so was the boyfriend. . . .

Dodie heard the front door ring. She fetched her turquoise robe and pulled it on. Her night was just beginning.

CHAPTER TWENTY-FIVE

When Tim awoke just before dawn, he glanced over to see Dodie sleeping and felt absolute happiness. He reached across the large bed to stroke her arm, then he slid close and kissed the side of her face, angelic in repose. He kissed her shoulder and her breasts and her stomach. When he got down farther she awakened.

"Where are we?" she whispered.

"Paradise," he said, touching her face.

"I thought about something last night but I forgot to tell you," she said, stretching, pushing his hands away. "Did you do a thorough check on everything forensic?"

"What do you mean?"

He sat up in bed and looked at her alluring body.

"I mean," she said, pushing her heavy hair out of her eyes, "I mean, is it possible to miss clues? You did initial examinations and so did the police and the police chemist, but isn't it possible to miss something?"

"Yes."

"Oh, well then, shouldn't you re-examine everything one last time?"

She smiled and knelt in front of him, running her hands up his blond hairy legs. She touched his penis, which grew hard under her hand.

"Don't let's get started," he pleaded, "because I've got to get to work. Really."

"We can't even play?"

"Not now, child," he said, moving away from her reluctantly.

"You could re-examine the *site*, isn't that what you call it?"

"That's appropriate," he said, "call it site, or call it closet."

Tim began to dress. He would go home to shave and change his clothes before he went to the office. He had several telephone calls to make in private and some notes to get together which he had left in his briefcase.

"I don't see what we could have missed, Dodie. We do a very thorough job."

"You went over everything?" Dodie said, slipping into her turquoise dressing gown. She was very hungry. She would eat a toasted bagel, scrambled eggs, bacon and stewed prunes for breakfast. She might even go to the club for brunch later.

"We found everything, I think," Tim said, "well, various things, as you know, but so far nothing fits conclusively. We're still working. We have fingerprints of a number of people but none of them proves anything in particular, just that they were there, but not when."

"The murderer could have worn gloves. I would have."

Tim began to laugh. Dodie had a rich imagination. She was far more complicated than he thought when he first spied her at Somerset Mall. She might like ice cream and movies but she had a side that was a lot trickier to understand, a streak of intelligence that surprised him. In fact, it seemed she was full of surprises.

"You're turning into a fine little scientist," he said.

234

"Want to join the medical examiner's office?"

"Sure, boss," she smiled, the dimples appearing on either side of her mouth.

"I'd like to stay here with you," Tim said, walking over to her, bending to kiss her soft lips. She put her arms up and around his neck and held him tightly, feeling his muscled body against her own.

"I wasn't very happy with Hank, you know," she said, "but I am with you."

He held her for a moment, then gently released her.

"I've got to go. I think your suggestion is good, by the way. Why not? I doubt we missed anything, but there's no harm in going over everything one last time. Some murders have been solved by new evidence coming to light. Tenacity is important. We want to know who killed your family, you can bet on it."

Dodie smiled grimly.

"I'm going to see my mother today to tell her I'm a widow. She doesn't seem to understand on the telephone."

"Give her a hug for me," Tim said. "Must go now, hon."

They kissed goodbye and he left her standing at the open door.

As soon as she closed the front door she called Doc. She thought he might go with her to the nursing home as Rabbi Stone had refused. She had not wanted Dickie to accompany her, not really, since she realized that Dickie had a thing for her and had even told Beverly that he wanted a divorce in order to be free for Dodie. Word got around quickly at Crestwood. There were those who lived for the sole purpose of passing on gossip, or "information," as they called it.

Doc was thrilled to hear from Dodie, having assumed she had dropped him as had all the other members, and immediately agreed to go with her to see her mother. She could count on him—this was the perfect time for a money pitch. He had to have fifteen thousand dollars by the end of the week or he would have to declare bankruptcy. The fact that he had not given a penny to charity in over a year was enough to get him thrown out of the club, but then to be followed by the public declaration that he was insolvent would surely ruin him.

"Dodie, sure, anything. Anything you want."

"Be here at one o'clock, Doc."

Doc noted the stern tone in her voice. He remembered her as having a soft voice, almost a baby voice, and this new quality was unsettling. She had seemed to acquire it shortly after Hank's death, as if she now had to be more grown-up. He did not know whether he liked the newborn Dodie. He did things for the old Dodie, the feminine, helpless Dodie, because he liked her. She was appealing. But what about this new Dodie? He wondered when the demands were going to stop. For the moment it was all right to do her bidding; this worked in his favor as far as getting the money. She could not refuse the paltry fifteen thousand he needed by the end of the week.

Promptly at one o'clock Doc Matthews's car pulled into her circular driveway. Dodie was at the door, dressed in a fashionable white mink full-length coat and matching fur beret. She ran outside, waved at her police escort and climbed into the back seat of Doc's car.

"You don't mind, do you, Doc? I'm more comfortable back here."

Doc smiled.

"Oh, no," he said, driving down the street and peering at her in the mirror. She was stretched out along the seat like a little queen.

"That car is following us," he said.

"Yes, they go wherever I go," Dodie said, unconcerned. "Maybe we should have taken the Rolls. We could have lost them."

"I need some money, Dodie," Doc began.

Dodie waved an imperious hand. "Don't be dull. I know, I've a check right here in my handbag."

"For how much?"

"Don't be greedy, Doc, it'll hold you for a few days. It had better. You know I can't just get large sums yet because I'm borrowing on my inheritance—I haven't actually received it yet."

"How much?" Doc asked, his voice trembling. He really needed more, but fifteen would tide him over, at least keep him out of the courts for the moment.

"Can't you drive faster, Doc? At this rate we'll get there tomorrow," Dodie complained.

Doc accelerated, still wondering how much the check was for. "Can we go to the bank now?" Doc asked.

"No," Dodie frowned, "it's not convenient. I told mommy I'd be there for tea. You know mommy loves her tea."

Doc groaned. She was playing with him.

"Can't you tell me how much you're giving me?"

"Ten thousand right now, Doc."

"Oh, no," Doc sputtered, "that isn't enough. I'll need at least five thousand more!"

"Well, really, Doc," Dodie said resentfully. "I'm not a Rockefeller."

"Nearly," Doc said. "I've done for you, Dodie. You could do for me."

"Doc, you're not going to bleed me for money, are you, dear?"

Doc said no more on the subject. He had some pride. Next week he could get more money. Adroitly, he changed the subject. They began to talk about gardens, which Dodie had told him she was interested in along with the French Impressionist art. She could talk about the care of roses for hours, and intended to rip up the Schwartz's landscaped gardens and replant them with her favorite flowers.

Dodie gazed ahead of her at the traffic. There were long distance trunks and little cars which obviously belonged to students on their way to the University of Michigan. She sighed. It must be nice to be a student. She had never been a student for very long . . .

The expressway was cleared of the snow which had come unexpectedly during the night. She hated winter. Her mind drifted back to the Schwartzes. She had seriously considered moving into the Wabeek estate but had changed her mind after making love to Tim in Rose's bed. She would never be able to get Rose out of her mind if she lived in that house. And the house was absurdly large, really too large for just two people. The best idea was to get rid of it, sell it. The property would fetch upwards of a million, possibly as high as three million . . .

Their conversation remained neutral until they arrived at the Little Mary Nursing Home in time for early tea with Mrs. Margolis in her newly decorated suite of rooms. Dodie had quickly shifted her mother into the main suite after Hank's demise. Money, she said, was made to be spent.

Doc eyed the suite of rooms with a jealous pang. The decor must have cost as much as Dodie was giving him. The rooms had been freshly painted in bright yellow, and the sheets, pillow slips, chintz drapes and upholstery were all done in a matching floral design.

"Mommy," Dodie cried, running into the bedroom and throwing her arms around a small, white-haired old lady.

"Who are you?" her mother said crankily.

"It's me, mommy, Dodie, don't you recognize me?"

Her mother was seated in a chair, staring up at her blank-eyed.

"Oh?" she said.

Mrs. Margolis turned her head and reached for her cup of tea. "I don't know any Dodie. Did you say Dodie?"

"Yes, mommy."

"What kind of name is that?"

"Sit down, Doc," Dodie said, "do you want tea or coffee? I'll get the nurse to bring some."

"Nothing, thanks, I'm not thirsty," he said.

Doc had never got used to hospitals or sick rooms. In one corner of Mrs. Margolis's room was an oxygen tank. The table next to the bed was covered with a box of tissues and various bottles of medications. Apparently, the nursing home was lax about locking up the medication, and it looked as if a careless attendant had left a bottle of Valium out as well as arthritis medication. This was against the law. Things were so different from when he was a young resident at a teaching hospital.

"How are you, mommy? Are they treating you nice?"

Her mother did not reply. She sucked on the lemon she had discovered in the saucer.

Doc inspected the old lady's face. Not much of Dodie in her except the large, dark eyes. They had the same out-of-touch look about them.

"I rang for the nurse. I wonder where she is," Dodie said. "I pay enough here, you'd think they'd come running."

"Yes, one would think that money talks," Doc added, "but it doesn't seem to talk loudly enough."

"True," Dodie agreed, "I've found that out myself. I thought being rich meant instant everything but it's not true."

"There are several nurses hanging around in the hall," Doc said, noticing an attractive pair of legs whip past the doorway. "Shall I get one?"

"I hired a private nurse for mommy. She must be somewhere around."

"I wish you'd go," Mrs. Margolis said, "I need to be alone." She spoke with a slight Slavic accent, and had the same high-cheek boned look as Dodie. He glanced at her. She was drooling. Did Dodie have the same genetic code? Would she end up like this too?

"We just got here," Dodie said.

"I don't want strangers here," Mrs. Margolis said.

"I'm your daughter."

Her mother glanced suspiciously from Dodie to Doc and back again.

"Is that your husband?"

Dodie laughed. "Hank died. I told you twice, mommy. Why can't you understand? Hank is dead. And his parents, too."

Mrs. Margolis shrugged and looked away.

"What do you want?" she muttered.

"Me? Nothing at all, mommy. This is Doctor Matthews, don't you remember him? You met him before."

"Too many doctors," she said, looking at him. "At least he isn't Jewish."

"Yes, I am," Doc asserted.

Dodie blinked back her tears, her mother's lack of recognition finally getting to her.

"Who are you?" Mrs. Margolis whined, bewildered. Her eyes darted around the room. "Where am I? Why am I here? I want to go home."

Doc went over to her and in his best medical voice, the one he had practiced for years in order to gain respect of his patients, said, "You're doing just fine, Mrs. Margolis. Is there anything we can get you?"

"A gun," she said.

"This is a nursing home, mommy," Dodie said reassuringly, "they take good care of you. You don't need a gun or any weapon. Isn't it pretty here? Don't you like these sheets?"

Mrs. Margolis made a wrenching sound from the depths of her chest. "No, no, it's ugly. Being old is ugly. My daughter was a blond with blue eyes."

"I've always had dark hair," Dodie said defensively.

Doc Matthews laughed.

"Stop that laughing," Mrs. Margolis suddenly screamed.

Weakly, she got herself out of the chair and limped to the emergency button and pushed it. Presently, two nurses entered the room.

"What is it, dear? It's time for a nap now. Get back into bed, dear."

Each took an arm and brought her to the bed, forcing her up and into it. They tucked her under the flowered sheets.

"Be a good girl," Dodie said, then turned to the nurses. "I'm her daughter, the one who pays the bills."

"Yes, ma'am," they said in unison.

"Maybe we should go?" Doc asked, "it's a long ride back and you've seen enough, Dodie."

"I've got to tell her about Hank and Buddy and Rose. I don't think she understands. I've got to tell her," Dodie said, pushing back tears of frustration. The visit had not gone at all the way she wished. Everything had gone wrong. Her mother had deteriorated since her last visit some months before.

"I think she's tired, come on, let's go," Doc said.

"Get out," Mrs. Margolis muttered, her eyes closed, "my daughter is a blond."

"Goodbye," Dodie said sadly, moving from the room in a daze. She followed Doc down the hall and to the administration office to take care of her mother's current bill.

When they got to the car she noticed Officer Gracey parked at a discreet distance, waiting for them.

"Let me drive, Doc, it will be faster," Dodie said, getting behind the wheel of his car. Doc was not thrilled with her driving but allowed her to do as she wished. He would shortly be the recipient of a much-needed gift and he wouldn't want her to change her mind. A change of heart would be the final disaster for him.

Dodie was trying desperately to keep the horror of the visit from overwhelming her. She felt like an orphan. Could it be possible her mother was telling her some last-minute truth?

"Maybe I'm not a Margolis, Doc?"

"Huh, what?" Doc said, looking at her *retroussé* nose.

"Maybe you're a Greek, or Italian, or an Irish girl?" he suggested.

"Damn you, Doc, I always counted on being what I thought I was. Now I have an identity problem. I could be a bastard," Dodie wailed, "or whatever that's called. It's possible. With my crazy mother I could be a bastard. This is terrible!"

Tears cascaded down Dodie's cheeks. She cried while Doc handed her tissues from the box he had taken from Mrs. Margolis's bedside.

"What does anything mean when your mother doesn't love you?" Dodie wept. "I often had the feeling when I was a child that I was doing something wrong. They were always whispering."

Doc knew she felt rejected but was at a loss for what to say or do. What could he do? He murmured sympathetic denials and let her cry. Sometimes a woman just had to cry. You had to let it run its course. Anyhow, they would soon be back at Crestwood Hills and he would be ten thousand dollars richer.

He touched her shoulder as she cried. This was a woman he had thought he knew, but now he was unsure.

CHAPTER TWENTY-SIX

"I've been trying to get Alana on the phone for two hours," Ben said, shaking his head with annoyance.

"Want me to try, sweetie?" Beverly asked, as she walked across her designer-decorated living room to Ben and took the telephone away from him. She dialed Jerry's office, listened while it rang ten times, then hung up.

"I wish I had her home number," Ben said.

"She'll get there eventually, she's usually late. She's a night person, I guess."

"A night person, a night person," Ben said, looking at Beverly's long legs. She was wearing a magenta skirt and matching blouse she had picked out when he took her shopping. The outfit had cost six hundred dollars from Linda Dresner's boutique, and Ben had paid cash which Jerry had advanced him. The amount of money was more than Ben had ever spent on one woman and made him feel slightly sick. Beverly had reassured him that spending money was what rich people did.

Ben looked around her living room, wondering how much had been spent here. It was okay when some other man was spending the money but he was not at all sure that he enjoyed the experience of parting with so much money just for clothes. This was a world far apart from frayed blue jeans and old sweaters, a world he had rejected. He still did not think it was necessary to squander on clothes. To spend on art or travel was one thing, but to squander on some rags that would probably end up at a garage sale seemed obscene.

"What are you looking at, my angel?"

"What did this set Dickie back?"

"You mean the decor?" Beverly said, arching her eyebrows. "Perhaps fifty thousand. I don't remember. Cynthia Edwards, the well-known New York designer, was flown in for consultations. We went to New York and bought everything there through her. I hate to part with it, darling, but I suppose I'll have to give it up, won't I?"

"I don't know about these things," Ben said.

"I saw the tiniest sign of guilt on Dickie's face before he left for his trip. I'll have to work on that, pet."

Ben paced around the living room. He wanted to speak to Jerry. He hated not knowing. Anything could have gone wrong, anything.

He suddenly looked at Beverly.

"Are you sure you want a divorce from Dickie? I mean maybe it's better for you if you stay married."

Beverly did not wish to respond to this remark.

"I'm so glad you're here, darling," she said, looking fondly at him. She was going to be extra-nice to Ben even though she had a dreadful feeling of imminent betrayal. Something was surely brewing.

She had spent the better part of the day getting ready for him: bathing and oiling her body, dressing, making up so she appeared perfect. She had rehearsed various modes of seduction—the dialogue, the movements. She had danced around her house choreographing the movements and then she had gone to her hairdresser, Bruno, a young French bisexual who was the rage among the members of the club. Every woman vied for his attentions.

"Give me the phone," Ben said, "I'll try them again. I have no patience for waiting."

He dialed Jerry's office again. At last he got the answering machine; then there was a click and Alana answered the phone.

"Where the hell is Jerry?"

"I've just been down to the Oakland County Jail with a writ of habeus corpus," Alana said breathlessly, "he's been arrested and they won't let him out. They said there was more evidence against him and kept him. Now I'm waiting for him to call. I'll try to get back to you, or you call me later."

Ben put down the phone. "Did you know that Fryman was arrested?"

"No," Beverly said, "what for?"

"I don't think it's for a parking ticket he didn't pay," Ben said. "Maybe he's the murderer."

Beverly smiled.

"I don't think he's nutty enough to kill anyone. He's awfully self-protective. He's more the white-collar crime type," she said.

"He doesn't have the guts. It takes guts to murder," Ben said, scratching his curly head. "Oh, Christ," he said, "I just thought of something weird. I think Dodie came to my apartment last night."

"*I* came to your apartment last night," Beverly said, "I think you must have dreamed about Dodie."

"No, stop, it's not funny. I really think she did. I remember it now. Funny, because I haven't thought about her all day. I woke up with a terrible headache . . . yeah, the glass of wine. The wine made me sick. But she was there. Of course she was. We've got a deal."

Beverly's heart began to pound with jealousy. She had imagined something like this happening but she had thought she could prevent it. The dreaded younger woman —*and* a younger woman with big bucks, the bucks Beverly no longer had.

"What's the deal?"

"She's giving up the will contest. So she said. I wonder if her lawyer has called Fryman yet?"

"Maybe we better get down to the jail to see him," Beverly said, "I don't know what's going on, do you?"

"I'm smoking a joint," Ben declared, sitting on her William Morris couch and searching for the rolling papers he thought he had in his jeans pocket.

"Your doorbell is ringing," he said to Beverly, who was standing over him like a guard. "Answer it. It can't be Dickie, he'd have a key. Were you expecting anyone?"

"No."

"So answer it already."

"Should I?"

"Maybe you shouldn't," Ben said, "I don't know."

"I don't know, I'll think about it," Beverly said. "Maybe it's a neighbor."

"I can't tolerate the ringing, Beverly."

"I'm getting bad vibes," she said.

"Yes, well, it's probably the press. They're besieging everyone."

"I know," she said, "the *Detroit News* has been here six times today. The guy's probably just come back."

"Send him away and we'll screw," Ben suggested.

"That would be nice."

"Do you want to?" he asked.

"Yes."

"I feel like some ice cream. I'd pay more for that than those clothes."

The front door bell rang continuously. Whoever it was did not appear to be giving up so easily.

"Go ahead, get rid of whoever it is and then we can go to bed," Ben said.

"Must I go?"

"Yes," Ben said assertively, "this is silly. Go, woman."

"Okay," Beverly said nervously.

"Go."

Beverly marched into the hallway and peered through the glass panel next to the door. There were several people out there but she could only see outlines through the translucent panel.

"Who's there?" she called.

"Police!"

Beverly yanked open the door. Outside stood two policemen. Behind them in the driveway were two police cars, flashers beaming, engines running.

"Yes?" she asked.

"Are you Mrs. Beverly David?"

"Yes, what can I do for you?"

She felt her legs trembling and her mouth go dry. The cops were big, heavy. They could lift her with one finger. She glanced around and saw that Ben was standing in the hallway.

"My God, something's happened to Dickie," she gasped. But if that was the case, what were those police cars doing outside?

"You're under arrest, lady, please come with us."

Beverly began to back into the hallway. As she retreated the two policemen moved into her house.

"I'll read you your rights, ma'am," one of them said.

Beverly felt dizzy. She looked around for help, for Ben. He was gone.

She looked at the lips of the policeman reading her her rights. Most of it was a jumble of words until she heard "for the murder of Po Lee."

"Po Lee? Me? Po Lee? Me?"

She kept repeating it, unaware of the silly rhyme.

"I didn't murder her. Not me, I didn't murder anyone."

"Come now," one of the police said in a kind voice, "you

can have a lawyer, you'll have a fair shake."

They led her to the waiting car in full view of at least half the neighborhood. Although the houses were spaced far apart, the noise of the sirens and the obvious marked cars had brought the neighbors out. Her closest neighbor, Mrs. Kurian, stood in her driveway gawking incredulous. Nothing like this had ever happened on Ardmoor Drive.

"This is crazy," she said to the policeman on her right. "Why me? Why not Ben Schwartz? He had more reason."

She was instantly sorry she had mentioned his name but she was not going to sit idly by and be convicted of a murder.

"I think the medical examiner has proof," the policeman said. "We do have a warrant for your arrest, lady."

"I was nowhere near the Schwartz house when the maid was murdered," Beverly said, taking a deep breath, knowing anything she said could be used against her in the divorce proceedings as much as in anything else. Alleged murderesses did not get much of a property settlement from a judge.

"I was in bed with Ben Schwartz until noon that day. Then he told me he had a doctor's appointment and left. I was in his bed; I can prove it. He's the one who left."

"Yes, ma'am, you can tell that to the detectives. I can't help you, ma'am. You'll get your chance to tell your side of the story. I'm just doing my job."

Beverly just stared out the window of the police car. The day was pleasant, warm, sunny. The sun was filtering through the window. You could almost play golf.

"I'm not going to be convicted of someone else's crime," she announced. "There are worse things than a penniless divorceé, worse things than being alone."

Beverly was hustled into the police station past a large group of gawkers who had already heard that the Crestwood Hills murderer had been arrested. Cameras flashed in her scared face. She was rushed through the outer offices and led into a bare room containing a small table and chair.

"Sit," one of the cops said.

"I'll stand, thanks," she said.

They left her alone. She walked around the room for a while, then grew tired and sat down in the uncomfortable chair. The whole thing was as unreal as a made-for-television movie.

When Tim Levine came into the room she was slumped dejectedly in the chair, wishing she had thought to bring cigarettes with her.

"I'd like to chat with you, Mrs. David, okay?" Tim said.

"Why not? I've got nothing to hide."

"You're entitled to speak to your lawyer first, if you wish."

"My lawyer is in jail," she said, fixing her hair, fluffing it up. She knew she now appeared ragged. She smiled seductively at Tim, who smiled back.

"I'm just a little housewife," she said, "I don't need a lawyer. I'll defend myself. I know I did not kill Po Lee. I know I am innocent."

"We've arrested you for the murder of Po Lee," Tim said briskly, thinking that the woman wore too much perfume. The scent was suffocating. "There may be further indictments. We know you worked with someone else, Beverly; that's what we want to talk to you about. Now, I'm being good to you, Beverly. After all, we're members of the same tribe, but when I finish in here the detectives will be at you and they're not as cordial. I believe my mother knew you. Midge Plotkin. Does that ring a bell?"

"Maybe," Beverly said. "Which school?"

"I believe you were in high school together. Central?"

"Midge Plotkin. Did she have red hair?"

"I think she had auburn hair, yes; it's gray now," Tim said, regarding her with probing eyes. She did not look like a murderer, but then again neither did those English people who tortured and killed children on the moors. Perhaps the archetypal murderer was not a monster but just an ordinary-looking person. Being wealthy and privileged did not always make for fine character . . .

"We have evidence to prove you were at the scene of the murder," he said.

Beverly looked genuinely puzzled, which he considered a fact in her favor.

"What evidence? You can't have any because I was never there."

"I don't really have to tell you, Beverly," he said gently, "but I will because there is nothing that can erase this evidence. It's good, strong forensic stuff."

"What is it?" Beverly said, terrified. "Tell me. What is it?"

"We have your hair," he said, playing on her sense of helplessness.

Instinctively, Beverly touched her head. They had her hair? What the hell was this guy talking about?

"We found bits of your hair in the closet where Po Lee was brutally murdered. We know it's your hair because it has been microscopically compared with the hair sample we took from you with your permission. There is no doubt it's your hair, you see."

He did not believe for one moment that Beverly would have strangled the maid alone, even if she thought it was Dodie. Beverly did not seem mean enough or strong enough. But Beverly *did* look like an accomplice, and Beverly could have been in that closet with the person who had actually put his hands around Po Lee's throat and squeezed.

"Hair varies from the base to the top," he said, "and hair that is dyed is actually easier to establish. The hairs in the closet match your hair. I'm sorry, but this will help us towards a conviction."

His voice grew louder, more dramatic. This kind of scene excited him nearly as much as determining the method of death and establishing the motive. It made him feel so professional. Beverly's eyes were frightened, and he could see he was getting through to her.

"Beverly," he said, lowering his voice to a near-whisper, "we're talking about first-degree murder—murder one."

"I need a lawyer," Beverly said. "I want a lawyer."

Tim stood against the wall looking down at her, his eyes accusing.

"You mean you have nothing to tell me? Beverly, you had better tell me everything you know."

"I know nothing," Beverly snapped, "get me a lawyer. I've got nothing to say."

Tim opened the door and beckoned in two detectives who had been standing in the hallway waiting their turn.

"Detective Langston, Detective Randolph," Tim said, "Mrs. David."

The detectives grunted some sort of greeting and looked at Beverly as if she had been already been convicted. She saw that they were not going to treat her as courteously as the medical examiner had done.

"I didn't go near that closet," Beverly said, "I was in bed with Ben Schwartz. He'll corroborate this. Then he got up and went to the doctor, or the dentist, I don't remember."

Tim nodded. Ben Schwartz might confirm it but this did not change the facts. He was not going to tell her that it was not only *her* hair which was discovered in that closet, but also Jerry Fryman's and Ben's and some assorted dog hairs. The dog hairs were puzzling because Dodie Schwartz did not have a dog. It was possible that the three of them, Ben, Beverly and Jerry, had brought a dog with them, or a couple of dogs. The reason why was yet another mystery.

"Let her call her lawyer, guys," Tim instructed the detectives. "She's all yours now."

He noted the look of terror spreading across Beverly's face. They might break her. She looked ready to spill the beans.

"One last thing," Tim said. "Have you seen Ben Schwartz today?"

"Ben Schwartz, Ben Schwartz," Beverly repeated, stalling, wondering what to answer.

"No," she decided to say, "no, why?"

"Nothing much," Tim said, "we've a warrant out for his arrest, too. We'll find him. You're sure you don't know where he is?"

"I'm sure," Beverly said, trying to swallow the fear that was clutching at her.

"Goodbye, Beverly," Tim said, and shut the door.

She wanted to scream at him to come back and protect her from those two *goyim* staring at her. She attempted a seductive smile at the heavier of the two. It didn't work. He didn't seem to notice. She smiled at the other, who was actually the more attractive of the two. He simply continued staring.

CHAPTER TWENTY-SEVEN

Tim sat at the police chief's desk looking through his notes. He did not really know if the case would get through the court and end in a conviction for Fryman, Schwartz and David. Hair fragments were not enough. Any bright lawyer could cook up number of ways to have such evidence thrown right out of court.

The connection between Fryman, David and Schwartz was still unexplained, unless they were in collusion on Hank's will in some way. But how to prove this? They had determined to get rid of Dodie—this much made sense.

The fact that Jerry had readily admitted to numerous other wills lent credibility to his explanation of where he was the day Po Lee was murdered. But in the case of Rose, Buddy and Hank, Tim could not get around the fact that Jerry had seen all three shortly before they died. Yes, Tim thought, there could be a conspiracy between Fryman, Schwartz and David to take over the Schwartz estate, eliminating the opposition one-by-one.

However, proving this to a jury beyond a reasonable doubt was another story. Tim's case had to be mostly circumstantial unless something concrete came to light soon. Though it was possible to convict this way, what he badly needed was a confession from one of them which implicated the others. He'd work on it. Jerry seemed the weakest link. Maybe he could get something out of him if he offered immunity. Plea bargaining was possible, too; he might not need to offer immunity. It all depended on how desperate Jerry was.

There were many loose ends that bothered Tim. Above all, the poison had not yet been determined. They had yet to try potassium chloride, insulin, curare, to name a few, and all three could be injected in lethal doses without any special problems. Soon they would figure this part out, but this still did not tell them *who* injected . . . Was Hank murdered by his own brother? And how did Doc Matthews figure in this? He must have falsified the death certificates; surely he knew they had not all three died of heart attacks . . . Tim's head was a whirl of unanswered questions.

Tim opened the door to where Beverly David was being held, and to his surprise the two detectives were laughing at something she had said. He closed the door without saying goodbye. Whatever amusing story she was telling them did not change reality: her hair was found in the closet.

He drove back to the medical examiner's office to consult the computer. Leona had left messages on his desk and he sifted through them. Patti called three times—must be important. A Robert Nam called twice. Dodie called. The Crestwood Hills police called. He looked at the time marked on the messages. Most were from the morning.

Before descending to the lab he went through his notes again. Maybe he had missed something important. Pieces of the puzzle were missing. Once he thought there might be two murderers because of the difference in the murder technique between Po Lee and the Schwartzes. He had not reckoned on three murderers. Of course, one person, on his or her own, could have planned and executed all the murders, changing methods for the sake of confusion. Or all three murders could be totally unconnected.

He wondered if he should follow his intuition, which told him that the murders of the Schwartzes and Po Lee were unconnected in terms of motive. His apprehension, his gut feeling, might be basically correct. Patti had taught him to follow his instincts. What if there were two murderers, or even three, unconnected, unrelated to each other in a conspiratorial sense?

He picked up the telephone and called Patti, who was still in Michigan, and left a message with the service. He was annoyed she was not at home. He had to discuss the case with her as he had done in the past; she had always been a help, smart and clear headed about everything except her personal life. When she was not personally involved, she displayed a formidable intelligence.

At times he felt an urge to discuss the details of the case with Dodie, but it might be considered unethical as she was still a suspect in the case, at least according to the police. Although the evidence against her was weak and basically circumstantial, she had not been dropped from suspicion.

This bothered him. So long as she was not dropped as a suspect their relationship had to remain casual, without any real intimacy. Yes, he badly needed a confession. Dodie was right—his personal life was being affected, and so was their relationship.

He walked downstairs to the lab, and remembered he was supposed to dine with Dodie. He picked up the telephone to cancel. At this point, work came first—he was on the edge of discovering something significant. He felt close to an answer as he sifted through the computer results. And the person he needed right now was Patti.

Dodie seemed disturbed that they were not going to

meet. She didn't understand that his real motive in solving the case, other than his professionalism, was for her. For them.

He drove immediately to Patti's parents' house and rang the bell. No reply. He walked back and forth on the sidewalk for half an hour, then decided to go home and keep calling her. When he got home, his mother was in her French mood and wanted to feed him. He politely refused, able to think of nothing but getting in touch with Patti. He dialed her number repeatedly, and finally she answered.

She said she would be over as soon as possible. He felt excited now. The two of them were going to get at the truth.

"Patti's coming over. We'll be going out later, but I want to talk privately while she's here, mom."

He ran upstairs to say hello to his father, who was sitting in bed watching an old Bette Davis movie.

Tim changed into old clothes, the ones he remembered that Patti liked. He ran a comb through his thick blond hair and glanced in the mirror. He had never thought of himself as good-looking, and when a woman said he was, he did not believe it. But he did not care. Faces and bodies came and went . . .

He heard the doorbell ring and his mother let Patti in. He left them alone for a few minutes to give his mother an opportunity to quiz Patti about California and her new boyfriend. He went downstairs to the kitchen and fixed some matzoh with jelly on it, gulped it down and then poured himself a glass of milk. His belly full, he went to greet Patti.

"Well," she said gleefully, "if it isn't the Jewish Sherlock Holmes."

"Let's go into the den," Tim suggested.

"Sure."

He followed her out of the room, observing that the blond streaks in her hair were gone, and her hair was dark again. She looked like the person he once knew.

"Settling down?" he asked.

"Not exactly," she said, turning to face him. They stood in the den looking at each other and for a moment he felt the same old attraction. He pushed it out of his mind. Now he had Dodie.

"I hope we'll always be friends, Patti," he said.

"Agreed," she smiled.

"Thanks for coming. I can use your help."

"I'm pleased you want it, Tim." Impulsively, she reached up and kissed him, just missing his mouth. The kiss landed on his chin and they both laughed.

"Do you have time?" he asked. "This is complicated to explain."

"Do I get a fee?"

"If you want one," he said.

"Of course not, silly."

"Okay, let's sit a while; later we can go out for a bite, if you like."

Patti made a grinding motion with her teeth and laughed again. "You're so serious."

"Murder is serious," he said.

"Right, let's get on with it, then. Go ahead, pick my brain all you want. I'm willing."

Tim gazed at the splash of freckles, the pale skin, the dark eyes. She had the perfect Irish face, the perfect Jewish brain.

CHAPTER TWENTY-EIGHT

"Lovely," Rabbi Stone murmured. He stepped into the icy cold shower, reached for the shampoo and poured it over his head. He sang as he shampooed, first in Hebrew, then in English. He hummed the chief motif from *Aïda*, then drifted into the finale of Beethoven's Fifth. He rubbed the soap over his body, luxuriating in the feeling.

So far this week he had been interviewed twelve times by the newspapers and radio. He had even appeared on early-morning television. He was a celebrity, something which he imagined he was not cut out to be but which had grown surprisingly pleasant. Donations were pouring in for the building fund. People he had never seen before came up to him and tried to shake his hand, and he had to apologize continuously for a bad cold so people wouldn't be so quick to touch him. Apparently he had made a couple of statements which his congregation considered sensible and calming. The members of Crestwood Hills had congratulated him for putting the Schwartz family murders into perspective, and were thinking of giving an award, a lifetime membership to the club in his name to any Jewish person in the community who helped solve the murders. This in itself was unheard of in the country club's annals. In a sense and quite ironically, he was aware that the Schwartz murders had brought him fame he would never have otherwise enjoyed . . .

Singing, he rinsed off, stepped out of the shower and wrapped a large red towel around his chilled body. He went out and into the bedroom, which was decorated in somber tones befitting a man of his dignity. Humming the Grand March from *Aïda*, he danced into the living room and then into the kitchen where he put the kettle on for tea. He got out a danish ring from the freezer, tore off a large hunk and put it into the oven to heat up.

He sipped his tea and tried not to think about that afternoon. The police had escorted him to the police station for two hours of relentless questioning, some of which he could not answer. He barely knew the maid, having only seen her on his rare visits to the Schwartz family. When they were satisfied with his answers they let him go. He thought that was the end of it, but the next day they had come to the house and searched it, taking away two of his sweaters.

Next day he was called to the medical examiner's office where they took hair samples, fingerprinted him again and questioned him for several hours until he was exhausted. Though he had done his utmost to cooperate, he would not enjoy repeating this experience. A homicidal maniac was loose among them. A terrible feeling that he was still a suspect lingered.

He was abruptly pulled away from his thoughts by the sound of the doorbell ringing. He walked into the hallway and looked toward the door. He wasn't expecting anyone but as far as the members of his congregation were concerned, it was always open house. He was the temple's spiritual advisor, and could be called upon at any time.

"Just a moment, please," he called, scurrying to the door, "be right there." He wouldn't want someone who needed him to leave.

He glanced through the peephole. A small, dark stranger stood there. Perhaps this was one of the younger members of the temple whom he did not know well, probably someone who rarely came to services. Yet a member of the temple must be served.

With a winning smile the rabbi pulled open the door.

"Good evening, son, can I help you?"

It was not a boy, but rather a man in his thirties whose appearance had a distinctly Oriental cast.

"Rabbi here? My name Robert Nam."

"Yes, I'm the rabbi, please, come in. What can I do for you?" The rabbi made a welcoming gesture but Robert Nam just stood there looking bewildered.

"Come in," the rabbi said, turning, thinking he would follow him. He suddenly looked down and spotted his half-naked state. "Oh, goodness," the rabbi exclaimed, having temporarily forgotten he was wearing only a towel around his waist. "Come in, please, and sit down. I'll put a robe on, please excuse me for a moment."

Robert Nam stood hesitating, then walked through the hallway and sat down in the rabbi's living room. Within moments the rabbi returned, robed.

"Would you like a cup of tea?" the rabbi asked kindly. "We can sit and talk in the library as we sip."

Robert Nam said, "I want talk about Po Lee."

"Po Lee? The maid? You must be her brother."

"I'm Korean. Po Lee Chinese."

The rabbi frowned. He did not quite see the connection.

"I take tea," Robert Nam said.

"Right, oh, good. Go into the library," Rabbi Stone said, "and I'll fix you some tea."

He went into the kitchen, his mind racing. Who had sent this person? It seemed the rabbi's destiny was to be involved in this sordid case. Fame or no fame, it was becoming tiresome . . . He put the cup of tea on a tray and took some cookies out of the cookie jar and placed them on a dish. Whatever the circumstances or whoever the person, the rabbi believed in good manners.

He placed the tray before the little man, his heart sinking. He did not want to know about Po Lee. He did not want to have anything directly to do with such evil. As the leader of the temple he knew he had an obligation to deal with life in the best possible way in order to set an example for others. Wasn't this going too far? If only he could make this little person vanish.

"Nice tea," Robert Nam said.

"There's more in the kitchen," the rabbi said generously.

"No, thanks, tea enough."

"Now what can I do for you?"

"I saw your picture on television. Want to talk you. Called medical examiner. Couldn't get anyone. Not home much. Work at club."

"You work at a club, you say?" the rabbi asked, hoping to make the conversation brief. He was beginning to feel uncomfortable.

"Crestwood Hills Country Club," Robert Nam said, "park cars there."

"Oh, yes?" the rabbi said. "Go on."

"Had date with Po Lee day she murdered," Robert Nam said. "Good woman but Chinese. Po Lee good woman. Pretty, too."

The rabbi began to get interested. This little man might know something.

"You saw her that day?"

"Not exactly."

Rabbi Stone looked frightened. The little man might know something—something horrible.

"She came to the door?"

"No, no," Robert Nam said, "did not. Did not. I ring

and ring. No one come. I leave."

"Oh," the rabbi was disappointed, "you left. So what?"

"Saw murderer."

"You saw the murderer; *you* saw the murderer?"

"I saw murderer," Robert Nam repeated.

"Would you recognize this person?"

Robert Nam, frightened, bewildered, nonetheless nodded yes.

"Sure," he said, "I find him. Po Lee good woman. Didn't deserve die."

"You're positive?" the rabbi asked.

Robert Nam nodded again.

"You can tell the police, then?"

"Yes," he agreed.

"We can go together," the rabbi affirmed.

The rabbi excused himself and rushed into his bedroom to get dressed. He was thrilled to be a hero at last.

CHAPTER TWENTY-NINE

Ben drove around without aim or purpose, trying to decide what to do, almost wishing the police would pick him up and make the decision for him. The immediate funds in his bank account were limited and his sole access to wealth, Jerry Fryman, was in jail.

Beverly's arrest had been a shock, too. He had listened while she talked to the police, and then had run out the side door and hid in the garage until they took her away. Listening to the news, he learned that he too was being sought. Evidence had come to light bringing about certain arrests, he had heard on two separate radio stations. Word had leaked to the media that hair from the alleged perpetrators was found at the scene of one of the deaths. He wondered which one they were talking about.

And then it came to him. The hairbrush . . . the hairbrush was missing from his bathroom. He had noticed its absence in the morning when he went to use it. Beverly said she hadn't seen it. But that was it! Beverly and Jerry had been arrested, and now they were looking for him. All three people had used the hairbrush. Beverly had taken it from

Jerry's office and forgot to return it.

Ben parked at the curb and stared at the pay phone, thinking that he ought to call up the police and anonymously tell them that Dodie had taken the hairbrush from his apartment. That had to be it—she had got hold of the hairbrush and planted the hair at the scene of one of the murders. He turned on the radio to find out whether there was more information. Too early for the local news. Anyway, he felt positive that Dodie had stolen his hairbrush. This had to be the reason she had come to his apartment; the business about the will contest had just been a scam, a distraction . . .

When he had called Jerry in the morning to inquire whether Myles Rush had been in touch, Jerry was already in jail. But Myles Rush had not called anyway—he was certain of this. Dodie never had any intention of speaking to Myles Rush about dropping the will contest. What she intended was to dope him up enough to be able to sail through his apartment looking for something she could use against him. She had found what she thought was his hairbrush, not realizing there would be hair in it from others. He laughed. It was a damned good thing Beverly hadn't bothered to clean out the hairbrush . . .

But Ben's laughter faded quickly with the realization that he could be convicted of murder through this phony evidence. Everyone was screaming for an arrest and he could end up being the scapegoat. Should he turn himself in? Evading the police was silent acknowledgment of guilt. If he went to the police station of his own accord he had a far better chance of showing them he was not the culprit.

Reluctantly, he got out of the car and walked toward a pay phone. He called a neighbor to feed the puppies. Then he dialed the police station. But when he heard a voice he hung up, returned to the car and drove away.

Not knowing what to do or where to go, he drove around some more and found he was in Doc Matthews's neighborhood. He decided to go over to Doc's and perhaps use his telephone.

Doc's face went chalk-white when he opened the door and found Ben standing on his porch.

"It's you? Come in." Doc poked his head out the door to see if anyone was nearby and watching. Satisfied they were alone, he allowed Ben to enter his house. "Let's go in the living room. What can I do for you, son?"

"Frankly, Doc, I'm here because I don't know where else to go."

"I don't think you should stay here for long. The cops have been here once already. They're searching all over for you."

"It's just a matter of time before they find me," Ben said nervously. "But I just don't like the idea of them locking me up, so . . ."

"Yeah, I know what you mean," Doc said, glancing at Ben's unshaven face. He *did* look like a criminal.

"I was thinking of turning myself in," Ben said, sitting down on Doc's couch, looking around the living room which was half-empty. There was no carpet and no pictures on the walls—his wife must have cleaned him out. There was a bleakness about the place which made Ben regret his having come.

"I think that's a fine idea," Doc said, nervously getting up and going to the windows to check whether there was a squad car outside. "That would save you a lot of trouble, because they'll get you anyway. Looks good," Doc said after a glance. "Want me to drive you?"

"Yes," Ben said. His mind was made up and the burden off his shoulders. Doc would drive him.

"I'm going to the club but I can drop you off on the way."

"You know Dodie took my hairbrush, don't you, Doc?"

"Huh?"

"Dodie, *your* friend Dodie, came to my apartment, doped me up and took my hairbrush. The police found hairs at the

265

scene of one of the murders. They say the hair is mine. Now if that isn't some kind of crummy frame, what is?"

Doc's eyes widened. Should he defend Dodie? Or had he already got himself too far into the Schwartz murders? For some time now he had suspected that Dodie might be involved in the murders, but when Po Lee was killed he had changed his mind. Was Dodie in on all the murders with another person? Doc was confused. He thought he had it all worked out, but when Po Lee was murdered he realized that the murderer might indeed be Ben Schwartz. He might have been wrong about Dodie all along.

"Let's go," Doc suggested mildly, not wishing to aggravate Ben. "Let's give the authorities a chance to iron out this stuff. We're not detectives."

He stared at Ben. Ben did not look like a murderer but what did a murderer look like? Lizzie Borden, a sweet-faced child, had axed her own parents . . .

Doz gazed around his depleted living room, wondering why Dodie had given him the check so readily. He had believed it was because he was subtly blackmailing her. But maybe she had given him the check out of kindness and not because she thought he had falsified the death certificates for *her*.

"Screw the authorities," Ben said, and followed Doc from the room and into the closed garage.

They drove quickly to the police station and Doc dropped an angry Ben off and drove away. Ben stood hesitating in front of the station, then marched in determinedly.

Incredulous stares followed him through the station. Detective Langston took him into a little room, blew smoke in his face and was rude. But Ben stuck to his story.

"She came to my apartment, tried to screw me, knocked me out with some dope and stole the hairbrush."

"But we found the hairbrush in your apartment," the detective said nastily. "We've got it; I think it's Exhibit 10D.

Ben thought about this. Maybe they had found the hairbrush. "Then she took the hair out of the brush. Can't you see it's the same thing? What would my hair be doing at the scene of a murder?"

"And Mrs. David's and Mr. Fryman's," the detective added. He continued to question him until Doctor Levine arrived, accompanied by a pretty woman. The medical examiner looked skeptical as he talked, but the girl nodded agreement and wrote in a pad.

"All right," she said, "I think this is enough for now."

Tim escorted Patti from the room and they retired to the police chief's office to confer.

She smiled at Tim. "Let's get rid of some of these suspects," she said, "unless you're positive that the ones locked up are the perpetrators. We don't have much evidence, Tim; come on, let's face it. Dodie Schwartz does have a good strong motive for the murders. Some thirty million worth. She might very well be putting the finger on Ben, why not? I would."

Tim clucked. She sounded as if she had been reading Raymond Chandler.

"Ben Schwartz is unreliable," he said. "He's a liar. The brush might not be Fryman's."

"Don't be stubborn, Tim, we must look at every angle now."

She yawned. She had been up late with Lyn at the airport. He had left for Los Angeles on the "red eye" special. When she saw him out of his California milieu she realized it was not going to work. He was a nice fellow but not really her type.

"Why don't we go over to the lab and have another go with the computer," Tim suggested.

"Okay."

She looked at Tim. She liked him as much as ever. Nothing had ever really ended between them—they could pick up where they left off. Only he did not seem interested in her in that way any longer. He seemed to want her ideas but nothing else. She would have to work her way back into his affections.

"Just a sec," she said. "If he can lie, why can't we?"

"How?"

"We'll take Ben Schwartz with us to the crime lab, show him around, show him the machines, the equipment, the slides with the blood samples, the hair samples, the whole bit."

"Yes," Tim said.

"It's evidence," Patti mused. "Anyway, this is our scenario. We tell him we have enough evidence on the four bodies, not just the maid's. We found scraps of this and that at the murder sites, in Rose Schwartz's bedroom and in Hank's house. We'll have to forget the golf course at this point; that would sound ridiculous."

"Do you think he'll go for it?"

"I do," Patti said. "He's scared. Did you see his eyes? He's only pretending to be cocky."

"What else?"

Patti was warming to the occasion; having a part in solving a multiple murder appealed to her. Maybe this was the way to get back into Tim's heart.

"We know they were overdosed. Let's tell him we now know the poison injected and we can trace it to its source."

"I wish we did," Tim said, "we've tried tests for hundreds of poisons with no results."

"You haven't tried potassium chloride or arsenic."

"No one uses arsenic any more," Tim interrupted. "That's Agatha Christie stuff."

"Maybe it's something simple, who knows," Patti said. "Anyway, what difference does it make, we're lying. So, we say we know the chemical—we've got the goods. If he's going to roast for one murder, he might as well roast for all."

"It's just the opposite," Tim said with exasperation. "If

268

he's being done for one, why would he admit to the other three? He'll keep his mouth shut."

"How about premeditated?"

"He'll never admit that he planned anything. We might have to plea bargain if we can. Anyway, let's go; we've nothing to lose and a little pressure might help."

"You're terrific," Patti said, "Now I remember why I went for you—you're terrific."

Taken with the affectionate tone of her voice, Tim brushed his lips against her pale cheek.

"If only you weren't betrothed to Lyn," he said jokingly.

"The betrothal is off, my lord," Patti said. "He's gone back to the West Coast."

"Oh?" Tim felt pleasantly satisfied, his faith in her restored. She wasn't going around the bend as he had thought.

"Good girl," he congratulated.

"Is that all you can say?"

"For now," Tim said, smiling.

"Did you realize, Tim," she said, changing the subject back to the murders, "Did you realize the injections given to all three Schwartzes were given intramuscularly, and that ten times more than the usual dosage was administered. Buddy Schwartz was dead within minutes."

"Yes," Tim said, "and there aren't many chemicals that will bring about such sudden death."

"Remember that case in New York state, the one involving the doctor?"

"I do," he said, "why?"

"Curare; wasn't he accused of injecting curare into terminally ill patients?"

"I'll have to look it up for details," Tim said. "But it's not that farfetched at this point, kiddo."

At that moment Officer Gracey opened the office door and looked in.

"Doc, you'd better get out here, that rabbi is here with

a little guy who claims he was outside Mrs. Schwartz's house the day the maid bought it. He says he can identify the murderer."

Tim followed the policeman down the hall eagerly. Rabbi Stone, accompanied by a small, dark man, stood at the front of the police station, a smug look on his face.

"Hello," he said importantly, "this is Mister Nam, a friend of the Schwartz maid. Po Lee, I believe?"

Robert Nam stepped forward to present himself. His voice was low, shy.

"A good woman," he said, "I saw who kill her. Saw with own eyes."

The little man pointed to his bright, dark eyes where tiny points of tears were beginning to appear.

Rabbi Stone slapped him on the back and pleaded, "Please, don't do that, not here."

He pounded him on the back and repeated his warning. Robert Nam immediately stopped crying and moved away from the rabbi.

"Let's go into the chief's office and talk this over," Tim suggested, flushed with the prospect of the case breaking. He glanced at the rabbi who was walking with them toward the chief's office.

"You can't go with us, rabbi, it's private at this point. Thanks for your help. By the way, how did you meet this man?"

"I went to house of rabbi," Robert Nam said.

"That's correct," the rabbi said, deeply disappointed that he would not be allowed to hear Robert Nam's information. Still, he would get the credit for discovering him.

"I call your office," Robert Nam said, "you don't call me."

Tim blushed, recalling the name. He had called several times.

"Okay, rabbi," Tim said to the rabbi who was still walking with them.

He opened the door to the office where Patti was waiting and ushered in Robert Nam.

"'Bye," he said to Rabbi Stone, firmly shutting the door. "This man thinks he saw the murderer of Po Lee," Tim announced.

"Wonderful," Patti said.

Tim reached into a folder and brought out a pile of photographs. He handed them to Robert Nam who sat down on a straight chair.

"Look through these," Tim said, "and see if you can find the person who came out of the Schwartz house."

Chapter Thirty

Tim was puzzled by Ben Schwartz's cooperative attitude in the lab. He had expected him to be rebellious, at the least, surly, yet he was polite and helpful. The first thing he was shown were the blood samples taken from all the suspects.

"We've got you right here, Ben," he lied, pointing to a slide.

Ben nodded. "Interesting," he said.

"And these fibers in here have been positively linked to your yellow sweater. You were wearing your yellow sweater, weren't you?"

"I often wear my yellow sweater but I don't remember exactly when," Ben said.

They walked around the lab with Tim displaying all the sophisticated equipment to determine motive, cause, place, time and culprit.

"You're not such a tough guy, are you?" Tim said, trying to irritate him. Instead, Ben shrugged.

"This is where we perform our autopsies," Tim said,

pointing to a table filled with all sorts of menacing instruments.

"This makes me sick," Ben said, "I've got a queasy stomach sometimes."

"But you kill animals, how do you explain that?" Patti asked, in a voice planned to intimidate.

"That's different," he said defensively, his shell beginning to crack.

Patti saw her opportunity and went on. "Your temper doesn't get involved in killing animals?"

"No," Ben said.

"You're joking," Patti said, laughing in his face.

Tim admired her technique. She would make a great prosecuting attorney.

"I know what you're trying to do," Ben said, "you're trying to trap me, get me to admit I killed my family. But I won't, babe, because it isn't true, dig?"

"I don't dig," Patti said, "I think it's well within your character."

"Better admit it," Tim said, "if you plead guilty we might be able to get something other than murder one. I'm not sure, though."

"I'm not admitting anything," Ben insisted.

Patti laughed in his face. He began to shake with anger, but did not say anything hostile or rude. He remained silent.

"If you confess to killing Po Lee—and we *know* you did it—" she said, "we might be able to help you with the others. But no confession, no deal. You'll be up for four life sentences."

"I'm not confessing to anything," he said.

"Someone saw you running out of the house," Tim intervened. "We know you did it. We have a witness."

"A witness? A liar—" Ben said.

"Hey, listen, man," Patti said, "you know something, if

you didn't waste your parents you could still inherit. But if a jury finds you guilty through circumstantial evidence linking your family murders to Po Lee, you've had it. You won't get a penny. You'll just be a bum floating around the world for the rest of your life."

"Floating in jail," Tim corrected.

"That's what I mean," Patti smiled.

"You did it, didn't you?" Tim asked casually. "You killed her by mistake."

"I did not kill anyone," Ben said helplessly.

"You could get off on murder one," Tim said again. "You could serve your time for the accidental death of Po Lee and get out eventually if you behaved. *If* you didn't kill the others."

Ben began to babble something unintelligible.

"What's he saying?" Tim asked Patti.

"I think he's saying he killed her. Yes," Patti said, "are you taping this?"

"Of course, but I think it's inadmissable evidence."

"It is unless you get the judge's permission beforehand, but at least they'll hear it," Patti said.

Ben continued speaking incoherently.

"Beverly told us plenty," Tim said. "We've got the yellow sweater, too, and a few other things up our sleeve."

Patti looked at Ben and then she leaned over to him and suddenly yelled in his ear.

"Shut your face, murderer, you killed your family, admit it, admit it!"

"I did not!" Ben screamed back.

"You did!" Patti yelled.

"I'm not confessing, there's nothing to confess. I did not harm my parents. I loved them. In my own way, I loved them."

"Would you write out a confession for the death of Po Lee?" Tim asked in a gentle voice.

"No, I will not. It's Dodie! That bitch stole my inheritance. They were my parents, my brother, my money! It was my family, not hers, but she's stolen it all away from me!"

"He's babbling again," Patti said quietly. "Take him up to your office and get this down on paper and get him to sign it."

"Right," Tim whispered, concealing his anxiety at what Ben was saying.

"Can I smoke a joint?" Ben asked, suddenly calm.

"I don't see why not," Tim said. "Come up to my office it's more comfortable, we'll get this all straightened out. You'll feel so much better, Ben."

"Yes," Ben said, following Tim and Patti.

As soon as they sat down in Tim's office, Ben took out a joint, lit it and toked deeply. "She screwed me out of my inheritance; she kept trying and she succeeded. She knew there was a fortune, she's no fool, she only acts that way. Hank left her everything, and nothing for me."

"You're positive?" Tim asked.

"The bitch," Ben said.

"This implies there's a will we don't know about," Patti said, jotting down some notes. "Are you saying what we know as Hank Schwartz's last will and testament is a forgery?"

"Yes," Ben said.

"Hey, hold on," Patti said. "Did Jerry Fryman cook up the forgery?"

"That's it," Ben said.

"You mean then that Dodie . . . Dodie Schwartz *did* inherit Hank's estate? God, we must get hold of that will," Tim said.

"It may have been destroyed," Ben said, not wanting Dodie to profit, not now.

"But," Patti said, "you must realize that *you* can't inherit Hank's money if you killed him."

Ben grimaced and shook his fist at her. "I didn't kill my

family. I didn't kill Po Lee, the poor thing. I didn't kill anyone and I'm not letting Dodie get away with this crap. If she's found guilty, *she* can't inherit. What the hell, I'll see *her* poor first."

"Why should we believe you?" Tim said nervously.

"Because it's the truth."

"You injected them, didn't you?" Tim said, attempting another tack. "You know how to administer lethal injections. You did a lot of killing at the Humane Society. We know all about it."

Ben stared at him, his face rigid. "We don't call it killing. It's a sacrifice. My God, wait a minute, I just thought of something!" Ben's mouth fell open. "It's a red herring. She killed her own maid, her own devoted maid, as a red herring. It would look as if she couldn't possibly have done it. Don't you see? Don't you understand?"

"*You* killed no one, you're saying?" Patti said aggressively.

"Yes, right," Ben shouted, his face reddening.

"I think you might be lying," Tim said.

"Hank thought I had something to do with our parents' death," Ben said, tears coming into his wild eyes. "I couldn't change his mind. She kept telling him and he believed *her*, not me. *She's* the liar, not me."

Tim felt a wave of nausea coming over him. Someone was indeed lying.

"It's possible someone else got rid of your family and Po Lee, not Dodie. Isn't that possible?" Tim persisted.

"No, it's not," Ben said. "Hey, man, if Dodie thought Hank put her in his will for the big bucks maybe she wouldn't have wasted him. She might have divorced him. She would have got plenty."

"Look, Ben," Tim said, "why don't you just come clean. You don't expect us to believe that stupid story, do you?"

Tim felt the anger rising inside himself. This case had

taken on monstrous proportions. Was the woman he was in love with a murderer?

"Look, you've got no real evidence against me. The yellow sweater is bullshit. How about Dodie's yellow sweater? Who doesn't have a yellow sweater from Saks?"

"What we need," Patti muttered, "is a confession . . . from Dodie." She looked at Tim for a response, but he was staring through the window, a look of stunned bewilderment on his face.

CHAPTER THIRTY-ONE

Doc Matthews stood in the hall that led to the dining room and thought that the day was not so bad. Although it was still winter, the weather seemed unusually warm. He had heard the club was thinking of having a Pro-Am tournament as part of the late winter festivities. Also, he had actually been invited to a cocktail party the Smiths were having for their new son-in-law, Max. His mood was high. The check resting in his pocket cheered him. He would be able to pay off a few of his creditors, keeping the most vicious of them at bay.

Walking tall, he proceeded down the hall toward his lunch date with Dodie. They had further financial matters to discuss, such as when he was getting the next installment. He had considered depositing the money in a Swiss account but had dismissed the notion as too grandiose. Since he had no real intention of living in Zurich he had better get the rest of his debts paid off so that he could continue to live graciously in the Crestwood Hills community without feeling like a leper. As it was, each time he entered the club he felt all eyes turn to him disapprovingly.

Well, he *was* the poorest member of the club. *Members only* really meant the rich only. The club was neither a democratic nor charitable institution. Money was the only game in town . . .

He walked into the dining room looking for Dodie, feeling self-conscious. He might be the poorest member, but he was dining with one of the richest. He found the nearest empty table and sat down. Though he preferred another in the bay by the gardens, he did not have the nerve to walk through the entire dining room to get there. He looked around to see if anyone was looking at him. He knew almost everyone in the room; the group did not vary that much.

He sneezed. The roses in the center of the table were triggering an allergy. He discreetly removed the vase from the table and placed it on the floor. He looked up to see Tina Fisher snickering. He reached for the vase, pretending to wipe it clean and admire it, then replaced it.

Doc studied the menu. He liked lunch at the club. The selection was immense and there were always hors d'oeuvres and the salad bar in the middle of the room. He decided on a small steak, medium-rare, and some potato skins, with fresh fruit for dessert.

He had heard the dues were going to be raised again. Was the club attempting to price certain members right out? He had heard the committee was going to boot out some members—Dickie David for one, now that he was the celebrated husband of a criminal in custody. His name was being smeared, which Doc felt sorry about. Dickie was a prince and didn't deserve such lousy treatment. Doc was glad *he* wasn't the one being smeared in that way . . . rumors ran rampant, exaggeration was filling people's minds. No doubt the women's card room resounded with speculation and gossip.

He looked up and smiled. Nat Kanterman was coming his way, possibly the only male friend he had in the whole club. Nat was the president, a friendly man, a lawyer who had an unblemished if rather uneventful reputation. Doc had never heard any gossip about him.

"Afternoon," Nat said, his blue eyes twinkling behind his glasses. He had a habit of looking affectionately at everyone.

"Hi," Doc said, starting to get up from his seat.

"No, sit, Doc," Nat said. He was diplomatic but assertive when necessary. "I want to talk to you. Maybe we could go to the men's card room?" Nat suggested. He had white hair which was thinning on top but which he wore surprisingly long for a member of Crestwood Hills. He was thin with long fingers, a discreet diamond flashing on his pinkie.

"Okay," Doc said agreeably, wondering what he was going to talk to him about. He knew he was in arrears for the dues. He had written a note to the committee explaining his problem and promising them that he would shortly be paying what he owed.

He followed Nat into the men's card room, which was empty. Nat hovered around the door, then decided to sit at one of the tables. Doc trotted after him. Passing the table that displayed the tiny chocolate bars always present for the card players, Doc helped himself to several, tucking a few into his pocket and unwrapping the others.

"Want one?" he asked, offering Nat a selection.

"No, thanks, Doc."

Doc sat down opposite him, munching on the chocolate. "If this is about the dues—" he began.

"No, no," Nat cut in, amiably, "it's not. We know you've had some financial problems since your divorce and we've been carrying you. It's not that."

Doc gazed at him wondering what it was. What could be so important that Nat would take him from the dining room into the men's card room?

"I hate this conversation," Nat said, "but as president of Crestwood Hills I have to do this. It's up to me."

"Go ahead," Doc said, becoming suddenly irritated at the pussyfooting. "Spit it out." He stared into Nat's face, sensing trouble. What could it be this time?

"The club is asking you to resign. I'm sorry, Doc. I've known you a long time and I like you, but I've been overruled. I wanted them to give you another chance, but they said no. There's nothing I can do. I hate to see a member asked to resign. I hate it."

Doc was not expecting this. "That heart specialist voted against me," Doc said miserably.

"I don't know who you mean," Nat said, "we've a number of heart specialists in the club."

"The bastard voted against me."

"They're preparing to get rid of some others too, Doc, it's not just you. No one has a vendetta against you."

"I worked hard to join this club. My friends—when I had them—all wanted me to join. My wife. Her brother. The initiation fee was twenty-five thousand. Do I get my money back?"

Nat fumbled in his pocket and brought out a handkerchief. "You know our policy, Doc. I *am* sorry."

"I may not be wonderful," Doc sputtered, "but I don't deserve this. I've got a check for ten thousand in my pocket. Will that help?"

Nat shook his head balefully. "There's nothing I can do," he said.

"How long do I have?" Doc asked, getting up.

"The end of the month," Nat said.

"Can I appeal the decision? I think my luck is changing, I can feel it."

"No, Doc, it's final. We examined the charter. We asked the old members. We even consulted our lawyer. You're out, I'm afraid, and there is no appeal."

Doc felt ridiculous, like a child sent into the principal's office, for a reprimand.

"This isn't fair," he said, "I didn't do anything wrong."

"I've never had to tell anyone to leave the club," Nat said gently. "I hope I never have to do this again. I have always regarded the members of this club as family. Most of us have known each other since childhood. We grew up together."

Nat was gazing at Doc, a pained expression on his face, and for a moment Doc felt sorry for him. He glanced around the card room. He would not be in here again. He walked out into the hall, determined to leave with his head held high. As far as he knew, he was the only member of the club ever to be asked to leave.

Doc looked back to say goodbye and scuttled back to the dining room to look for Dodie. She was sitting at a table, dressed in golf attire, a man at her side. She noticed Doc and waved.

When he got to the table she introduced the man as Myles Rush, her lawyer. He was large, imposing and had a crooked smile. Doc felt weak in the knees and in no mood to make polite conversation. He wanted to tell Dodie what had happened, but now that Myles was present this was impossible.

"Myles and I were discussing the estate," Dodie said, smiling. "I thought you might like to meet him."

Myles gave Doc the once-over and promptly dismissed him. "This little girl is going to have a lot of money. We have to be careful with it. We want to protect her, don't we? She is a woman alone, after all."

"All alone," Doc echoed forlornly, thinking of himself. His days were numbered. Where would he find friends, patients? He could not imagine not going to the club. He reached for a white linen napkin and wiped his brow. The room was crowded and overheated. The warm November weather had brought everyone out.

"She says you want money to invest in your practice," Myles continued, "and we are willing to lend it—but at a proper interest rate. Of course, it will be less than the bak."

Doc nodded. He did not feel like discussing investments. His mind was elsewhere.

"Perhaps you can come over to the office." Myles said.

"Yes," Doc said.

"What would you like to drink?" Myles asked Dodie.

"Perrier with a twist of lemon, I think," she answered.

"You're not certain," Myles said in a loud, jovial voice. "In that case I shall order you a double martini. Bet you've never had one in your life, young lady. I remember you said you don't drink."

"She does not drink," Doc intoned, a wave of self-pity coming over him. It was all so unfair.

Myles called the waiter. Shortly, he was putting down double martinis in front of the three of them. Dodie picked up the glass, hesitated a moment, then drank.

"What the hell," Doc said, lifting the glass to his lips.

"To us," Dodie said.

"Members only," Doc said.

"That excludes me," Myles said, laughing.

"Exactly," Doc muttered, finishing off the martini. He got up.

"Excuse me, I'll leave the two of you to your present indulgence. I've got to go now."

"Oh?" Myles said, pumping his hand. "Well, if you say so. See you at the office then, Doc."

"Uhm," Doc said, "and if you need any medical attention, injections or whatever . . ."

He skulked away without looking back.

Doc drove away slowly, realizing that this was the last time he would ever be at Crestwood Hills. Word would go around the club like wildfire. There would not be a single member who did not know he was kicked out the door. He could never go back there.

Right now he felt hungry. He had been cheated out of his

steak. He decided he would indulge himself at Burger King. He found one at Maple and Telegraph and drove into the window line. He would take the burger and fries back to his office so he could open his mail to see if there were any checks from patients. The line was long but he had plenty of time. Where was he going, anyhow? Just to the bank and the bank was open until four.

It occurred to him that he could cash in the ten thousand and leave for Mexico. He loved Mexico—the hot food, the hot women. Mexico City was a sophisticated, international city. His money would last a few months, maybe longer. He would have time to think about what he wanted to do. He could sell his house. He would not get much out of it after the paid off the second mortgage, but it would be something.

He waited patiently while the cars ahead of him slowly moved up the line. Yes, it might be wise to clear out. There was nothing holding him here any longer. His wife was gone, his friends had disappeared and now he was an outsider in the community.

Doc paid the pretty girl at the window and reached for the bag containing his lunch. He smiled a pleasant goodbye to the girl who was staring at him through the window.

Driving to his office he thought of more plans. He would close the office, informing the few remaining patients that he had gone on an extended vacation. He would write the owners of the building to see if he could get out of the lease, and if they refused he would break it anyway. The house would be sold in his absence by a real estate agent. Then too, Dodie would be good for money. The ten thousand was just the beginning. He might even be able to live indefinitely in Mexico, or wherever the American dollar went far. He believed her when she said her money was tied up. She was good for the future, when the enormous sum she inherited would be coming her way.

Life was not all that bad. Yes, it was grossly unfair, but

he was a survivor and he would survive his dismissal from the club. After all, country clubs weren't *everything*.

He left his car in the carport, and juggling the bag with his lunch, located the office key. As he approached the door he thought he heard someone typing in his office. Stopping, he listened intently. He swore he could hear the distinct clickity-clack of the typewriter keys. It was not possible; his secretary was long gone, having quit because he owed her four months' pay. Was this some kind of practical joke?

Suddenly the typing ceased. All was quiet within. Strange and baffling. He must have imagined it; he was under a heavy strain. It was not every day he was kicked out of Crestwood Hills. Not every day he decided to abandon his life altogether and start a new one. He would not be all that surprised if he was hearing things.

Fumbling, he finally managed to stick the key in the lock and open the door to the office. He walked in, half expecting a red head with long legs, chewing bubble gum and typing up a storm. He put his lunch on the table. He checked the ladies' room. Empty. He felt silly. He was alone and there was no typist.

Picking up the bag of food he walked into his private office. Something was lying on his desk. It looked like a letter of some sort. He leaned over to see what it was. Putting the bag down he brought out his glasses:

TO WHOM IT MAY CONCERN:
I, Doc Matthews, have decided I can't go on bearing the guilt over the deaths of my friends, the Schwartzes. I apologize to everyone for helping those poor people to an early grave. May God forgive Ben Schwartz!

The letter was signed with his name. Doc felt puzzled, and he removed his glasses, then put them back on. He reread the letter. All of a sudden, he heard a noise behind him. He turned to see what it was. A shot rang out, hitting him in the chest. He slumped against the desk, pushing the hamburger, fries and Coke onto the floor where they spilled over the worn carpet.

Doc never got to eat lunch.

CHAPTER THIRTY-TWO

"Be back in about an hour," Jerry Fryman said, letting his secretary out of his car. "Call Doc and let him know I'm on my way so he doesn't go out." Alana slammed the car door, nodded and ran toward the front of the office building.

She had brought the writ of habeus corpus to the jail only to discover that fraud charges had been brought against her boss. He was allowed to post bail of fifty thousand dollars and told to keep in touch with the police station every day.

With the discovery of the will fraud, he was in serious trouble, though somewhat less serious than murder. He might be able to wheedle his way out, turn on the charm for the jury. He would have to use all his special lawyer's knowledge of the art of persuasion to get out of this one. In the interim he had to be extra cautious, making certain that every single thing he did was above board. He could no longer afford the tiniest infraction of the law. This even meant he could not go down to the art museum in search of girls. His entire life had to be curbed—they would be watching him . . .

The jail experience had been ugly. For a Harvard-educated lawyer to be locked up with a stinking drunk was a painful absurdity. And when the drunk vomited right near his expensive Italian shoes, he had cried out in alarm to the guard. The guard had not seem interested and the vomit and the drunk remained until the next morning when the drunk was taken, unwashed, right before the judge for his sentencing.

The terrible food he had been given, together with his anxiety, had gone straight to his ulcer. His stomach was killing him. As soon as they released him, Jerry decided he would once and for all go to Doc and let Doc examine him . . .

He did not bother to park in the lot but left his car by a yellow line, unlocked, and ran into the building. Doc's office looked closed at first glance. Usually, Doc's door was open so that patients could go in and sit down in the waiting room.

Jerry tried the door. To his relief it opened. Inside, the waiting room lights were turned off. He sat down in the gloom to wait for Doc to appear. He knew the secretary had left some time ago, so he did not expect to see her. Doc had been carrying on all of the office chores alone.

Jerry sat for five minutes, then got up. His stomach ached fiercely. What if he needed an operation? Where was Doc, anyway? He wanted to get this examination over and return to his office where a mountain of work awaited him.

Dickie David had called him ten times from Florida where he had gone on a business trip, and each time left the same message. He was concerned about the whereabouts of his wife, having not yet learned she was in jail. Jerry would have to get in touch with her as soon as he could. She was probably languishing in there, miserable and frightened. He could probably get her out on bail when he learned the charges. Unless she had been arrested for murder one and they had some kind of fantastic evidence and would not grant bail, he felt quite certain she would be let go. Doctor Levine had told him that Beverly was arrested, but he refused to tell him the exact charges. This was when Jerry was a prisoner; now that he was a lawyer again he could demand an answer. They had to tell him the truth. But first things first.

He got up and walked down the hall. Passing a cubicle where patients were treated, he went in and turned on the light. He might as well use the telephone while he was waiting. Doc wouldn't mind. He reached for the yellow phone and dialed his office. It took Alana five rings to answer, which aggravated him.

"Alana," he snapped, "where were you? What takes so long?"

"Sorry, boss," she said, "I'm talking to some of your clients. They're sitting here waiting. Will you be long?"

"I haven't seen Doc yet," he said. "Who's there?"

"Dickie David and his wife," she answered.

"Dickie's in Florida."

"Not anymore, he's right here. Want to talk to him?"

"Beverly's in jail," Jerry said.

"No," Alana insisted, "well, not unless this one is a clone. It sure looks like Beverly."

"Oh, they let her out," Jerry said.

"Seems so, yes."

"Tell them I'll be back soon."

Jerry hung up. Where was Doc? He was beginning to feel better now that he was out of jail. People needed him. His clients were waiting. He had to get back to his own office; he had an important job to do. He left the cubicle and was about to leave the office when he thought he might as well say a quick hello and goodbye to Doc. He walked rapidly to the door where Doc's secretary used to sit and pushed open the door.

What he saw on the floor did not immediately imprint itself on his brain. He was not expecting Doc to be lying in a pool of ketchup, french fries, and a Whopper. He stood above Doc, gazing blankly down at him. Was that blood? In Doc's hand was a small gun which looked like a water pistol.

"Oh my God," Jerry said, the truth hitting him. "Oh, Jesus, he's killed himself."

He reached down and pulled the gun away from Doc as if the gesture would bring him back to life. The gun was not the kind children play with, he observed morbidly, and now his fingerprints were all over it. He pulled his handkerchief from his pocket and tried wiping the gun handle. Then, coming to his senses, he grabbed the telephone and dialed the operator.

"Connect me to the police, quick, there's been a death," he yelled into the phone.

It seemed an eternity before the police arrived. Jerry did not know what to do with himself. He stared out the window in the front of the building and waited. He avoided the room Doc was lying in.

Two policemen, service revolvers drawn, leaped from the patrol car and raced inside.

"I didn't do it. I didn't do it," Jerry said helplessly, recognizing one of the cops he had seen at the Crestwood Hills station. "I just found him in there," he said, waving the gun around, "I only came here because I've got a serious ulcer . . ."

One of the policemen snorted and threw a look to the other.

"Keep him company, Mark, I'll see if there's really a body. I think he's kind of nutty," he whispered and went to have a look around. In a moment he returned.

"Okay, just come along quietly," he said to Jerry, clamping handcuffs on him. They took him to the waiting car.

CHAPTER THIRTY-THREE

Tim did not want to hurt his mother's feelings by refusing the brown paper bag filled with peanut butter and jelly sandwiches, but he really didn't want them. He and Dodie planned to eat at the club after they finished their golf game.

"You'll get hungry out there on the course," his mother warned ominously.

"I'm in a hurry, mom, and not hungry. I already ate lunch. And I'll be eating later."

"Hope it works out," Mrs. Levine said, disappointed that he was not taking the sandwiches. "You're sure you don't want these?"

He shut the door while she was talking. She would forgive him later. He ran to his car, noticing that what had begun as a warm winter day now looked overcast. The forecast predicted rain. He put his clubs in the back of the car, wishing this were just a normal rendezvous with a girlfriend.

He drove toward the club thinking about Dodie. This was the first time she had been on the links since Buddy

Schwartz had his fatal attack. In the last few months she had let her golf go by the boards in just the way he had let his job go. It was not that he wasn't working diligently on the Schwartz murders—he was. But, lately his heart was not in it the way it used to be. If only he could have the assurance that Dodie had not viciously, willfully murdered her in-laws and husband. *If.* But there was nothing definite with which get her off the hook. And Po Lee? It was possible Ben Schwartz was right. Dodie could have murdered the maid to distract the police and the medical examiner's office from herself.

Ben Schwartz had said he was with Beverly David the day Hank was killed, and Beverly had agreed. He had told Tim the story of the hairbrush, and when Tim privately questioned Jerry Fryman he had said, yes, his hairbrush was indeed missing. The explanation was crazy but plausible, which then made it impossible to hold Beverly for murder one. She had the perfect excuse. So far. Now that Doc Matthews had killed himself—or been murdered—Beverly would certainly be questioned again. She was out of jail when he died. Doctor Fenton, the first medical examiner to examine the body at the scene of the crime, said it was nearly impossible for the doctor to have committed suicide because of the angle of entry of the bullet. No one shot himself in the chest. In any case, Jerry Fryman's fingerprints were all over everything. As he was found standing with a near-smoking gun in his hand, he was arrested. His excuse was patently ridiculous, but what could *his* motive be for getting rid of Doc?

Tim did not feel perplexed, however. He believed all would fall into place as soon as he could get the last pieces of the puzzle assembled. He was on the verge. Once and for all he had to determine Dodie's role in this. *Was she a murderer?* The words made him shiver, but since Patti had accused him of avoiding a confrontation with Dodie he felt it was his duty to do just that. Confront. Not only to satisfy himself but to do his rightful job as a medical examiner.

He had admitted to Patti that he had become lax in his duty because of a romantic attachment to Dodie. Patti was stunned. Though she had walked out on him, she now saw *him* as the betrayer. Now he was about to confront the woman he wanted to love and thought he had and perhaps still did. He was praying for her, praying she was as innocent as he wanted her to be.

Tim arrived at the club eager for their golf date, eager for the reckoning. Although the day was cool and a light rain had begun to fall, he imagined the golf course was a good setting for what he had to know. He gave his car to the parking attendant, took his golf bag and went into the club. She must be in the locker room getting ready, he supposed.

There was a distinct air of excitement which he perceived as soon as he entered the club. People were running from room to room laying floral decorations on every table. Must be a wedding. The first person Tim saw was Dickie David, who was coming from one of the bars, a harried look on his face. When he saw Tim he stopped.

"Well, Doctor Levine," he said, embarrassed, "my wife is out of jail, but I'm afraid she's run off somewhere. She left me a note saying she was checking into the Hyatt-Regency but she's not there."

"I'm sure you'll find her," Tim said soothingly, looking around for Dodie. He had his own problems and was not in a position to help this man. "You'll find her," he said, wondering if Dickie might know where Dodie was. "And Dodie Schwartz? Do you know *her* whereabouts?" He had no time to lose—not anymore.

Dickie's cheeks turned red. "She's in a funny mood. In the bar." Dickie pointed towards the room he had just left. "In there," he said, "she isn't used to drinking. She . . . ah . . . she's not the Dodie I know." And with that he swung off towards the entrance of the club.

Tim took a deep breath. He turned and walked towards

the bar. The room was empty except for a bored-looking bartender who was staring down at a solitaire hand.

Tim made a quick trip to the ladies' card room where two tables of women were at play. No one had seen Dodie. No one seemed at all interested. He went to the nearest phone and called her home. No answer. He then tried Wabeek. No answer. As a last resort he walked through the various lounges which the members of the club were decorating with mad enthusiasm. Finally, he checked the dining room where late lunch and tea was being served. There was Dodie, sitting alone, sipping from a large glass.

He stopped. She was beautiful, her dark hair set off by a stunning white wool golf outfit, a kind of jump suit that zipped up the front. The suit fit her body snugly so that her round, firm breasts were outlined seductively. Slowly, she raised her eyes to him and his heart skipped a beat.

"Tim," she called, smiling, "come on in, the water's fine."

He put his golf bag down. When he sat next to her he saw immediately she was drunk. Her eyes were bloodshot and had a curious glazed look about them.

"I know I can't handle it," she giggled.

"Well, we can't play golf," he said.

"No, no, I'm fine. I'll sober up. I need some fresh air, just some fine Crestwood air. I had lunch with my lawyer . . . stayed all afternoon."

"Jerry Fryman?"

"He's not my lawyer," Dodie laughed, "he's in jail."

"Yes, he's in jail. He got out for a few hours, but now he's back in."

"Good."

"He shot Doc Matthews."

"Shot Doc Matthews?" Dodie said, trying to focus her eyes.

"Yes, and we also found a check on Doc for ten thousand dollars from you."

"From me?"

"Yes."

"Poor Doc, poor, poor, Doc," Dodie said, tears coming to her eyes. She wiped them on her sleeve and gazed at Tim, who was watching her carefully, waiting for any tangible sign of her guilt.

"Why?" she asked, "why did he shoot him?"

"We don't know yet," Tim sighed heavily.

"Everyone has to die," Dodie said.

"You still want to play golf, Dodie?"

Dodie got up. "I'm feeling better, let's go," she said. "We can't bring Doc back. Maybe he's better off."

"Better off?"

"He had no money, no woman, nothing. He put phony stuff on those death certificates."

"He did? How do you know that? Tim asked.

"You told me so. They were murdered, weren't they?" Dodie said. "May I have my check back?"

"I believe it's part of his estate now," Tim said, "I can't just give it back, Dodie, that would be unethical."

"You're so proper," she said, reeling away from the table. "That's what I like about you."

Dodie suddenly whipped her head around and caught the eye of Eileen Ferentz, who was gawking at her from another table. Other members at other tables were also looking, some with sneaky, irritated glances, others with obvious disdain. Jack Goldstein's mother rose imperiously and left the room. Dodie giggled and stuck out her tongue.

Tim got up and took her arm.

"You look ill," he said kindly. "Why don't I take you home?"

"I'm playing golf," Dodie insisted. "I'm good, you'll see, and I haven't played in ages. Didn't get to go to La Costa this winter."

Her voice was husky. Tim did not want to have a scene in the Crestwood Hills dining room, just in case he had been totally wrong about Dodie, just in case one day they would really be together, the unfortunate past forgotten.

"Please," he begged, "I'll take you home. We can play tomorrow when you feel better."

"No way" she said, wrinkling her nose and moving off away from the dining room. He tried to keep up with her, but she ducked into the ladies' room. In a moment she reappeared with her golf bag.

"Let me take it," Tim said, struggling with the two bags.

Dodie walked unsteadily to the entrance, paying no attention to the other members who watched her drunken departure.

Outside the rain was beginning to fall in earnest.

"My clubs are rusty," Tim said, thinking that perhaps the rain would bring her into focus. The rain was as good as a cold shower. "You'll have to tell me which clubs to use in the beginning. I've almost forgotten which ones to use."

They walked down towards the green, Tim's arms aching from the load of the two bags. He surveyed the first hole.

"Looks impossible," he said.

"It is," Dodie said reassuringly. "That's where Buddy fell . . . after the bee sting."

"Hey, it's raining hard, don't you think we should forget about this?"

"No," Dodie said, poking around in her bag for the right club. She took out an iron and approached the tee. She swung with perfect control but did not come into contact with the ball. The effort caused her to fall down on the wet grass. Tim ran over to help her up.

"Are you okay, Dodie?"

She glanced up at him and smiled. He was so kind . . .

"Why don't we sit on the bench under that tree," Tim suggested. "Let's talk a while."

Dodie put up her lips to be kissed. "I love you," she said. "Do you love me?"

"Yes, I love you, Dodie, but you *must* tell me the truth."

"The truth," Dodie said drunkenly, "of course I will. I can trust you, can't I?"

Tim felt scared. He did not want to hear the truth, not really.

"Let's sit under the tree," he repeated, feeling that somehow that simple little act would make everything normal.

"My father was a terrific pharmacist," Dodie said, "I don't care what she says."

"Who?"

"My mother. She told me I wasn't his."

"Whose?"

"My dad's. She said I was another man's child," Dodie whispered huskily. "She's a liar."

"I'm sorry, sweetheart, when she told you maybe she was ill. It's probably not true. Old people say things they don't mean sometimes."

"I think it's true. I'm a bastard."

Tim patted her affectionately on the shoulder.

"I think we should go in now," he said.

"He's a liar," Dodie said.

"Who?"

"Ben Schwartz."

"Yes," Tim said nervously.

"Ben Schwartz is the murderer," Dodie said.

"Dodie, Dodie, sweetheart, I have something to tell you, it's urgent, please listen! Ben is insisting that *you* helped him murder his parents and Hank, and the Chinese maid was killed just as a cover-up. To keep us off the track, don't you see? Of course, this is premeditated murder. He says you're the one who injected his family. Is that true, sweetheart?"

Tim wanted desperately to gain her confidence. He suppressed his own feeling of anxiety. The tack he was on was working, the pieces were coming together. Shortly the puzzle would be done.

"You were his accomplice, sweetheart, weren't you? You can tell me, it's okay."

Dodie smiled crookedly.

"You're beginning to sound like Humphrey Bogart and anyway, Ben is still a liar, always bragging, always competing. Who the hell does he think he is?"

She was feeling giddy, dizzy. Out of the blue a sexual fantasy was coming over her. With bleary eyes she gazed up at Tim—or, was it Buddy? . . .

"Go on," Tim encouraged, "tell me the rest of it, Dodie. Why is Ben a liar?"

"He's a liar," she said, opening her eyes wide, seeing only Tim. "He had nothing to do with Hank's death or Buddy, or Rose, or Po Lee's, nothing. Why should he get credit? He always wants the credit. He was always competing with poor Hank."

"*Who* should get the credit, Dodie?" Tim asked, his voice shaking.

Tim's impulse was to tell her to shut up, to tell her to ask for a lawyer, but now he had to know the truth. He still cared for her, but he had to know the truth about the Schwartz family murders and about the Chinese maid.

"Can I trust you, sweetheart?" Dodie said, her voice almost mocking.

"Oh, yes," he answered, wondering how she could not notice his alarm. He looked into the sweet, wet face, the dark, luminous eyes, the dimpled mouth he had kissed so many times, and felt a keen sense of loss.

"I do know how to inject," she said in a conspiratorial manner. "I've known for years, goodness, it's easy. Daddy used to inject all the diabetics on Calvert Avenue. He taught me. I learned from the master."

"Oh, I see," Tim said, "you injected your in-laws and Hank, too. Is that right, Dodie?"

"Yes, sure, right."

"With what?"

"Curare—works almost immediately, and you can inject it into the muscle. However, with Rose I injected it right into the vein. She was asleep. Hank was more difficult. I had to get him partly undressed. I seduced him, I guess, and while we were having sex I injected him. He thought I had bitten him and seemed to like it for a minute. It was over fast."

Tim stared at her in horror. Words came to his lips but he was unable to speak. He wanted her to say she was joking, that none of it was true, that she was making it all up just to be perverse.

"Did I do something wrong?" she asked in her innocent voice.

"Oh, no," he said, pushing out the words, trying to look calm and reassuring. "And Po Lee?" He held his breath, still hoping she might laugh, or even cry, and say she had made up the whole awful story to tease him.

The rain was running down Dodie's face. And all at once she became aware of the horrified look on Tim's face.

"I don't know if I can trust you," she blurted, getting off the bench, backing away.

"Sure you can," Tim said, "trust me." He continued to sit.

"Oh? All right, yes, good."

She edged over to him and in a childlike whisper began to speak. "I thought it was a good idea to throw everyone off. I told you I'm strong. Strong as a guy." She giggled. "Po Lee didn't know it was me. I was dressed like a guy. I was wearing a yellow sweater, one that looks like Ben's. Just in case she survived, she would have thought it was Ben, see?"

Tim nodded.

"See?" Dodie repeated, "I got her from behind at first . . ."

"Yes," Tim interrupted, "you're a strong girl."

He was staggered by her story. He got up. His knees felt weak.

"Two people in love should tell each other everything," Dodie said.

Tim shook his head, unable to think of anything further to say. They stood facing each other in the rain.

"You're not sympathetic," Dodie suddenly cried, "I can see by the look on your face. You don't care! You don't love me! You don't care anything about me! You were so different from all the rest. I don't belong here. I don't belong with you. I didn't belong with Hank. I only married him for his money, and I deserve it! I deserved the money! I should have been rich. My mother thought I should have been rich!"

She began to slip away from him.

"I can't trust you," she screamed, and ran to her golf bag which Tim had propped against the tree. He ran after her, sliding in the muddy grass.

He saw what she was aiming to do and tried to avert her action by grappling with her, but she had already grabbed an iron and with extraordinary energy was raising it over her head. The club struck him on the side of the head and sent him reeling across the wet ground, blood oozing over his face.

Dodie did not look back. She fled over the green, looking for a place to hide. She must get somewhere, fast. She knew that near the eighth hole there were a number of fancy houses. The people who lived in that area were all members of the club. She could take shelter, and when it stopped pouring she could go back to the club for her car. Maybe someone would drive her there.

Her feet were soaked and the water was a nuisance as it squashed around in her shoes. She bent and took them off. Running barefoot was much easier. She leapt across the course until she came to the eighth hole. Just north of it were the houses. The first house looked deserted. She couldn't remember who lived there. Was it the Plotnik family, or the Haffners' house? She tried the garage but could not get in. She ran down the course to the next house. All doors were locked.

Then she remembered something excellent. Mignon Teedberg's daughter was having a bas mitzvah today and Mignon lived two houses away. Dodie started to run and fell into a muddy pile of leaves. Her clothes were caked with dirt. She attempted to brush herself off but only succeeded spreading the muck around, covering her hands, her face, her hair. By the time she arrived at the Teedberg home the mud and the rain had caused the blood to completely soak the front of her golf outfit.

She rang the bell. Inside a reception was going on. She could hear the merry sounds of the party. She rang and rang. Apparently, no one could hear her through the din. She went around to the side of the house and peered through the french windows. Yes, a gay fête was happening. Black waiters in white uniforms with red cumberbunds were offering trays of hors d'oeuvres among the many guests. Dom Pérignon was being served. She peeked around, stretching her neck to see the dining room. It was filled with food: crepes of all sorts made to order, caviar, hot canapés, smoked salmon and pressed duck. She smiled. It was quite like Crestwood Hills: the same people, the same food. She even recognized the Korean boy who parked the cars . . .

Everyone was dressed in his or her finest. Women wore their diamond earrings and men star sapphire pinkie rings and gold neck chains. She knocked on the window. She knew everyone in there. There was no reason to stand outside in the pouring rain.

No one noticed Dodie pressing her face against the window. She decided to go around to the back of the house and try the garage door. She was tired and thirsty and the vision of the food was making her mouth water.

The garage door was wide open and she went in without any problem. The kitchen door was left open. She walked over and looked in the kitchen, the hub of activity. Servants were rushing back and forth for glasses, more champagne and more hot hors d'oeuvres. Dodie counted the help—fourteen in all.

She stood regarding the scene. If she crept forward and helped herself to a plate, would anyone notice? She was not doing anything wrong. After all, she had been invited to the party but declined in favor of her golf date with Tim.

All of a sudden, Mignon marched into the kitchen, saw her and screamed.

"What's that? *Who's* that?"

Mignon was wearing a white silk dress with lace collar and cuffs and matching shoes which tied around her ankles in little bows. She looked like the person being honored, rather than her daughter. Dodie stared at her disapprovingly.

"Jesus, oh, God," Mignon screamed, "what's the matter with you? Were you in an accident? It's Dodie, isn't it?"

Everyone in the kitchen stared at Dodie, eyes wide.

"Who, me? I wonder if someone might drive me back to the club? I got caught in the rain."

Mignon stared incredulously at her.

"Stay here," she warned, "I'll get help." She rushed out of the kitchen, slamming the door.

The kitchen help tried not to look at Dodie, who was standing quietly in the corner, but could not help rolling their eyes.

Mignon quickly returned.

"The police are all over the place, God in heaven, Dodie, you're ruining my party. What did you do? They're asking for *you*. There's an Officer Gracey outside—you better get right out there. Did you have an accident?"

Dodie grimaced, then ducked out the door to the garage praying the keys would be in the ignition of the Cadillac. She yanked open the door and got in. She got out and climbed into the Porsche. Someone was pounding on the kitchen door from the inside, and on the garage door from the outside.

She jumped out of the Porsche and through the side door. Police seemed to be everywhere. There was hysteria in the air. Amidst the parked Cadillacs, the Mercedes-Benzes, the BMW's, the Rollses, police cars were sprinkled all over, flashers going wildly, creating a carnivallike atmosphere. This must be the most colorful social event of the season, she thought happily.

She dashed around a police car and headed for a Cadillac. The key must be tucked in there somewhere. She would have no trouble in getting away.

Behind her several policemen were approaching. An ambulance careened forward, for a moment distracting her. She stopped, frozen to the spot, thinking they might try to force her into it. To her surprise Tim stepped out. His eye was puffed out and his face was bloody.

"Tim!" she shouted gaily.

"Into the police car!" he ordered, his face a stony mask.

"Why should I?" she asked.

"Please, Dodie, *please,* " he said, his manner softening.

"Okay," she agreed, complacent as a child.

The police bundled her into the car.

"Hey," she called out, laughing as she rolled down the window. "Del and Danto Tannenbaum, remember? The poor relations. I told you about them."

Tim stood in the rain, his eye beginning to throb, a terrible headache overpowering him. He stared at her. What did she mean?

Shakily, he climbed back into the waiting ambulance, and realized what she was telling him . . . The poor relations would inherit the Schwartz millions. Unless, of course, Ben contested the will—and Beverly David would make sure he did.

Tim laughed at himself. He was beginning to think like a member of a country club.